BLUETICK REVENGE

ALSO BY MARK COHEN

The Fractal Murders

BLUETICK REVENGE

MARK COHEN

New York   Boston

Copyright © 2005 by Mark Cohen

Mysterious Press
Warner Books

Time Warner Book Group
1271 Avenue of the Americas, New York, NY 10020.
Visit our Web site at www.twbookmark.com.

The Mysterious Press name and logo are registered trademarks of Warner Books.

Printed in the United States of America

First Edition: July 2005

10   9   8   7   6   5   4   3   2   1

Library of Congress Cataloging-in-Publication Data

Cohen, Mark.
    Bluetick revenge / Mark Cohen.— 1st ed.
        p. cm. — (Pepper Keane series)
    Summary: "The second mystery featuring private eye Pepper Keane, a former JAG
with a diet Coke addiction, who becomes the target of an outlaw biker gang"—Provided by
the publisher.
    ISBN 0-89296-800-1
  1. Private investigators—Fiction. 2. Motorcycle gangs—Fiction. 3. Motorcyclists—Fiction.
I. Title.
    PS3603.O367B58   2005
    813'.6—dc22   2004030822

In memory of Dexter S. Cohen and George Vandenberg

Acknowledgments

I want to thank my agent, Sandra Bond of the Bond Literary Agency, for her professionalism and her unwavering belief in me. (Well, she might have wavered a little as the deadline approached, but she now knows we are capable of a fourth-quarter comeback.) I want to thank my editor, Kristen Weber, for her patience and guidance. (She flatters me with her praise of my imagination; I fear that someday she will visit Nederland and learn that my depiction of the town and its characters is entirely accurate.) Finally, I want to thank Mysterious Press for having the courage to take a chance on a quasi-vegetarian private eye who lives with his dogs (Buck and Wheat) in the mountains, reads philosophy in an attempt to make sense of life, and has strong convictions on the subject of cola.

BLUETICK REVENGE

The greatest happiness is to vanquish your enemies, to chase them before you, to rob them of their wealth, to see those dear to them bathed in tears, to clasp to your bosom their wives and daughters.

—Genghis Khan

1

I'D BEEN SCOPING the place for a week. That seemed a long time, but this wouldn't be a traditional dognapping. Not that I had much of a basis for comparison. I had never dognapped before, though I had taken a few catnaps.

I focused my binoculars on the area between the cabin and the million-dollar mountain home. They were a good fifty yards apart. It was an old two-room cabin and its windows were protected from the winter wind by faded pine shutters. But for a dozen empty antifreeze containers piled near the door, there was no sign the cabin was in use.

The animal was chained to a tall pine about halfway between the cabin and the residence. He had maybe thirty feet of slack. He lay in a plywood doghouse, his muzzle resting near its entrance. His expression showed boredom and sadness. The water in his metal bowl had long since frozen.

There were two Harleys parked in front of the home—the fewest I had seen yet. I'd been there four hours this day and seen only two men. One was about fifty and looked like Jerry Garcia a few years before his death. The other was a lanky ponytailed man in his early thirties, who walked from the house to the cabin every few hours with a machine pistol in one hand. Both displayed tattoos on their faces and hands, and they probably bore more beneath their winter clothes. Neither fit Bugg's description. I decided I would make my move tonight.

It wasn't quite dark enough. I walked through the dense pines about a half mile back to the F-150 I'd parked just off a county road. Had anyone looked through the shell into the back of the truck, they would have seen a chain saw, a few dozen logs, and some camping gear. My hope was they would assume I had been cutting firewood.

I placed the binoculars on the passenger seat, then removed my parka and tossed it into the truck as well. If things got hairy, I didn't want bulky winter clothes slowing me down. A down-filled vest over a flannel shirt over a high-tech undershirt would keep me warm enough. I clasped my hands together, then brought them to my mouth and blew on them to keep them warm. Tiny clouds of mist spiraled before me as I exhaled. It was the third Tuesday in November—Thanksgiving was two days away—and though there was little snow on the ground, there was moisture in the air. The thermometer in my truck showed twenty-six degrees.

It was overcast. No stars were visible and the moon was nowhere to be seen. As the last remnants of the day's light vanished, it became wonderfully dark. There would never be a better time to do it.

I climbed into the truck, placed the keys in the ignition, and started her up. I waited a few minutes, then exited the vehicle, leaving the driver's door slightly ajar, but not enough to cause the dome light to come on. If someone came along and stole it in the next twenty minutes, I'd be shit out of luck. Chances of that happening on a Tuesday night in a national forest were slim. I checked my Velcro shoulder holster; the Glock was still there.

The hike back to Bugg's secluded mountain home took ten minutes. The wind hadn't changed, so I was able to approach without the dog picking up my scent. The trees surrounding the home had been cleared to a distance of one hundred feet in an effort to make it more defensible in the event of a forest fire. I stopped before I hit the clearing and surveyed the area one last time. I donned a black ski mask to protect my identity, then got down on my belly and started crawling toward the dog. He was awake but resting on his side with a vacant look. I was within twenty feet when he raised his magnificent head and scanned the area. I didn't want him barking. Still on my belly, I removed a roast beef sandwich—one I had purchased at the B&F just for this purpose—from my vest pocket and tossed it at him. Then I sprinted.

He let out two melodic barks, then went to work on the meat. I unhooked the chain from his collar and snapped my leash into place. With the dog now under my control, I started running back to the trees. He ran alongside, as if we'd been friends for years, gulping the sandwich as we went. As we hit the trees a man inside the home yelled, "Fuck!"

We continued toward the truck. I heard a door slam. Floodlights suddenly illuminated the house and cabin, but I was back into the trees by then. "Something's going down!" the man yelled. "Check the cabin." One of the Harleys roared to life. I continued running, dodging the pines as best I could. It was incredibly dark in the forest, and my forty-something face took more than one hit from low branches weighed down by accumulated snow. The bike noise grew faint as the rider headed to the highway.

The dog dropped what was left of the sandwich and tried to go back for it, but I yanked the leash hard. By this time I had my second wind and was running at a good clip given the darkness and rough terrain. It was a good thing I had the dog with me, because mountain lions can be unforgiving if you startle them.

I smelled the exhaust from my truck, then saw the truck itself. I reached the truck and opened the driver's door. The dog jumped right in and I followed suit. Headlights off, I drove down the dirt road at a moderate speed toward Colorado Highway 72 just west of Ward. All I had to do was make the highway without coming into contact with the bike.

I was less than two hundred yards from the pavement when a single headlight appeared and started toward me. Think fast, Pepper, I told myself. I didn't want to shoot the guy, but I didn't want him to get a look at my truck either. I could have clipped him with the truck, but somebody might have noticed the damage to my vehicle and put two and two together. I punched the accelerator and went straight at him. When I was twenty yards away I turned on my brights. He held one hand up to his eyes to dim the glare. It was Jerry Garcia. I blasted my horn and swerved to the right just as I met him. He took a nasty spill and ended up in the drainage on the side of the road. I killed my headlights, turned right at the pavement, and headed home to Nederland.

I had trouble sleeping that night. Dognapping gets my adrenaline flowing. This is particularly true when the dog is a champion bluetick coonhound owned by the leader of the Sons of Satan.

2

AT NINE THE NEXT MORNING I was enjoying a cup of hot coffee in the plush reception area of the downtown Denver offices of Keane, Simms & Mercante. My cup had the firm's logo emblazoned on it. I had known "Big" Matt Simms more than fifteen years. We had formed a law firm after I had left the U.S. attorney's office. Matt was now a prominent attorney and the managing partner of what had grown to be a nine-person firm. I had left the practice of law some years back, primarily because of burnout, but my former partners had voted not to change the firm's name. They did not do this out of affection for me; they did it because the firm had invested a lot of money in that name over the years. Or, as Matt had so eloquently summarized the decision, "I don't want to have to pay some fucker to design a new logo."

"Would you like more coffee, Mr. Keane?" the receptionist asked. She was a tall brunette with pouty lips and fine cheekbones. Late twenties. Her dress was made of satin or something like it, and the vertical black and white stripes of the fabric only served to accent her curves. I had seen her once or twice before when visiting Matt in connection with the projects he occasionally asks me to undertake. She was beautiful but maintained a certain formality she felt was expected at a first-rate law firm, and I suspected that had deterred many a man from asking her out.

"More coffee would be wonderful," I said. She retrieved my cup and saucer, then returned with a fresh cup. I started reading the *Rocky Mountain News*. The big stories concerned Islamic militants, a new report on global warming, and tax cuts for the rich. "Thank God for cabernet and antidepressants," I muttered.

A few minutes later Matt strolled toward me and extended his hand. A former offensive lineman at Colorado State, Matt stands six-two and weighs in at about 270 pounds. His ego is even bigger. We shook hands.

"Thanks for coming on short notice," he said. His collar was unbuttoned and his sleeves rolled up, his brown, wavy hair a bit disheveled. "How was the drive in?" He had already turned around and was heading for his office. Not even looking at me.

"Glad I don't do it every day," I said. It is forty-six miles from my mountain home in Nederland to downtown Denver. "The traffic is unbelievable."

"Tell me about it," he said. "If I didn't have three kids in high school, I'd move downtown." Matt lives in Cherry Hills Village, an exclusive suburb with an exceptional school system. It is home to many doctors, lawyers, and overpaid athletes.

Even before we hit his office, I smelled the aroma of a cigar. It's supposed to be a smoke-free building, but Matt possesses a healthy disregard for rules. Not coincidentally, it's a trait shared by most of my friends.

I entered his corner office first and he closed the door behind me. Matt sat in the executive chair behind his mahogany desk, and I sat in one of the burgundy leather chairs in front of it. Our perch on the thirty-seventh floor of the Qwest Tower provided a nice view of the city on this sunny winter morning. The snow-capped Rockies glistened in the distance. I had been looking at the same mountains since the day I was born, and though Denver had grown from a sleepy little cow town on the plains into yet another land-devouring urban cancer, I took comfort in the fact that the mountains remained more or less unchanged.

"I appreciate your help with this," he said. "The dog means a lot to my client. She's under tremendous pressure, and the dog's her only friend." I said nothing. "Did you have any trouble?"

I shook my head. "You think I never stole a dog before?"

He reached into his desk drawer, removed a white envelope, and handed it to me. I thumbed through it. It contained twenty hundred-dollar bills. "That cover it?" he asked. He picked up half a stogie from a ceramic ashtray—one his kids had probably made years ago—inserted one end into his mouth, and lit the other end with a gold-plated lighter. It reminded me of Roger Miller's old song "King of the Road": . . . Smoke old stogies I have found, short but not too big around . . .

"Two thousand is fine," I said. I placed the envelope in the pocket of my blue blazer.

"To get right to the point," he said, "some things have happened and I need your help." I folded my hands and waited for him to continue. "I've kept most of this from you because I thought your role would be limited to getting the dog, but it's become more complicated." He paused to consider his words.

"Start at the beginning," I said.

"Right," he said. He puffed on the cigar. "I don't do as much criminal law as I used to," he said.

"Who needs it when you can bill corporate clients three hundred bucks an hour?" He nodded in agreement.

"When I do take a criminal case," he continued, "it usually involves some kind of white-collar crime. Antitrust, regulatory offenses, things like that." He leaned forward and placed his hands on the desk, still holding the stogie in his right hand.

"About a month ago a woman named Karlynn Slade came to see me. Turns out her common-law husband is Thadeus Bugg, the leader of the Sons of Satan."

"The guy I stole the dog from. You told me this before."

"You know anything about the Sons of Satan?"

"Just what you told me," I said. "It's a biker gang that consists mostly of thugs who live in the mountains. Bugg lives a few miles out of Ward, about fifteen miles north of Nederland. Way out in the boonies. He's got a meth lab in a cabin behind his house, by the way." There could be no other reason for the abundance of antifreeze containers and the periodic trips to the cabin by the man with the machine pistol.

"He has meth labs all over the West," Matt said, "and that's just the tip of the iceberg. These are bad guys. They're into drugs, prostitution, fencing, weapons, loan-sharking, and murder for hire. Some are on the fringe of the White Power movement. They're not the largest gang in Colorado, but they are the most violent." He paused. I'd seldom seen him display anything other than supreme confidence, but this morning I detected concern.

"The feds have gone after Bugg before," he continued, "but they've never been able to make anything stick, because key witnesses keep turning up dead. They think he played a role in the death of an ATF agent in Wyoming about six months ago."

"Didn't they kill one of their own a few years back?"

"A guy named Rankin, a probationary gang member. Bugg somehow found out he was working for the feds. They found his body in his cabin. He had been secured to a support beam with radiator clamps, then blow-torched. His dick was in his mouth when they found him."

"I remember that," I said. "They never identified a suspect."

"And they probably never will," he said. "The Sons of Satan are like brothers. The penalty for betrayal is a slow, painful death. That's why each member has 'SPD' tattooed on his left wrist. You can't look at your fuckin' watch without being reminded of what awaits those who are disloyal. There are men sitting in maximum-security prisons as we speak because they'd rather spend the rest of their lives behind bars than betray the Sons of Satan."

I sipped my coffee in silence as I stared out at the city. I despised the Sons of Satan and others like them, but I felt grudging admiration for the value they placed on loyalty.

"Anyhow," Matt said, "this broad comes to me because the day previously two FBI agents visited her and told her she was going to spend a long time in prison if she didn't become an FBI informant."

"What do they have on her?" I asked.

"Enough to make life unpleasant," he said. "She lived with Bugg for seven years, knew what he was doing, and used his money to buy lots of nice things for herself. I spoke with the new U.S. attorney after she retained me, and he made clear that the Sons of Satan are number one on his priority list. He's got his eyes on a Senate seat, and he's going to use the Sons of Satan to beef up his law-and-order credentials. They're going to nail Bugg on something eventually, and when they do they'll indict her for aiding and abetting, accessory after the fact, conspiracy, and misprision of felony. She also ran a blue-collar prostitution ring that provided just about anything you can imagine to working men up and down the Rockies, so they've got her on conspiracy to violate the Mann Act if nothing else."

"She have a date for New Year's?" I asked. Matt forced a smile.

"She comes to me and doesn't know what to do. She's not thrilled with the prospect of prison, but if Bugg finds out she's working for the feds she'll end up in a fifty-five-gallon drum at Monster Joe's Truck and Tow. It's not really my cup of tea and I'm thinking I should refer her to someone else, when she opens a briefcase filled with twenties, fifties, and hundreds."

"How much?" I asked as I sipped my coffee.

"Over three hundred thousand," he said.

"That's a lot of blow jobs," I said.

"Very funny," he replied. "It's drug money. As soon as the feds left, she took all the cash she could find in the house and went into hiding."

"Then she decided she needed an attorney?"

"Yeah, the money is in my safe." He swiveled in his chair and gestured to show that the safe was in the credenza behind his desk. "It's possible she took even more and just hasn't told me about it. I guess Bugg doesn't like banks. Anyhow, it didn't take long for me to realize she had a serious meth habit, and I knew the feds would consider her more credible if she got clean, so I urged her to enter a treatment program. There's no way she can go back to Bugg, but she could still be of immense help to the feds. I told her the Witness Protection Program was her only chance, but she'd have to be drug free. She pitched a fit, so I told her to find another lawyer. She finally agreed to enter a thirty-day residential program on the condition that I get the dog for her."

"And recalling that I am unemployed and moderately adventurous, you hired me to snag the dog formerly known as Prince for your kinky, drug-addicted, dog-loving client?"

"Yes," he replied. I finished my coffee and he asked if I wanted more. I said I did, so he punched the intercom button with one of his beefy fingers and asked the receptionist to bring me a refill.

"How is Prince?" he asked.

"He's fine," I said. "His lot in life has improved greatly in the last fifteen hours. He's asleep on the couch in my basement."

"You didn't leave him outside?"

"Can't," I said. "Don't want word getting out that I recently acquired a bluetick coonhound. Dog like that would stick out in Nederland."

"How come?" he asked.

"When's the last time you saw a hippie hunting raccoons at eight thousand feet?" Nederland sits 8,236 feet above sea level. It is widely known as one of the last hippie towns in America, though it is also populated by cowboys, miners, professionals who work in Boulder, and the occasional ex-Marine JAG who just wants to live in a small mountain town and not be bothered by anyone. Ninety-nine percent of the dogs in Nederland are descended from malamutes, huskies, or wolf hybrids.

"I get your point," Matt said. "Does he get along with your dogs?"

"Seems to," I said. I have two dogs, Buck and Wheat. Buck is a cross between a Great Dane and a Rhodesian ridgeback. Wheat is purebred schipperke and resembles a black fox.

The receptionist brought my coffee and took back the empty cup and saucer. I flashed my pearly whites and thanked her. She remained pleasant but professional. "Cold," I said, after she had departed.

"The coffee or Theresa?"

"Theresa."

"I thought you had a girlfriend," he said.

"I do," I said. "I was just making an observation."

"Anyhow, she's not your type."

"My type is hard to find," I replied.

"I'll bet," he said. "You can get beauty and brains if you're lucky, but beauty, brains, philosopher, and redneck is hard to come by."

"I'm an enlightened redneck," I said. "I own a gun, but I vote Democratic."

"Getting back to the business at hand," he said. I met his eyes to signal I was listening. "While Ms. Slade was in treatment, I worked out an agreement with the U.S. attorney. She gets immunity but has to tell all in front of a grand jury, then testify at trial. When it's over, they'll relocate her and give her a new life."

"Do the feds know she took money from Bugg?" I asked.

"I'm sure they've heard she took some money," he said, "but they haven't really asked about it and I haven't volunteered it. It may come up as they begin to prep her for the grand jury, but for now I think they are content to let her keep whatever she took as long as she cooperates. And they understand that I need to get paid somehow."

"Sounds like you earned your money," I said. "She stays out of prison and starts life over with three hundred grand."

"That's what I thought," he said, "but when I went to visit her a few days ago, she was having second thoughts. She'd been in jail when she was younger and wasn't looking forward to being babysat by federal marshals in a Ramada for the next year or two while the feds build a case."

"I don't like what I see coming," I said.

"It would just be for a few weeks," he said. "I'm working on an arrangement that will enable the feds to relocate her now and just bring her back when she has to testify. That has to be approved by some deputy assistant something or other at the Justice Department, and that takes time. In the meantime, I need someone to protect her from Bugg—and from herself." I let out a long sigh.

"There are people more qualified than me," I said. "Security professionals, bodyguards, retired cops." He sat up straight and looked me right in the eyes.

"I've practiced law for nearly twenty years," he said, "and I've employed a lot of those types. Most of them are dumber than shit.

You read Wittgenstein for fun and have more balls than anyone I know."

"It doesn't sound like this is going to involve much philosophical analysis," I said.

"No, but you'll be well compensated."

"How much did you have in mind?"

"I was thinking two thousand a week," he said. "And as much money as you need for expenses. She left Bugg with little more than the clothes on her back, so she'll need some new clothes and some personal items." He looked at me, waiting for an answer. His eyes give him only slightly less moral authority than the Uncle Sam portrayed in those wonderful World War I recruiting posters.

"All right," I said.

"Good."

"When do I meet her?"

"In about twenty minutes," he said. "She finished treatment this morning. My paralegal is headed over there now to pick her up."

3

THE DRIVE BACK to my mountain home was tense. Karlynn and I had not gotten off to a good start. After Matt had introduced us and told her I had recovered Prince, her first words had been "What kind of name is Pepper?" That was strike one.

"It's the name my parents gave me," I said. She sighed, then sat down in one of the chairs opposite Matt's desk and lit a cigarette without asking. That was strike two. Matt's cigar was one thing, but cigarettes were another.

Matt and I took our seats, and he explained what was happening with the feds and what my role would be. FBI agents had interviewed Karlynn at the treatment center before finalizing the immunity agreement. Those agents and federal prosecutors would question her again several times in the next few weeks, and those sessions would lay the foundation for the case against Bugg and the Sons of Satan. Her statements would provide the probable cause needed to obtain permission to install wiretaps and to subpoena bank and phone records. Then the feds would begin building a case from the bottom up. "If things go as planned," Matt told her, "you and Prince will be living a new life before the end of the year." That sounds like more than a few weeks, I thought. When it was time to seek indictments, Matt continued, the feds would bring her back to testify to a grand jury. Then they would make arrests. The first trials might not take place until a year later.

As Matt began to tell her about my background and qualifications, I sized her up. She was five-five and weighed only about 115. Blue eyes. Her breasts were disproportionately large for the rest of her sleek body. Her dark, stringy hair was of medium length. She wore tight, faded jeans, a pale yellow T-shirt with the name of a bar emblazoned across it, and black boots with spiked heels. No makeup that I could detect. About thirty-two years old, I guessed. She turned and looked at me.

"You don't look like a bodyguard," she said. I wore tan slacks, a blue oxford shirt, a navy blazer, and cordovan loafers. No tie. At five-ten and 215 pounds, I was hardly small, but nobody was mistaking me for a professional wrestler.

"Mr. Keane can handle himself," Matt assured her, "don't worry about that." He paused to make sure he had her attention. "The important thing is for you to stay drug free and to cooperate with the feds. If you screw this up, Karlynn, there's not going to be anything that I or any other attorney can do for you. Do you understand?" She nodded like a teenage girl trying to pacify her parents.

"I mean it," he said.

"I heard you," she said.

Now, as we headed west on the Boulder Turnpike in my truck, she sat in silence and smoked a cigarette. At my insistence she'd cracked her window and was holding the cancer stick up to it. I was listening to Jim Rome's nationally syndicated sports talk show. The show has a vernacular of its own, and regular listeners are referred to as "clones." I suppose I'm a clone, though I've never called the show. Much of the show consists of clones putting down other clones, and it is often downright hilarious. Currently we were listening to Roger in Buffalo suggest that Clarence in

Oakland should spend less time calling the show to explain why the Raiders would win the Super Bowl, and more time looking for a job.

"Can we listen to something else?" Karlynn said. From her tone you'd have thought I'd been forcing her to listen to it for months. This is going to be a fun couple of weeks, I thought.

"Sure," I said. "Anything except rap or heavy metal." She fiddled with the radio until she found a classic rock station. Another ten minutes passed before she said anything.

"So you were in the army?" she said.

"Marines," I said.

"Same thing," she said. Ordinarily that would have been strike three, but for two thousand a week I could cut her some slack.

"No, it's not the same thing," I said. "The army fights land wars; the Marine Corps supports naval operations." She just stared out the window.

We came into Boulder on Twenty-eighth Street, and I pulled into the Boulder Mall. The indoor mall, not the one on Pearl Street. It's a dying mall, and only a few stores remain. The city of Boulder has been trying to figure out what to do with it for years, but the city council has been more concerned with human rights abuses in Tibet and making sure the rest of the world knows that Boulder is a nuclear-free zone than it has been with sales tax revenue. "What are we doing here?" she asked.

"Shopping," I said. "This is where you get your clothes and whatever else you need." I found a space, put the truck in park, and cut the engine.

"I don't need anything," she said.

"Look," I said, "I live in a house two miles out of a small town, and it's a town a lot of your biker friends like to visit when things get a little dull back at the old amphetamine ranch. You're not going to be able to waltz into town whenever you need a carton of cigarettes or some Tampax."

"Fuck," she said. She opened the door, got out, and slammed it shut. I shook my head.

"You might want to buy some hair dye, too," I said. "Bugg and his goons are looking for you."

We entered the mall through the Foley's entrance. Foley's is a department store once known as May D&F. I think the "D&F" stood for "dry goods and furnishings," but that's just a guess. It might have stood for "downtown and freakin' expensive." Though it was still a few days before Thanksgiving, the store had its Christmas face on. Fake pine trees adorned with bells and tinsel were strategically positioned, each with colorful packages beneath it. Karlynn went straight to the lingerie section and I followed. She began sifting through a bin of pastel panties as I stood watch. "Do you have to watch me buy underwear?" she said.

"Part of the job."

"Try not to enjoy it too much," she said.

When she'd finished in lingerie, I followed her through the store as she selected jeans, shirts, and a few personal items. I paid for everything. Matt had given me ten thousand in cash. When we finally went to pay for her purchases, the cashier thought we were married and told me I would receive a free set of perfume and lotion for my wife if I opened a charge account. "We won't be together much longer," I said.

By the time she had finished shopping, it was nearly one and I was hungry. "Want something to eat?" I asked.

"I'm not hungry," she said.

"Mind if I hit the food court?"

"Whatever," she said. I started walking in that direction. She waited a moment, then ran as best she could in her boots until she was beside me. I carried several shopping bags in my left hand, leaving my right hand free in case I needed my Glock. She carried the third bag. The food court was surprisingly busy given that few stores remained at the mall, but I found an empty booth and placed the bags on one of the benches. She followed suit.

The rectangular food court had once boasted a dozen vendors, but competition from a newer mall in nearby Broomfield had taken its toll. The Broomfield City Council does not care about Tibet or nuclear weapons. There were now only three vendors, the other spaces boarded up. I handed Karlynn a twenty and told her to get whatever she wanted. I got in the pizza line, ordered two slices with mushrooms and a large diet Coke. When I returned to our table, she was not there. I slowly scanned the area until I'd turned 360 degrees, but she was nowhere to be seen. Damn, I thought, I'm going to have to be more careful.

I set my food down and began walking the perimeter of the food court. I checked all three establishments. Just when I was really starting to worry, I saw her walking down a long passageway toward me. She'd been using the restroom. She saw the look on my face.

"You think I took off on you?" she asked. I studied her face and manner, but she showed no signs of drug use.

"That crossed my mind," I said. "I told you to get some food; I didn't tell you to go to the bathroom."

"I don't need your permission to take a piss," she said.

"No, but you need me to protect you from Bugg and his scum-bag friends, and I can't do it if I don't know where you are." We started walking toward our table. She stopped at the Greek place, purchased a gyro and an orange soda.

We sat across from each other, not saying much. "You married?" she finally said.

"No."

"Kids?"

"No."

"Girlfriend?"

"More or less."

"She live with you?"

"No."

"How's she gonna feel about me staying at your place?"

"That's a damn good question," I said. Fortunately, Jayne Smyers, PhD, associate professor of mathematics at the University of Colorado, was in the middle of a nine-month stint teaching fractal geometry at Peking University and wouldn't be returning until Christmas, at which time we hoped to share ten wonderful days with each other. Peking University is in Beijing, which was known as Peking until the 1980s, when translators began using the pinyin system of romanization of Chinese. For reasons unknown they still call it Peking University rather than Beijing University. Maybe the person in charge of the university was a 270-pound cigar-smoking Chinese man who didn't want to have to pay some fucker to design a new logo.

"What about you?" I said to Karlynn. "What's your story?" She said nothing, didn't even look at me. "I was just making conversation," I said. "If you don't want to talk, that's fine."

"There's nothing to tell," she said. "I left McCook, Nebraska, the day I graduated from high school, and took the bus to Omaha. I met Thad in Sturgis seven years ago and I've been with him ever since. Then the feds came after me, and you know the rest of the story."

"You left him after one visit from the FBI," I said. "I think you already had one foot out the door." She lit a cigarette, then pursed her lips and released a stream of smoke with the expertise of a woman who'd been smoking a long time.

"He's a prick," she said. "I loved him once, or thought I did, but the gang is everything to him now." I nodded. "He drinks too much. Stays out for weeks. Treats me like shit."

"He beat you?" I asked. In the light of the food court I had noticed some faint yellow discoloration beside her left eye. She ignored the question, and I went back to work on one of my pizza slices.

"He didn't used to," she finally said. I sensed she felt shame for letting him treat her that way.

"He beat you a lot?" I asked.

"Can we talk about something else?"

"Sure," I said. "You have any family?"

"There's another great topic," she said. She took a drag on her cigarette, this time releasing the smoke more slowly. "My brother Lyle is doing twenty to life in Lincoln for second-degree murder." She put the cigarette down and resumed eating.

"That's it?"

"Christ," she said, "you're as bad as the feds. My mom was a drunk and died of cirrhosis. My dad still lives in McCook, I guess, but I haven't seen him in years and I hope I never see his sorry ass again." I took the hint, finished my second slice of pizza, and began getting ready to leave.

"Oh, shit," she said. She turned her head away from the food court entrance so that she was facing the wall on the closed side of our booth.

"What?"

"That man over there. That's Anvil. He's one of Thad's enforcers." I looked toward the entrance and saw a bearish man. He stood six-four and must've weighed 260. His complexion was ruddy and pockmarked. About thirty years old. His scraggly red-blond hair reached nearly to his shoulders. He wore black boots and a black leather jacket with the Sons of Satan emblem across the back. He had a slight beer belly, but a belt made of bicycle chain prevented his tattered jeans from slipping too far down.

"Did he see you?" I asked.

"I think so," she said. She was using her soft drink cup to shield her face from him.

"I'll take care of it," I said. "If something happens, grab the bags and walk—don't run—to the truck. I'll meet you there." I turned to look at the man. He looked right at me and began walking deliberately in our direction.

"Be careful," she said. "He's crazy."

Now he was at our table. "Well, looky here," he said in a deep and gravelly voice, "Bugg's gonna be real happy when I tell him I saw his little whore having lunch with a cop." What can I say? People see my dark, closely cropped hair and my thick build, and they think I'm a cop. She lowered her cup and glared at him.

"He's not a cop, Anvil," she said, "so go away."

"Is that your real name," I said, "or just a nickname?" He ignored me and glared back at Karlynn. "The reason I ask," I said, "is that I'm kind of interested in how people get their names."

"Nobody's talkin' to you," he said.

"I mean, was your father a blacksmith or something—"

"Go away, Anvil," Karlynn repeated. He leaned over, placed his beefy hands on the table, and looked at me. It was hard to miss the "SPD" tattoo on his wrist.

"You the guy that took Bugg's mutt?" he whispered. "Cuz if you are, Bugg's paying five large to the man who ices you."

"Of course, sometimes a cobbler will use an anvil," I said. "Was your father a cobbler?"

"You're real funny, mister," he said. "Maybe I'll just kill you right here." He opened his jacket to reveal a large knife in a leather sheath attached to his belt.

"I doubt it," I said. I opened my blazer to reveal my Glock 17. "See ya around, Anvil," I said.

He took a few steps back, then pointed his index finger at Karlynn and said, "You're dead, bitch."

4

WE ARRIVED AT MY HOME at midafternoon. Buck and Wheat greeted us at the door. Prince started barking as soon as we entered. Karlynn ignored my dogs, followed Prince's voice straight to the basement, and began stroking his head. Then she knelt down and caressed his floppy ears as he joyfully licked her face. It was a side of her I hadn't seen.

"He needs to go out," she said.

"Just for a minute," I said. "I don't want my neighbors knowing I've acquired another dog."

"What neighbors?" she said. I live in a log home a few miles out of Nederland, on the edge of the Roosevelt National Forest. Three thousand square feet on an acre lot. Nederland, population 1,894, is seventeen miles west of and three thousand feet above Boulder. My nearest neighbors, a pair of aging hippies named Luther and Missy, live a few hundred yards west of me in an old summer cabin they have converted into a year-round residence. We are separated by a fair number of pines and aspens, so it's easy to accept the illusion of privacy, but they share the house with others, and the composition of the group is constantly changing. I never know when one of them might light up a joint and go for a walk. And there are plenty of other homes hidden behind the trees in the mountains surrounding Ned. Not to mention hikers, hunters, fishermen, skiers, campers, miners, squatters, fugitives, and some dreadlock-wearing kids who call themselves "The Rainbow People."

"There are more people up here than you think," I said, "and word spreads fast in a small town." I walked upstairs and they followed me to the back door. "Will he stay near the house," I asked, "or should I tie him to something?"

"He won't run away," she said. I opened the door and let all three dogs out. We watched Prince bound among the trees for a moment. He was a well-muscled hound, about eighty pounds, with plenty of black or blue specks adorning the white areas on his back, ears, and sides. His head and ears were predominantly black. There were patches of tan over his eyes and on his cheeks. After a few minutes I opened the door and Prince trotted up to it, so I let him in, leaving Buck and Wheat to play outside. "I'm so glad you got him," she said.

"Is he really a champion?" I asked.

"Sure is," she said. "He won awards for tracking, too."

"Because it didn't look to me like he was living the life of a champion," I said.

"I bought him as a present for Thad," she sighed. "About two years ago. From a breeder in Arkansas. Thad grew up in Arkansas and was always going on about getting a bluetick coonhound and hunting raccoons like when he was a kid. So I bought him a dog that had been trained by a professional. Cost me fifteen hundred bucks." She stopped, but I got the impression she hadn't finished what she had started to say.

"And?"

"And," she said, "Thad takes him hunting now and then, and sometimes they enter tracking competitions, but other than that, Thad doesn't pay much attention to him."

"The dog's been neglected," I said. "A short-haired hound like that shouldn't be kept outside in the winter, not in this climate. He shouldn't be chained up with no room to run. And he should have fresh water; the water in Prince's bowl was frozen solid."

"I know," she said. "It made me sad, the way he treated Prince. In his own way he loves Prince, but that's how he was raised. If the dog's not helping you hunt or track or do some chore on the farm, you chain him up and forget about him." I said nothing, but she knew I had something on my mind. "What?" she demanded.

"Nothing," I said.

"No, what?"

"You didn't mind that he was a murdering drug dealer, but you didn't like the way he treated the dog?"

"Jesus Christ," she shot back, "I don't need you to judge me. I can get that from the feds." I started back to the living room. "I've been doped up for seven years," she added, "so give me a break."

"All right," I said, "forget I mentioned it. Let me show you around." I gave her a tour of my home, showed how the kitchen was organized, taught her how to work the remote, then led her upstairs to the guest bedroom and let her dump her belongings. "There's a bathroom in there," I said. "If you need anything, let me know." I left her there and went to my study on the main floor.

I hadn't held a salaried job since leaving the practice of law, but I kept busy. I did investigative work for my former law partners and most anyone else who could pay me. I worked out every day, spent time at my brother's gym in Denver, read lots of philosophy in an attempt to make some sense of this thing we call life, and sometimes showed up at a karate class taught by my best friend, an unemployed astrophysicist named Scott McCutcheon.

I sat at my desk and pondered what to do. The Anvil incident concerned me because word would be out that Karlynn was still in the area and keeping company with a man matching my description. We were lucky it hadn't happened in Nederland. Once they knew I lived up here, it wouldn't be hard to find me.

I picked up the phone and dialed Matt. A woman answered and told me he was in a meeting. I asked her to interrupt. My need to speak with him was not urgent, but I abhor phone tag. After thirty seconds of elevator music, Matt came on the line.

"We need to revisit the money issue," I deadpanned.

"A deal is a deal," he shot back. "You're stuck with her. The two of you having fun?"

"Yeah, she's a laugh a minute," I said. "I pull you away from something important?"

"No, what can I do for you?"

"After helping Ms. Slade buy lingerie this afternoon," I said, "I had the pleasure of meeting a gentleman named Anvil. Anvil is an acquaintance of Mr. Bugg, and he told us Mr. Bugg is most unhappy with Ms. Slade. He also indicated Mr. Bugg has put a five-thousand-dollar bounty on the head of the gentleman responsible for stealing his canine companion. I'm paraphrasing, of course, but I thought it might be prudent to ask you for copies of any documents in your possession pertaining to Anvil or Bugg or the Sons of Satan."

"You done?" he asked.

"Yes."

"Because that was entertaining. If you've got more, I want to hear it. It beats the hell out of going over tax returns with the IRS."

"I'm afraid that was it," I said.

"Okay," he said. "The answer to your question is that prior to finalizing an agreement on behalf of Ms. Slade, I insisted—as any competent attorney would—that the feds provide me with sufficient documentation to convince me they had a case against her. I'll have a courier deliver copies to you tomorrow."

"Tomorrow's Thanksgiving," I said.

"Friday, then."

"Okay," I said.

"I don't know how much it will help," he said. "Most of the reports I have pertain only to Karlynn and the prostitution operation. You can't show them to her, by the way. That would contaminate her testimony. She has to testify from her own personal knowledge. The feds don't want some slick half-Jewish defense lawyer arguing she was just parroting what she'd read in their files." It was a rare example of Matt making an attempt at humor. Self-deprecating humor in this instance. His father was Jewish and his mother a Baptist from Alabama. Or as Matt likes to say, he's half Elijah, half *Kaw*liga. Elijah, for those who don't know, was a Jewish prophet, and Kawliga was a wooden Indian made famous by Hank Williams.

"I understand," I said.

"Hey, before I hang up, what kind of shape is Anvil in?"

"It didn't come to that," I said. "Anvil's cards weren't very good. He decided to fold and play another day."

"You take care," he said.

"Roger that," I said.

It wasn't quite time for dinner, so I picked up a book I'd been reading, leaned back in my chair, and put my feet up on the desk. Presently I was working my way through *Zen and the Art of Motorcycle Maintenance*, by Robert Pirsig. I'd read it many times before, but it's a wonderful examination of philosophy and well worth rereading every few years. Philosophy had interested me since college, and I had even tried graduate school for a year.

Later, when I left the practice of law, one of my goals was to study the entire history of philosophy from pre-Socratic Greece right up to the twentieth century. I attained that goal, though by the time I got up to American pragmatism I had forgotten what distinguished the stoics from the epicureans. That's one of the dangers of studying philosophy. You're never quite done.

I heard water running and assumed Karlynn was taking a shower. Sometime after five she and Prince wandered into my office. She wore a new pair of jeans and what sure as hell looked like one of my size 44 white cotton T-shirts. Her hair looked a little less stringy, and I could see how she might make it into the "good-looking" category with a little bit of effort. "I'm bored," she said.

"My job is to protect you, not entertain you."

"Whatcha reading?" she asked as if I'd said nothing. I held up the book so she could see its title.

"I didn't know you were into bikes," she said.

"It's not about bikes," I said. "It's about values."

"Oh."

"If you see one you like," I said, "feel free." Two of the walls in my study are lined with books, mostly books on philosophy and some fiction by authors such as Edward Abbey and Thomas McGuane. She glanced at a few of the titles, then scanned the rest of the office. It's only about two hundred square feet, but it's more than adequate. I'd furnished it with a mahogany desk and added color by creating a cactus garden atop the matching credenza against the south window.

"You must like bears," she said. The other walls boasted several paintings of grizzly bears, including an original by Robert Bateman that I had purchased after one particularly profitable year during my legal career.

"Bears are cool," I said. "In my next life I want to be a grizzly. I want to live on the Alaskan coast and eat salmon and berries all day."

"Is that you?" she asked, pointing to a framed black-and-white photo of young Pepper in full boxing regalia. It was clear she was going to continue to make conversation, so I put the book down.

"That's me," I said. She moved closer to the photo. Beneath the photos on a small silver band, was an inscription: "Capt. Pepper Keane—Heavyweight Champion MCB Camp LeJeune for 1984. An officer AND a lawyer—who'd have thunk it?"

"Most heavyweights are taller," she said. That definitely should've been strike three, but I'd heard it so many times that I'd become more or less immune to it. She wasn't going away, so I removed my feet from my desk and stood up.

"I guess we should feed the dogs and make some dinner," I said. She followed me to the kitchen. I let Buck and Wheat in, then handed her a large metal mixing bowl and told her where the dog chow was. "I've been feeding him in the basement," I said, "so he won't fight with my dogs." While she was doing that, I ushered Buck and Wheat into the garage and fed them. Then I returned to the kitchen and started boiling water for spaghetti.

She returned from the basement and stood against the counter while I chopped tomatoes, onions, mushrooms, and garlic. "Joe Frazier is only five-ten," I said. "And Tyson isn't even six feet." She didn't respond. I melted some butter in a frying pan and slid the vegetables into it.

"You one of those men who like to cook?" she asked.

"No," I said, "I'm one of those men who like to eat." Then I opened a jar of Ragu and poured it into a large pot. I dumped some cabernet into it, then squeezed a little lemon juice into the mixture, and finished by sprinkling in some ground cinnamon and clove. "Pepper's secret recipe," I said.

After dinner we watched TV. I sat in my recliner. She and Prince sat on the couch, with Buck and Wheat on a rug near the fireplace. As best I can recall, we watched a medical drama, a legal drama, and snippets of *Scooby-Doo* during commercials. I like *Scooby-Doo*. At ten-thirty, after the sports news, I stood and announced, "I think it's time for me to hit the hay."

"Do you want some company?" she asked.

5

THE SADDEST THING was not that she had been willing to sleep with me after knowing me twelve hours, though that was sad. It was not that I had stayed up until one a.m. attempting to convince her I was not rejecting her, though that was sad, too. The saddest thing was that I had been tempted. I had a wonderful woman in my life, but I had been tempted to sleep with Karlynn Slade. Why? For the novelty of it? Simply because I was a man? Or was I subconsciously mad at Jayne because she'd opted to spend nine months teaching in the People's Republic of China? I would let those questions percolate.

Despite my lack of sleep, I woke before she did. By seven I was sipping coffee at the long oak dining table and reading the *Rocky Mountain News*. The dogs had already been out, and all three now lay beside me on the hardwood floor. The paper reminded me it was Thanksgiving, and I gave thanks I'd had the good sense not to sleep with Karlynn Slade.

Not that there was anything wrong with her body. That was fine, but there was a lot wrong with her mind. I'd spent more than two hours trying to explain that to her. "I don't think that's a good idea," I had said. I saw the hurt in her eyes as soon as I'd said it, and knew it was just a matter of time until the tears began to flow.

"Aren't you attracted to me?" she asked from her seat on the couch. A dangerous question under the best circumstances. A potentially lethal question when asked by a recovering meth addict coming off a relationship with the leader of a sadistic biker gang.

"You're very attractive," I said, "but I'm being paid to protect you."

"So?"

"I can't do that if my judgment is clouded."

"I could rock your world," she said.

"It's not hard to do," I replied.

"You think you're better than me, don't you?" Another dangerous question.

"No," I said patiently, "I don't think I'm better than you." I paused to consider my words. "I think we are two very different people. And I think you're vulnerable right now because you're under tremendous pressure. You've just spent thirty days in a treatment program and your body is still adjusting to being drug free. Your husband wants you dead and the feds are threatening you with prison unless you testify against him and give up the only life you've ever known. You're scared, and I don't blame you. It's natural to want to latch on to someone else under those circumstances."

Then the tears came. I walked over to the couch, sat down beside her, and held her hands. "I'm not a bad person," she sobbed.

"I know that," I said. "I knew that as soon as I saw you with Prince." She looked down at him and continued crying.

"My life is such a mess," she said. I walked to the bathroom and carried back a box of tissues. She took a few and wiped her eyes.

"How old are you?" I asked. "Thirty? Thirty-two? You've got your whole life ahead of you."

It had gone on like that for several hours. During that time we

talked about everything from her codependency to my career as a
Marine Corps JAG. She seemed to enjoy listening to my anec-
dotes and tales of my travels. Alaska particularly fascinated her as
I recounted an adventure that had taken Scott and me from the
rainy coastal areas in the south to the barren tundra of the North
Slope, where my seventy-year-old mother still works as a nurse
for the U.S. Public Health Service. She thought I was joking
when I told her there is a Mexican restaurant in Barrow, three
hundred miles above the Arctic Circle. I think it's called North of
the Border.

Today was a new day. She was a redhead now. She came downstairs sometime after eight wearing a pair of my gym shorts,
another one of my T-shirts, and a scowl. This vision inspired me
to start singing the theme song from *The Mary Tyler Moore Show*.
"Who can turn the world on with her smile? Who can take a
nothing date and suddenly make it all seem—"

She glared at me, and I interpreted that to mean she did not
appreciate my humor or my singing, so I stopped.

After enjoying her first cigarette of the day in my unheated
garage, she poured herself some coffee and joined me at the table.
"I never used to drink this shit until I went into treatment,"
she said.

"Coffee's a comparatively harmless addiction," I said. I had finished the paper, except the crossword puzzle, and slid the rest of
the paper over to her. I needed an eight-letter word for "coward"
and couldn't think of one.

"Is today Thanksgiving?" she asked.

"Sure is," I said.

"We should do something special."

"I promised a nephew I'd have Thanksgiving dinner with him,"
I said.

"Am I going?" she asked.

"I guess so," I said.

"You don't sound too excited," she said.

"It's not you," I said. "Nancy's kind of flighty." Last year she'd insisted on making a goose for Thanksgiving, and it had been the stringiest fowl I'd ever sampled.

"Who's Nancy?"

"My nephew's mom."

"Your sister? Or your sister-in-law?"

"Neither, she was married to my cousin."

She looked puzzled. "Then he's not really your nephew," she said. "He's your second cousin."

"I know," I said, "but I call him my nephew because he's only fourteen."

"So Nancy was married to your cousin?"

"Yeah."

"They're divorced?"

"My cousin's dead," I said.

"Oh." I told her the short version. My cousin, Hal Keane, had been a high school chemistry teacher, a football coach, and a reserve officer with the Denver Police Department. He had died four years ago in a gun battle with a couple of punks he'd caught pistol-whipping a Nigerian immigrant. My brother and I had been close to Hal during our youth, when we had lived within a few miles of each other, but we'd drifted apart as we'd grown older and fashioned our own lives. I didn't even know he'd been a police officer until after his death.

Nancy had been a guidance counselor most of her adult life, but she'd earned a master's degree in social work after Hal's death and moved from Denver to Boulder more than a year ago. Since then I'd taken on the role of an uncle to their son, Jimmie.

I walked to the kitchen, poured myself another cup of coffee, and resumed my seat at the table.

"Tell me about Bugg," I said.

"What do you want to know?"

"Does he have any family?" She allowed a bitter smile.

"The gang is his family."

"Aside from that?"

"He's got a brother in Arkansas—Tommy. They don't see each other much, but they talk on the phone every week." She sipped her coffee. "He's got an ex-wife named Linda out in California somewhere."

"Any kids?"

"He had some kids with Linda, but he doesn't have any contact with them. They're probably in their twenties by now."

"Poltroon," I said. The puzzle master would have to do better than that to stump Pepper Keane.

"Huh?"

"An eight-letter word for 'coward,'" I explained.

"Oh," she said.

"What does Bugg do for fun?" I asked.

"You mean, like, hobbies?"

"Yeah."

"I'd list drinking as number one," she said.

"Anything else?"

"I don't know," she said. "He likes the outdoors. Hunting, fishing, tracking—all that shit. I hate that whole mountain-man thing, but he knows these mountains inside and out. He's big into survivalism, too; he's got a generator and a six-month food supply in his basement. He even has food, weapons, and money hidden all around the West in case he ever has to make a run for it." I studied the crossword and sipped my coffee.

"Does he have any ties to the White Power movement?" I asked.

"Not really," she said.

"What about Anvil?"

"Anvil hates everybody," she said.

"I heard some of the Sons of Satan were big into White Power."

"A few of the guys talk about it," she said, "but they're not, like, skinheads or anything." I nodded.

"Bugg have any skinhead friends?"

"I wouldn't call them friends," she said.

"He does business with them?"

"Sometimes."

"Drugs?" I asked. She nodded.

"Some of them buy their shit from us," she said, "and sell it to their crowd." The "us" bothered me, but she'd been shacked up with the gang's leader for seven years, and I supposed the Sons of Satan had been her only family.

"He do any other business with them?" I asked. She stared at the table and said nothing. I had struck a nerve.

"Tell me," I said. "Please."

"They do some of the dirty work," she said, still looking down.

"Dirty work?" Now she looked right at me.

"Like when Thad wants someone killed or roughed up."

"Why do the Sons of Satan need outside help?" I asked.

"They don't," she said, "but Thad thinks it's safer. He used to say, 'Why put a brother at risk when I can pay a skinhead five hundred bucks to off someone?'" I watched as she walked to the refrigerator and retrieved a carton of milk for her coffee. My shorts definitely looked better on her. "One time he paid them to beat up a Mexican who fucked up his bike," she said as she resumed her seat. I asked her to elaborate. Bugg had taken a vintage Harley to a repair shop. The kid working on it had accidentally scratched the paint. "Why are you asking me all these questions about skinheads?" she asked.

"No reason," I said. "I'm just trying to learn about Bugg and his crew." I didn't tell her that skinheads had killed my cousin. He'd killed one with his pistol, but the other—the one who'd shot him—had somehow avoided capture and disappeared. One day later an anonymous man telephoned a local radio station, claiming he was responsible for the killings. He said my cousin's death should serve as a warning to white cops that protect niggers and faggots. Four years had passed and the authorities had all but given up.

6

THANKSGIVING AT NANCY's was about what I'd expected. She'd invited a few others to her Boulder home, but I'd never met any of them. Two of the guests were female therapists who rent space in the building where her office is located. One was in her late thirties and looked a little like a young Jaclyn Smith; she was tall and had long, dark hair punctuated with just two or three strands of gray. She wore tailored black linen slacks and a sheer white blouse. Her makeup was perfect. She said her name was Kendra Carlson. The other therapist was younger and plain-looking. Her name was Charlene, but everyone called her Charly.

Then Nancy introduced a lady from the neighborhood and her two young sons. Both boys had blond hair and looked to be four or five years old. There was a bookish, mildly attractive young blonde woman who said little. Nancy said she was "a friend," and I suspected she was one of Nancy's clients. Or maybe a lonely heart from Nancy's Unity church. The only other man was a chiropractor in his mid-forties who appeared to be Nancy's current love interest. He was tall and thin but lacked muscle tone. His light brown hair was starting to recede. His name was Tim.

Karlynn Slade looked out of place in her tight jeans, pink T-shirt, and black leather boots. I noticed a small turquoise heart tattooed on the inside of her left wrist. Nancy was dying of curiosity. "Who *is* she?" she'd asked after cornering me in the kitchen. Nancy is about five-six and stays in shape playing tennis. She looked good in her red corduroy dress. "Did you and Jayne have a falling-out?"

"I thought you'd be more supportive, Nancy," I said. She punched me on the shoulder.

"Who *is* she?" she repeated. I gave in to a little smile.

"She's a lady with a checkered past," I said. "I'm babysitting her until the U.S. Marshals can set her up in the Witness Protection Program." She studied my eyes to determine whether I was joking.

"You could've warned me," she said.

"I should have canceled," I said, "but I wanted to see Jimmie. I'm sorry." She rolled her eyes, then picked up a tray of vegetables and carried it to the living room, where she had assembled an array of munchies for her guests to enjoy while awaiting the Thanksgiving feast.

I decided to have a drink, but though Nancy's refrigerator contained a variety of new age beverages, it contained no Coke. I made myself a rum and organic cola, which was the best I could do under the circumstances, then moseyed into the living room. The two therapists were talking with each other, using terms such as "inner child" and "creative self." The quiet blonde was with them, looking interested but saying little. The neighbor kept asking Nancy if she needed any help. The little boys played with Lego blocks. Karlynn sipped ginger ale and studied the many knickknacks Nancy had collected over the years. The chiropractor stayed close to Nancy. Jimmie came down from his bedroom and stuck to me. I sat down on the oversize beige sofa, picked up the remote, and clicked on the TV. The Lions were playing somebody in a game that had NFC playoff implications.

"Your mom dating him?" I asked my nephew. Jimmie sat down beside me.

"Sort of," he said. He wore a Broncos cap—backwards of course—but I saw strands of his thin, dark hair beneath it.

"You like him?"

"He's okay, I guess," Jimmie said. "He's not into sports, though." In addition to teaching chemistry, Jimmie's dad had coached football, and Jimmie had been raised to love sports. He played running back on the freshman football team and planned to go out for baseball in the spring.

"Sports aren't everything," I said. "If he's good to your mom, that's what counts." He nodded like a boy is supposed to when an uncle imparts wisdom. He's tall for his age, but thin like his mom.

"Is that your new girlfriend?" he asked, pointing to Karlynn. Now she was studying the books in Nancy's bookcase.

"Not exactly," I said.

"Who is she?"

"You promise not to tell?"

"Sure."

"Her husband is the leader of a motorcycle gang. She's paying me to protect her."

"Really?"

"Honest injun," I said.

"Wow."

After a half-hour or so, Nancy announced, "Dinner is served." Everyone filtered into the dining room and took seats around the highly polished rectangular walnut table. I sat at one end of the table, with Jimmie to my right and Karlynn to my left. The chiropractor sat at the other end. Nancy made several trips from the kitchen, finally sashaying back in carrying a colorful tray bearing what appeared to be Cornish game hens.

Nancy asked Tim to give a blessing, and to his credit it was mercifully short. I smiled as I remembered a prayer Scott Mc-Cutcheon had taught me. He liked to say, "The Lord giveth, and the Lord taketh away. And if that ain't a square deal you can kiss my ass."

We began passing trays of food around the table. Aside from the birds, there was stuffing, green bean casserole, cranberry-orange salad, candied yams, and fresh sourdough bread with real butter. Short conversations erupted and evolved. When a topic had been exhausted, Nancy would say something to start a new conversation. The good-looking therapist kept eyeing me, wondering what I was doing with someone like Karlynn. "What do you do, Pepper?" she finally asked.

"Little bit of everything," I said.

"A man of mystery," she replied. "Tell me more." She conversed with the enthusiasm of a woman who'd just finished a *Cosmo* article on how to snag a man by focusing the conversation on him.

"You won't get much out of him," Nancy teased. "He's not very talkative."

"I used to practice law," I said, "but I got burned out."

"Well, you're much too young to be retired," she said playfully.

"I stay busy," I said.

"Doing what?" she asked. Mostly dognapping, I thought.

"I do some consulting," I said, "and odd jobs here and there." She possessed a wide mouth, like Julia Roberts, and her smile betrayed lots of white teeth.

"He's a private investigator," Jimmie said.

"Eat your beans," I said.

"So," the good-looking therapist said, "you chose to leave a profession that is highly regulated and requires long hours in favor of one that allows you to make your own rules and set your own schedule." I sort of smiled because she had hit the nail right on the head. Or at least one of the nails.

"Don't try to analyze him," Nancy teased. "You'll learn more than you ever wanted to know about Western philosophy and you'll lay awake at night pondering free will versus determinism or some such thing."

I looked at Nancy and sipped the last of my drink. "It's an important issue," I said with a straight face. "For instance, did you choose not to keep any Coke in the house so that I would have to mix my rum with this foo-foo organic cola, or did the big bang set in motion an unalterable chain of events that made any other outcome impossible?"

"You know," Nancy said to me, "you're not nearly as funny as you think you are."

I laughed, and since it appeared everyone had finished eating, I started clearing the dishes. When Nancy got me alone in the kitchen, she mentioned that the good-looking therapist had been Miss North Dakota about twenty years ago. "The fairest maiden in Grand Forks," I said.

After the pumpkin pie had been consumed, I played a few games of Battleship with Jimmie, then surrendered my seat so he could play against Tim. I claimed the empty recliner and resumed watching football, but soon fell asleep.

Karlynn and I stayed until around eight and began our drive back up the mountain to Nederland. It was dark and the truck was cold. She lit a cigarette and cracked her window.

"You liked that woman, didn't you?" she asked.

"Which one?"

"You know which one."

"I told you, I already have a girlfriend."

"The one that left you?"

"She didn't leave me," I insisted. "She took a sabbatical so she could teach in China for a year."

"You like the brainy ones, don't you?" I didn't answer. It was another one of those dangerous questions. If I said yes, that would launch her into "I'm not smart enough for you." If I said no, I'd be lying. The truck had been running for several minutes, so I turned on the heat. "I don't think she's your type," Karlynn continued.

"Why not?" I didn't think Karlynn Slade knew me well enough to decide what my type was, but I wanted her opinion just for the entertainment value.

"She's too high-maintenance," she said. "I'll bet it took her twenty minutes to get her makeup on." She turned away and blew some smoke toward the open window.

We drove on in silence. When we were halfway up the mountain, snowflakes began to descend and I shifted into four-wheel drive. Karlynn continued staring out the window, evidently deep in thought.

We arrived home before nine, but it was eleven on the East Coast and too late to call Jayne. We entered my home and found all three dogs waiting at the door with their tails wagging. Karlynn let them out while I went to my study to check my messages. There was only one. I hit Play. A male voice said, "Hey, this is— uh—Thad Bugg over in Ward. I need to hire a private dick. Gimme a call at four five nine three two nine nine."

7

I PRETENDED TO GO to bed at ten-thirty. I followed my usual nightly ritual. Changed into boxers and a T-shirt. Brushed my fangs. Washed my face. Swallowed a rust-colored pill containing one hundred milligrams of an antidepressant known as imipramine. Then climbed into bed with Buck and Wheat. Buck turned around three times and flopped down on my left. Little Wheat licked my face, then curled up beside me on my right.

When I was certain Karlynn was asleep, I got out of bed, walked down to the kitchen, and made some hot tea with lemon. Then I went to my study to think it through. The first question I asked myself was how Bugg had obtained my name. I'm not listed in the Yellow Pages. Either it was a setup or he'd seen one of the business cards I'd posted on bulletin boards in gas stations and mini-marts along the Peak-to-Peak Highway, from the casino-infested towns of Black Hawk and Central City in the south to the remote towns of Jamestown and Allenspark in the north. But for it to be a setup, he'd have to know I was protecting Karlynn. And he had no way of knowing that. Except maybe for Anvil. I was fairly confident Anvil had not seen Karlynn and me enter my truck; I'd been careful about that. If Anvil hadn't seen us enter my truck, he couldn't have obtained my plate number.

Without my plate number he couldn't have learned my name. Karlynn had told him I was not a cop, so he might've suspected I was an investigator, but that alone would not have helped him much—there are hundreds of people calling themselves investigators in the Denver and Boulder phone books. I wasn't certain, but for the time being I accepted the proposition that Bugg's call was legitimate.

The next question was why Bugg wanted to hire me. Was it to find Karlynn, the dog, or both? Or something else altogether? The only way to know was to call him. The safe bet was to ignore him, but he'd surely hire someone else—and that could be a problem for me. A big problem. I didn't need anyone roaming around Boulder County asking questions about Karlynn or a bluetick coonhound. I had to call him.

The final question was whether I could use this to my advantage. The answer was obvious. It was an opportunity to learn what he knew about Karlynn and the dog. With a little luck, I'd pick up some information that might help the feds put Bugg and the Sons of Satan away. On top of that, I could probably take Bugg for five or ten grand in cash without lifting a finger.

That night I had another dream about Joy. Joy was a law school classmate I had lived with for several years, but she had died in a freak auto accident before graduation. I still carried a torch for her, even though she'd been dead more than twenty years. In the dream we were walking through a ritzy shop, looking at extravagant china and crystal. She would see a piece she liked, pick it up and examine it, then put it down and look for another. She bought one and we drove away in a Ford Taurus.

I woke up early Friday, made coffee, then read the paper at the dining table. I wore my usual morning attire: a white T-shirt, tan shorts, and my Adidas flip-flops. It was cold and windy outside but toasty inside. Prince was on the floor beside me, gnawing on a bone. Buck and Wheat were curled up near the fireplace. I tried to remember the details of my dream and interpret it, but I could make no sense of it. In fact, I was pretty sure Ford hadn't introduced the Taurus (or its cousin, the Mercury Sable) until several years after Joy's death.

At eight I phoned Matt and told him about the phone message from Bugg and what I was thinking. "Don't do it," he said. "The feds don't need your help. They'll have boatloads of evidence by the time this thing comes down."

"Is there any legal reason I can't do it?" I asked.

"For starters," he said, "you'd be guilty of criminal fraud. You'd be taking Bugg's money under false pretenses. He could press charges. Or sue you."

"He'll be in prison," I said. "Besides, I have a hunch he's a big believer in 'alternative dispute resolution.'" Matt was not amused.

"Karlynn could sue you, too," he added. "If something goes wrong and she gets hurt, she'd blame you. She'd say it was a major-league conflict of interest, and she'd be right."

"Only if I really intended to do what Bugg wants me to do," I said.

"What about Anvil?" he said.

"He could be a problem," I admitted.

"And what about Karlynn? Who's going to watch her while you're meeting Bugg?"

"I've got a friend who can help," I said. "Scott McCutcheon. Former Navy SEAL. Fifth-degree black belt." There was a long silence.

"You really gonna do this?" he asked.

"My inner child is telling me I have to," I said.

"Can I do anything?"

"Don't tell the feds," I said. "If I give them information, it's going to be my decision."

"Fuck," he said. "Be careful."

Karlynn wandered downstairs sometime before nine and poured the last of the coffee into one of the colorful mugs I keep in the kitchen. I'd purchased eight ceramic mugs while visiting my mom in Alaska, and each displayed a colorful Inupiat design. She wore a pair of cutoff jeans and one of my long-sleeve oxford shirts. My closet was apparently her closet. She looked a little down. "Something wrong?" I asked as she sat down across from me.

"Aside from the fact that I have no life?"

"Karlynn," I said, "I can't imagine what you're going through, but I'm sure it's stressful. The unknown always is. You'll get past it."

"I just don't want to spend the rest of my life waiting tables in a city I've never seen."

"Think of it as an opportunity," I said. "You said your life was a mess. This is a chance to start over. You don't have to do drugs or run a prostitution ring or hang out with men that beat you. You can try different things, find out what interests you, maybe go back to school. Start a family, if that's what you want."

"Who'd be interested in me?" she replied. I'm not a psychologist, but I had worked with hundreds of young men and women in the Marine Corps—many from families on the lower end of the socioeconomic ladder—and I felt sure Karlynn had a self-esteem problem. I told her so and suggested she might take advantage of our time together by contacting a therapist. She had plenty of time and money, and I told her I'd be happy to drive her to as many appointments as she wanted to schedule. "I'll think about it," she said.

Just then Prince raised his head. He looked alert. He raced to the bay window in the living room and began barking wildly, as if a regiment of raccoons had just marched past, all flipping him the bird in unison. I stood up, grabbed my Glock from the counter, and walked to the window. Karlynn looked to me for instructions. "Just stay put a minute," I said. A small pickup was making its way up the dirt driveway. There was a logo on the driver's side, but I didn't recognize it and couldn't read the writing. I saw one man in it—a young white man with short hair.

As the truck neared the house, I was able to read the writing beneath the logo: "A-1 Courier Service." The driver parked the truck and got out, holding a large padded envelope. The truck had commercial plates. I laid the pistol down on the end table beside the couch and went to the door. "You Mr. Keane?" the man asked. Upon closer inspection of his haircut I noticed a rattail hanging from the back of his neck. He seemed surprised I was in shorts.

"Yup," I said. He handed me a large padded envelope, then held out a clipboard and showed me where to sign. The label on the package told me it was from Keane, Simms & Mercante. Then I remembered, Matt had promised to send copies of the FBI materials the feds had provided.

"What is it?" Karlynn asked.

"Just a book I ordered," I said. "I'd forgotten about it." I took the package to my study and placed it in one of my desk drawers. Then I walked back to the kitchen. "I guess I'll take a shower and get dressed," I said. "Then I've got a little work to do in my office."

"I don't know what to do," she said. She sounded like a fourth-grader trapped inside on a rainy day.

"Why don't you make a list of all the things you've never done that you would like to do?" I suggested.

"What good would that do?"

"Sometimes it helps to write goals down," I said. "That's what all the success gurus say."

"Do you?" she asked.

"Sort of," I said. "About fifteen years ago I made a list of one hundred things I'd like to do during my life." I realized my mistake too late.

"Can I see it?" she asked. What the hell, I thought.

"Sure," I said. I retrieved the list from my desk and handed it to her, then went upstairs to shower. By the time I was dressed, Karlynn had gone back to her room. I heard the sink running and assumed she was washing her face or brushing her teeth. I went into my study and locked the door. Then I removed the package from the drawer and sat at my desk.

The first document was a memo from Matt to me on the firm's white linen letterhead:

FROM: Matt Simms
TO: Pepper Keane
RE: Thadeus Bugg and the Sons of Satan

As you requested, I have enclosed copies of all documents in my possession pertaining to Ms. Slade's case and the Sons of Satan.

After speaking with the U.S. Attorney and the agents in charge of the investigation, my impression is that the feds are focusing on three things in connection with Bugg. First, they believe he played a role in the death of an African-American ATF agent in Lander, Wyoming, last May. That agent, Steve Lowell, had been investigating a Sons of Satan chapter in central Wyoming in connection with some explosives stolen from one of the ski areas in Jackson Hole. (The ski areas use explosives to trigger avalanches before some bonehead skis into a high-risk area and causes one.) They found Lowell's body in a wilderness area up there. The coroner said he'd been beaten to death with a blunt object.

The second prong of their investigation is the Rankin murder we talked about. Rankin was a small-time hood and a probationary member of the Sons of Satan. Two years ago a Denver police officer stopped him for a traffic offense, ran a check, and found out there was a federal warrant out for him on a credit card fraud charge. Rankin immediately offered to help the feds nail Bugg and his gang on drug charges in return for a walk on the fraud charge. The feds agreed and released him on a $10,000 bond so he could return to the gang. Bugg arranged for a bondsman to post bond. Rankin was found dead the next day. The feds think Bugg somehow found out about Rankin's plans and had him killed, but it's possible the gang killed him as a precautionary measure. Or not at all, though that seems unlikely.

The third focus of the investigation concerns the gang's production and distribution of methamphetamine as well as their involvement in distributing other drugs. The FBI believes Bugg is a major regional supplier, but they haven't been able to get any help on that from anyone in the Sons of Satan organization. They are counting on Karlynn to change that.

Bugg has a lengthy criminal history, and I have enclosed a copy of that. He has not been convicted of anything serious in more than ten years, but he served thirty days last summer on a DUI charge. The feds interviewed his cellmates, but that didn't produce any leads.

With respect to Karlynn, I have enclosed copies of all FBI 302's pertaining to her. Most of these are summaries of interviews with women who engaged in prostitution for the gang. I've also enclosed a copy of Karlynn's criminal history.

I hope this helps. I wish I had more for you. If you want some general information about motorcycle gangs and their culture, you can find plenty on the Internet.

I had been a federal prosecutor in Denver many years ago, so I knew that Form 302 was the form FBI agents use to summarize witness interviews. The feds had interviewed seven women known to have engaged in prostitution for the gang at one time or another. They described the structure of the prostitution operation. Each woman was affiliated with a gang chapter, and the chapter was responsible for protecting her and making sure the gang got paid. Karlynn's role was to keep a stable of willing women and to serve as something of a bookkeeper. She protected Bugg's interests by making certain each chapter sent twenty percent of their prostitution revenues to him. Customers called an unlisted number and described what they wanted. That information was forwarded to Karlynn, who selected the girl, set the price, and relayed instructions to the customer. The girls and the local chapter were each supposed to receive 40 percent, though most women interviewed said it had seldom worked out that way.

Karlynn Slade's criminal history was remarkable only because it was better than I'd expected. She'd been picked up for shoplifting a couple of times before she was twenty. She'd twice been convicted of prostitution in Omaha, getting probation the first time and thirty days the second. She'd served six months on a bad-check charge at the age of twenty-five. And that was it. No felonies.

Bugg's criminal history was more interesting. The printout showed him to be forty-five years old, with more than a half-dozen aliases. The physical description listed him at five-eleven and 250 pounds. Red hair, green eyes, freckled complexion, with a long scar along his left arm and numerous identifying tattoos. Similar to the description Matt had provided when he'd first asked me to snag Prince.

He had commenced his adult criminal career at the age of eighteen in Arkansas, where he'd been arrested at various times for misdemeanors such as shoplifting, assault, obstruction of a police officer, resisting arrest, and drunk driving. He'd served six months in the county jail, then enlisted in the Marine Corps at twenty-one. The Marine Corps wasn't as picky back then as it is today.

Upon his completion of boot camp, the Corps assigned him to Camp Pendleton, near San Diego. Less than a year later a court-martial convicted him of assaulting an officer and sentenced him to six months' confinement and a bad-conduct discharge.

He had apparently stayed in California, because the printout showed numerous arrests and convictions in that state over the next fifteen years. Many of the offenses were misdemeanors such as drunk driving, theft, and assault, but he'd served eighteen months at Folsom on a forgery charge and three years in a federal prison for interstate transportation of a stolen motor vehicle. He had once been arrested for attempted murder in Riverside, but the charge had been dismissed due to insufficient evidence. At some point he had moved to Colorado. The Boulder County sheriff had arrested him less than a year ago for assault with a deadly weapon, but the DA dropped the charge after the alleged victim refused to testify. The final entry was the drunk-driving conviction Matt had mentioned in his memo.

I placed the documents in the padded envelope and locked them in my desk drawer. I didn't know much I hadn't already known. Bugg was physically powerful, fond of alcohol, and extremely violent. I dialed his number.

8

SATURDAY MORNING. I was in the bathroom off the master bedroom. The phone rang just before seven. I ran to the bedside table, pressed the speaker button and said hello.

"Hi, sweetie," Jayne said. "Why do you have me on the speaker phone?"

"Need both hands to finish dying my hair."

"I should have known," she said. "What color are you going for?"

"Black."

"Isn't that somewhat unnecessary in that black is your natural color?"

"I've got to get rid of my stripe," I replied.

"But I like your stripe," she protested.

"Me too," I said, "but I'm meeting someone in a few hours and the stripe has to be gone."

"Why?"

"Because Anvil knows what I look like, and he probably told Bugg."

"Tell me you're making this up."

"It's simple," I said. "Anvil's a big goon I ran into the other day at the food court after I helped Karlynn buy lingerie. He threatened to kill me with a knife and I threatened to put seventeen rounds into his—"

"Who's Karlynn?" she demanded.

"Karlynn is Bugg's common-law wife. She's sleeping in my guest room as we speak." Stone silence. "Bugg is the leader of the Sons of Satan motorcycle gang," I continued. "Karlynn stole three hundred grand from him and I'm supposed to babysit her until the feds are ready for her to enter the Witness Protection Program."

"Is there anyone else sleeping in your house I ought to know about?"

"Not unless you count Prince."

"Who's Prince?"

"Prince is a bluetick coonhound I liberated from Bugg. I'm told he has excellent tracking skills. Karlynn won't enter the Witness Protection Program without him."

"Who are you meeting this morning?"

"Bugg."

"Why?"

"Not sure," I said. "My guess is he wants to hire me to find Karlynn."

"Oh, my God!" she exclaimed.

"But he might want me to find the person that stole his dog," I added. "According to Anvil, Bugg will pay 'five large' to whoever 'ices' the dog thief."

"Jesus," she muttered.

"I miss you," I said softly. There was a brief pause.

"I miss you, too," she said. "I'm worried about you."

"Let's have phone sex," I said. "That'll take your mind off of it."

"It's not funny," she scolded. I knew better than to say anything. She was genuinely concerned and felt I wasn't taking her concern seriously. Five very long seconds of silence passed before she said, "What did you do for Thanksgiving?"

"Took Karlynn to Nancy's house, drank rum and organic cola, ate like a pig, and fell asleep watching football."

"Did she have other people over?"

"A few, but nobody I knew," I said.

"Anyone interesting?"

"Not really," I said. "How was your Thanksgiving?"

"It was wonderful," she said. "A friend invited me to join her and we had dinner with a French couple who live in a nice home near the American Embassy. They had the cutest little girl. They adopted her from China."

"Prince is kind of cute," I said. "For a hound."

"I'm sure he is," she replied. "Is Karlynn?" This was not a direction I wanted the conversation to take.

"She's a biker chick," I said. "'Cute' is not a word you would use to describe her."

"How would you describe her?"

"She's six feet tall, weighs about two hundred pounds, no teeth," I said. Jayne laughed.

"Does she have a hump on her back?" she asked.

"Two humps," I said. "Her friends call her 'camel.'" There was another short pause.

"It's cold here," she said.

"Fifteen degrees here," I said. "And windy."

"Sometimes I fear we're growing apart," she said.

"I'm here; you're there," I said. "We're doing the best we can."

"We're talking about the weather," she pointed out.

"I'm sure even Jean-Paul Sartre and Simone de Beauvoir talked about the weather on occasion," I said.

"They never married, did they?"

"They felt it was bourgeois," I said, "but you're missing the point."

"Which is?"

"Even the strongest relationships have ups and downs, and the fact that you're on the other side of the planet doesn't help."

"Are you mad at me for leaving?"

"Maybe a little," I admitted, "but when I look at it objectively, I realize I'm being selfish."

"I'm sorry," she said.

"Don't be," I replied. "You're doing something you have always wanted to do." I paused, then added, "Hell, I'd love to live in China for a year too, but I don't speak Mandarin, and even if I did, I doubt the university offers any courses I'm qualified to teach. Imagine the things I could teach those kids in a week. The poor bastards probably don't even know who Jerry Jeff Walker is or how to throw a nice spiral."

"It's a frightening thought," she said. "I *do* love you," she added.

"I know," I said. "Enjoy your time there and don't worry about us. You'll come home for Christmas and things will be fine."

We talked another five minutes and she became more chipper as she told me about her classes, her research, and her faculty colleagues. Jayne is one of the nation's leading experts in a field known as fractal geometry—the study of irregular patterns. She loves her work. And I suppose that is one of the things I love about her.

I had met Jayne Smyers more than a year ago when she had hired me to look into the mysterious deaths of three math professors—all specialists in fractal geometry. That case, which came to be known as "the Fractal Murders," had lifted me into the upper echelon of private investigators in the region, but during the course of working for Jayne I had fallen in love with her. And being an expert in geometry, she saw the need for symmetry and so fell in love with me.

"I'm monopolizing the conversation," she said at last. Her tone was apologetic.

"I was hoping if I let you talk you'd eventually find your way back to the phone-sex thing," I said. She laughed.

"I love you," she said again. "Please be careful."

Scott McCutcheon. Unemployed astrophysicist. Former Navy SEAL. Fifth-degree black belt. One-time field goal kicker for the Colorado Buffaloes. Brad Pitt with a receding hairline. I thought about him as I sipped coffee at a small table beside the fireplace inside Nederland's Pioneer Inn this cold Saturday morning.

We'd known each other since before kindergarten, and he was still my best friend and spiritual cut man. I felt reassured knowing he was watching Karlynn while I sipped coffee in the mountain-rustic decor of the Pioneer, stared out at the falling snow, and waited for Thadeus Bugg.

I picked up a spoon and studied my reflection in the convex side of the stainless steel utensil. The stripe was gone. My hair is black, but I've always had a small tuft of white just above my right temple. It's a genetic fluke known as mosaicism, though some people call it a witch's stripe. In preparing to meet Bugg it had occurred to me that I had better rid myself of this distinctive trait. Anvil had probably told Bugg of his encounter with Karlynn and me at the mall, and in describing me the stripe would have been one of the first things he mentioned.

Bugg showed up at 8:45—fifteen minutes early. But I'd been there since 8:15 on the theory it's always best to arrive first in these situations. I had positioned myself to have a good view of the door, and there was no mistaking the leader of the pack when he walked in. He matched the description on his criminal history, except he weighed far more than two-fifty. He was fat but also big. Like a big-time fullback who had decided to live off pizza and beer for six months.

He walked in as if he owned the place, and looked around. His red hair was thick and scruffy. He had the massive head of a rottweiler, and the front of it revealed the red face of a man who knew how to drink. He wore jeans, a sweatshirt covered by a denim jacket, and steel-toed work boots. Because Nederland's winter population consists largely of telecommuting yuppies, aging hippies, and unemployed snowboarders, I was the only man in the place who looked like a former Marine JAG. I wore chinos and a cowboy's tan corduroy jacket with my Polar Bear Club patch on it. The stone fireplace provided plenty of heat, so I didn't need the jacket, but it kept the Glock out of view. Bugg saw me and walked toward my table. "You Keane?" he said.

"Yeah," I said. I extended my hand but didn't get up. He shook my hand and sat down to my left. A young waitress in dreadlocks approached us. Bugg ordered black coffee and a stack of hotcakes. I asked for a bagel with cream cheese. She poured his coffee right away, refilled mine while she was at it, then headed to the kitchen with our order.

"Fuckin' cold out," Bugg said in a gravelly voice.

"Yeah."

"This is all confidential, right?"

"Yeah." Strictly speaking, that's not true. There is no privilege for statements a client makes to an investigator. Not unless the investigator works for the client's attorney.

"You know who I am?" Bugg asked as he laid his big forearms on the table. I noticed he hadn't shaved in a couple of days.

"I know a little," I said.

"Does it bother you?"

"Depends on what you want me to do."

"I want you to find my fuckin' wife," he said. "That bother you?" I shook my head and sipped my coffee. "What's it gonna cost?" he asked.

"Seven-fifty a day, plus expenses."

"Pretty steep," he said. I sipped my coffee and said nothing. "How much up front?" he finally asked.

"Depends on how difficult the job is," I said. "Tell me what's going on."

"What's going on is that I've been with this lady seven years and she up and disappears on me." He had just a trace of a southern accent, and I remembered he'd grown up in Arkansas.

"When?" I asked.

"'Bout a month ago."

"Why'd you wait this long to hire an investigator?" I asked.

"Thought I could find her on my own," he said.

"How'd you get my name?"

"Does it matter?"

"I guess not," I said.

"Saw your card at the store over to Ward," he said. There is only one store in Ward. "Store" is a generous term. It's a little place in a hundred-year-old building that sells batteries and beer. Ward is a mountain town with a population of less than two hundred. It's where you live if Nederland isn't eclectic enough for you. It used to be a mining town, but today the population consists mostly of bikers, survivalists, anarchists, and the Rainbow People. I guess there are still a few miners over there.

"What's your wife's name?" I asked. I removed a gold-plated mechanical pencil from my pocket and turned over the paper place mat so I'd have something to write on.

"Karlynn Slade," he said. "K-A-R-L-Y-N-N."

"You know her date of birth?"

"Yeah, lemme think—it's June fifth, nineteen sixty-eight." The day Sirhan Sirhan shot Robert Kennedy. I remembered it. Remembered seeing it on the black-and-white Zenith TV in our southeast Denver home. Remembered staring at the same television a few days later as the funeral train rolled across America.

"What does your wife look like?" I asked.

"She's about five-five or five-six. Dark hair, nice body."

"You have a picture of her?"

"Yeah," he said. He reached into one of the pockets on his denim jacket and handed me a photo of the two of them smiling in front of a motorcycle. I couldn't miss the "SPD" tattooed on his left hand as he handed me the photo. I studied the photo, pretending I'd never before seen the woman. Karlynn's smile was forced.

"Is this recent?" I asked.

"This summer," he said. "Go ahead and keep it."

"You have any idea why she took off?" I asked.

"Who knows?" he replied. He rolled his head around several times as if bothered by neck pain. The dreadlocked waitress appeared with his pancakes and my bagel. He poured a generous portion of maple syrup over them and began to eat. After she'd left, he said, "Christ, I don't understand why the girls in this town wear their hair like that." I shrugged and spread some cream cheese over the bagel. I don't understand dreadlocks either, but I thought it funny someone like Bugg considered it a sign of the decline of Western civilization.

"She must've had a reason for leaving," I said. "If you want me to find her, you have to be honest with me."

"Things ain't been so good between us," was all he said.

"Then why do you want her back?" I asked. The question annoyed him.

"We've got some things to settle," he said. This time he slowly swiveled his massive head from left to right several times. Were it not for the fact that he wanted me dead, I might have given him the name of Nancy's chiropractor boyfriend.

"Does she have any family?" I asked.

"She's got a brother in prison in Nebraska. Her father lives in McCook. You know where that is?"

"Yeah."

"She wouldn't go there, though."

"Why not?" I asked.

"He molested her when she was a kid," he said as he lifted another forkful of pancakes to his mouth. "All the fuckin' time. That'd be the last place she'd go."

"She have any friends I might want to talk to?"

"Her only friends are bikers. I've got that covered."

"Girlfriends?"

"Just some women we ride with. They'd tell me if they'd seen her." I didn't necessarily buy that, but I let it go.

"What about a rival gang?" I asked. He paused to consider it.

"Maybe," he said. "She likes meth."

"Does she have any money?" I asked.

"Why do you want to know?"

"A woman with money behaves differently than one without it," I said. He nodded.

"She's got more than enough to get by," he said. "She took a lot of cash when she left."

"I can't make any promises," I said.

"Hey, look," he said. "I understand you can't make any promises. All's I'm asking is that you give it your best shot."

"Five thousand up front," I said.

"That's a lot of jack," he said. "How you gonna earn it?"

"I'll talk to some friends in law enforcement, see if she's been picked up anywhere, see if they've heard anything. Then I'll circulate some posters with her picture and my phone number on them. After that I'll look at the meth angle, see if she's tried to score any."

"You best be careful if you're gonna ask questions in those circles," he said.

"I can take care of myself," I said. I said it in a way that left no doubt I was confident I could lick any man in a fifteen-mile radius, including him. He looked at me as if he couldn't quite believe what he'd just heard, then allowed a trace of a smile and plunged his fork back into his pancakes.

"Something else you should know," he said.

"What's that?"

"Me and her, we had a dog. A purebred bluetick. Best hunting dog I ever had. Really good tracking dog, too."

"Yeah."

"My wife really loves this dog," he said. "More than she loves me." I nodded. "'Bout four days ago some fucker walks right up to my house, steals the dog. Damn near kills one of my guys." I asked him to relate the details and he did. Fortunately for me, none of his men had gotten a good look at me or my truck.

"You think she was behind it?" I asked.

"Had to be," he said. "I don't know who she got to do it, but I'd love to get my hands on that sorry son of a bitch." I told him that was a good lead, and promised to follow up on it. No mention was made of Anvil's sighting of Karlynn, so I assumed Anvil hadn't yet gotten around to telling Bugg.

We continued eating and sipping coffee, both of us watching

the snow accumulate. It was a wet snow, not typical for this time of year. When Bugg had finished his pancakes, he leaned back and said, "So how'd you get into this? Were you a cop?"

"I was never a cop," I said.

"Military?"

"Marines," I said.

"I was in the Corps," he said as he sipped his coffee. "Infantry," he added. "What did you do?"

"Logistics," I lied. Given that he'd ended his military career by spending six months in the brig, I felt it best not to mention I'd served three years as a JAG.

After collecting five thousand in cash from Bugg, I drove to the post office to check my mail. There was the usual assortment of credit card offers as well as the seasonal barrage of catalogs. I put them all in the recycling bin, then headed home. Prince greeted me at the door, with Scott and Karlynn right behind him.

"How'd it go?" Scott asked. He wore jeans, a T-shirt with Japanese characters on it, and some old running shoes. He's a lean six-footer, weighing 170 pounds on a good day. But he doesn't have an ounce of fat on him, and his build is impressive. That's what happens when you begin each day with five hundred push-ups.

"Piece of cake," I said as I removed my jacket. "I think he likes me." I stomped each foot into the welcome mat a few times to prevent myself from tracking snow into the house.

"What did he want?" Karlynn asked.

"He wants me to find you," I said. I went into the living room and sat down in my recliner. They followed and sat on the couch.

"Did he say why?" she asked.

"He said the two of you had some issues to settle. He mentioned that you took some cash, but didn't say how much." Her face showed something that wasn't quite a smirk. I summarized my breakfast with Bugg and commented on his command of the English language.

"Don't let that fool you," Karlynn said. "He's smart. He's a lot smarter than you think."

"Does he have a neck problem?" I asked. "He kept rolling his head around."

"He does that when he can't show anger," she said. "He's going to kill me. He's not even going to try to find the money. He's just going to kill me." She said it as if she was resigned to it.

"First he has to find you," I said. "Then he has to get past me."

9

MONDAY. DAY SIX with Karlynn Slade. We were seated together on a mocha leather sofa in the lobby of the downtown Denver office of the FBI. She was about to give another interview to the feds, and I was about to spend the next two hours continuing to read *Zen and the Art of Motorcycle Maintenance*—one of the few philosophy books ever written that are actually enjoyable.

It wasn't my first time in the Federal Building. I had worked as a federal prosecutor in Denver after leaving the Marine Corps. Later, in private practice, I had occasionally taken on a case in federal court. But the caseload in federal courts consists mostly of drug cases, and I had tired of the war on drugs and eventually left the practice of law altogether.

After my cousin's death the feds had stepped in to assist the Denver police in investigating his death and the killing of the Nigerian immigrant. I had visited the Federal Building once or twice after Hal's death. Though I had not been close to Hal since we were kids, I had followed the investigation into his death and had accumulated an extensive file.

A door opened and two agents stepped out. The male stood six-two and had a good build. Not a day over thirty. He wore gray slacks, a white shirt, black wingtips, and a leather shoulder holster. A nondescript paisley tie hung loosely around his neck. His hair was sandy and cut short. He was chewing gum.

The female had fair skin. She was slender, perhaps five-six and 125 pounds. Closer to my age. She wore black gabardine slacks and a very plain powder blue blouse with a scoop neck. Her gun was on her hip, and her hips were a bit wider than you'd expect to see on a slender woman. Her nails were not painted, but she had applied some type of high-gloss coating to them. She wore her mahogany hair in what might be called a modified bob; she'd allowed it to grow a little longer and fuller in back. Not bad-looking for a federal agent.

"Hi, Karylnn," she said. "How are you doing?"

"Fine," Karlynn said without enthusiasm as she stood up.

"You remember Special Agent Livingston?" the female asked.

"Yeah," Karlynn said. They acknowledged each other with a look that told me there had been tension between them.

"Who's he?" Livingston asked, now looking at me. I stood up.

"Pepper Keane," I said. "I'm her ride."

"Pepper?"

"Yeah."

"You a bodyguard or something?" he asked.

"Jack of all trades," I said.

"Well, Jack, you'll have to wait out here."

"Figured I would," I said. "Brought a book to entertain me." I held it up so they could see it. It was the original hardcover edition.

"Never heard of it," Livingston said. I nodded and refrained from suggesting that he consider reading something other than *Guns & Ammo*.

Karlynn followed them into the inner sanctum of the operation, and I resumed my seat on the couch. I had the room to myself, though I could see a Hispanic female receptionist answering the phone in a work area separated from the reception area by a counter and a sheet of bulletproof glass. Aside from that, the lobby was comparable to what you might find in any upscale office building. Thick crimson carpeting covered the floor, and dark paneling adorned the walls.

After ten minutes I felt thirsty and asked the receptionist for directions to the nearest pop machine. She told me, so I walked out past the elevators into a lounge area and bought a diet Coke, then returned to the lobby and resumed reading. Every so often I would see an agent enter or leave. There had been a time when I knew every agent in the Denver office, but transfers and retirements had taken their toll, and I didn't recognize any of the agents passing through the lobby. Maybe that was a good thing. I had once prosecuted an FBI agent for beating a confession out of someone, and for quite a while thereafter I hadn't exactly been a popular figure in the Bureau's Denver office.

Perhaps another twenty minutes had passed when the door opened and Karlynn came out saying, "I don't have to put up with this shit." Both agents were behind her.

"Karlynn," the female said, "he didn't mean it that way. But we have to ask these questions."

I stood up and looked at Karlynn as she came toward me. "What's wrong?" I asked.

"What's wrong is that this guy's an asshole," she replied. Livingston looked at the female agent and rolled his eyes. Karlynn found a cigarette in her purse and lit up, notwithstanding the brass NO SMOKING sign affixed to the wall.

"Karlynn," the female said, "let's just start over, okay?"

"I want him in there with me," Karlynn said, referring to me.

"We can't do that," Livingston said. "It's against the rules."

"Then you change the fucking rules," she shot back. "C'mon," she said to me, "let's get out of here." I put my hand on her shoulder. A gentle human touch can go a long way toward calming an irate person.

"Why don't we call Matt?" I suggested. Karlynn sighed; the agents said nothing. "Is there a phone I can use?"

"You can use the one on the wall," the female said. "Dial nine to get out." I walked to a tan phone mounted on the wall and punched in Matt's number. He came on the line and I explained the situation in general terms.

"Livingston can be a little overbearing," he said.

"Roger that," I said.

"Can they hear you?"

"Yes."

"On a scale of one to ten, with one being unconscious and ten being nuclear, where's Karlynn at?"

"Seven," I said.

"Do you mind sitting in on the interview?" he asked.

"Not at all," I said.

"Put Adrienne on," he said.

I looked at the female agent and said, "He wants to speak with you." She walked toward me and I caught a subtle whiff of perfume as I handed her the receiver. I don't like it when a woman's perfume overpowers my olfactory, but she'd chosen a light fragrance and applied it with such caution that it was barely noticeable.

"Hi, Matt," she said. I heard only her end of the conversation. "That's about the size of it . . . This is nothing compared to what she'll face on the witness stand . . . I know that . . . We can always rescind the deal . . . It's against policy . . . Talk to me . . . All right . . . All right . . . Thanks, Matt . . . You too." She placed the receiver back in its cradle, then looked at me and said, "You can sit in with us." Karlynn shot Livingston a look and he rolled his eyes again.

The female extended her hand to me and I shook it. "I'm Special Agent Valeska," she said. "This is Special Agent Cliff Livingston." He came forward and I shook his hand.

"Mr. Keane was a federal prosecutor," she told her partner. "I think we can bend the rules a little."

They had the receptionist issue me a visitor's badge, then led us through a maze of hallways to an interview room. It was about ten by fifteen and very plain. The paint was off-white. The carpet was tan. The ceiling was suspended. The rectangular table was topped with a walnut laminate. The chairs were metal and uncomfortable. I took a chair in a corner and opened my book. But Livingston began the questioning in his booming voice, and it soon became apparent that I was not going to be able to concentrate on my book while sitting only a few feet away from the three of them.

"All right," Livingston began, "I want to ask some more questions about the Sons of Satan." He handed her several dozen mug shots and surveillance photos. "Do you recognize any of these men?"

"I recognize all of them," she said. He took her through them one by one while Adrienne Valeska took notes on a legal pad. The feds were trying to construct an organizational chart for the gang. Some of the men had nicknames such as Throttle, Pig, and Monster. All were members of the Sons of Satan. One of the surveillance photos featured my old friend Anvil, though his legal name was apparently Robert Alton Pugh. Livingston's questions about Anvil were typical of the questions he asked about the others.

"What can you tell me about Anvil?" he asked.

"He's one of Thad's enforcers," she replied.

"What does he enforce?"

"You know, rules. Like guys who get out of line or people who don't pay."

"Have you seen him assault people in that capacity?"

"Not very often," she said. "I've seen him get in bar fights, but if he's really going to hurt someone he usually finds a way to do it where there won't be any witnesses."

"Has he ever killed anyone?"

"Not that I know of," she said.

"How long has he been with the gang?" Livingston asked. She shrugged.

"Maybe two years," she said.

"Does he work?"

"He doesn't really have a job, but he works on computers and stuff. And he likes books."

"Where did he come from?"

"I don't know," she said. "He never talks about it."

"What else can you tell us about him?"

"He's crazy," she said with a bit of a snicker.

"Why do you say that?"

"I don't know," she shrugged. "It's like he's got two different personalities. Sometimes he's real quiet—just sits by himself and reads—but sometimes he just goes off on people. He lives alone in this little cabin up by Jamestown and doesn't have many friends. He spends a lot of time on his computer. He keeps to himself mostly, but he's very loyal to Thad."

We took a break at some point, during which Karlynn smoked a cigarette and I hit the men's room. Then I went to the lounge to buy another diet Coke and ran into Adrienne Valeska. She asked how I knew Matt and I told her. I also told her I was just baby-sitting Karlynn Slade as a favor to Matt and that the feds couldn't get her into the Witness Protection Program soon enough for me.

"Karlynn will be a good witness," she said. "We've wanted Bugg for a long time, and I think we're finally going to get him."

"I hope so," I said. "For your sake."

"You should hope so for your sake as well," she replied. "Outlaw gangs account for forty percent of the drug trade in Colorado."

"I like your perfume," I said. "Is it Joop?"

"You need to work on your changeup," she said. "Why don't we see if they're ready?" I shrugged and followed her back to the FBI's suite. I figured she had male agents and prosecutors hitting on her every week and had learned to go into a professional mode whenever a man tried to make conversation. Before entering the interview room, she turned to me and whispered, "It is Joop."

Karlynn and Livingston were already seated at the table. Valeska and I took our seats and Livingston resumed his questioning.

"All right," Livingston said to Karlynn, "do you recognize this man?" He handed her a 5 × 7 black-and-white photograph of a handsome black man in a coat and tie. She studied it while Valeska continued taking notes.

"No," Karlynn said.

"Never seen him before?"

"No."

"During your time with Bugg did you ever hear him refer to any law enforcement officer by name?"

"I'm sure I did," she said.

"Do you remember any specific names?"

"Not off the top of my head," she replied. "A lot of times he would just say 'that guy' or 'that fucker,' something like that."

"Did you ever hear him refer to a man named Steve Lowell?" It was now clear that the black man in the photograph was Lowell, the ATF agent killed in Wyoming about six months ago.

"Not that I recall."

"Did you ever hear any other member of the Sons of Satan mention that name?"

"Yes," she said.

"Who was that?" he asked.

"I don't know his name. He was from Wyoming."

"What did he say?"

"He told Thad that Lowell had been taken care of."

"When was this?"

"Last summer sometime."

"Can you be more specific?"

"I don't know," she said, "June or July."

"Where did that conversation take place?"

"At a bar in Rollinsville." Rollinsville is a town of a few hundred people six miles south of Nederland. A lot of westbound trains pass through it before entering the Moffat Tunnel and heading down the other side of the Continental Divide into Utah, Nevada, and ultimately California. The town boasts only one bar—the Black Bear.

"Would that be the Black Bear?" Livingston asked.

"Yes," Karlynn replied.

"I'm going to show you some photographs. Please look them over and tell me if the man who told Bugg that Lowell had been taken care of appears in any of these photos." He handed her several mug shots. By this time I had more or less been sucked into the whole thing, so I moved my chair closer to the table. The men in the mug shots all looked like felons.

"That's him," Karlynn said, pointing to one of the mug shots.

"Are you positive?"

"Yes."

"Had you ever seen that man prior to the time he told Bugg that Lowell had been taken care of?"

"Yes."

"How often?"

"I've probably seen him a dozen times, mostly with Thad. He comes to Denver a lot. We went up to Wyoming a couple of times—Thad likes to visit other chapters. I saw him at Sturgis once."

"And you don't know his name?"

"I already told you I don't," she said. "Everyone calls him Mongoose."

"Did you know what Mongoose meant when he said Lowell had been taken care of?"

"I had an idea," she said.

"What did you think he meant?"

"I thought it meant that Thad had ordered someone to be killed."

"Why did you think that?"

"I don't know," she said. "I could just sort of tell."

"Did you ask Bugg what it meant?"

"I didn't have to ask," she said.

"What was Bugg's reaction when Mongoose told him Lowell had been taken care of?"

"He really didn't have one," she said. "It was just another business matter."

"A business matter?" Livingston said, his voice full of scorn. "He thought murdering a federal agent was a business matter?"

"Ease up," I said, "she didn't kill the guy." He looked at Valeska.

"You see," he said, "this is why we're not supposed to let guys like him sit in on these things."

"Let's just move on," Valeska said.

"All right," Livingston sighed, "at any point did Mongoose say how Lowell had been taken care of?"

"He said something about someone named Skull. Skull had done a good job, something like that." Livingston and Valeska looked at each other. The revelation of Skull's involvement was new.

"Do you know who Skull is?" Livingston asked.

"No. He was just some guy Mongoose found."

"Had you ever heard of Skull?" Karlynn let out a little laugh.

"You hang out with bikers," she said, "you're gonna meet a few guys named Skull." She had a point. The name sounded vaguely familiar even to me.

"Well, had you ever heard Bugg or Mongoose mention Skull before?"

"No."

"You're positive?"

"I'm positive," she said. Livingston decided to move on.

"During the period prior to Mongoose telling Bugg that Lowell had been taken care of, had Bugg said anything that led you to believe he wanted someone killed?"

"No," she said.

"Had he expressed concern about anything with respect to the Sons of Satan or any of the Wyoming chapters?"

"Well, I knew something was going on. He spent a lot of time on the phone with Mongoose and some other guys from Wyoming just before that man was killed. He went up there several times. Lander, Riverton, that area. Mongoose is the boss up there."

"What did you think was going on?"

"I don't know," she said. "Some kind of trouble."

"What kind of trouble?"

"Like maybe someone up there was asking too many questions."

"What made them think that?" he asked.

"Thad can smell a cop or a snitch a mile away," she said. "It's like he's got some kind of radar—he can just tell."

10

GIVEN KARLYNN'S ASSERTION that Bugg could smell a cop or a snitch a mile away, I figured I'd better do something to convince him I was earning the five thousand dollars he'd given me. So I spent Tuesday morning putting up posters all over the Peak-to-Peak region while Scott stood watch over Karlynn at my home in Nederland. Each poster was $8^{1}/2 \times 11$. The top half showed a black-and-white photo of Karlynn. Beneath that was a physical description as well as my name and telephone number.

I plastered the casinos in Black Hawk and Central City and went as far south as Idaho Springs. Then I went north as far as Estes Park. I didn't worry about the area west of the Peak-to-Peak Highway because it contains no towns and very few roads. The Continental Divide takes care of that.

To the east of Nederland is Boulder. I figured I could place some posters down there in the afternoon while Karlynn met with her new therapist—the former Miss North Dakota, Kendra Carlson. Karlynn had approached me about it Monday evening. "Maybe it wouldn't be such a bad idea for me to see a shrink," she had said. I called Nancy and she recommended Kendra. I wasn't sure how Karlynn would take to doing therapy with the woman she'd described as being too high-maintenance for me, but Karlynn's impending entry into the Witness Protection Program didn't allow much time for therapist shopping. Nancy had given me Kendra's home number and I had set up an appointment for the next afternoon.

Now the three of us—Karlynn, Scott, and I—were in the waiting area. Karlynn was pacing, Scott was reading *Sports Illustrated,* and I was just sitting with my eyes closed and trying to remember where I'd heard the name Skull before.

The door to Kendra's office opened and a middle-aged woman exited. She had just finished crying. Kendra bade her farewell and encouraged her to call if she felt the need. Then she looked at us. She wore green tailored slacks, a white blouse, and black pumps. She had styled her long, dark hair with a bow that matched her slacks. Her makeup was still perfect. Karlynn was right—Kendra was high-maintenance, at least in terms of the time spent on her personal appearance. On the other hand, feminine beauty can make up for a multitude of shortcomings. Probably why they call it makeup.

"Hello, Pepper," she said as she extended her right arm. Her red nails were perfect, and her smile was wide and gracious. I stood to shake her hand, and Karlynn followed suit. "Hello, Karlynn," she said. Karlynn shook her hand as well. Scott glanced up to size up Kendra, looked at me, then went back to his magazine. "Well," Kendra said to Karlynn, "shall we get started?" Karlynn looked apprehensive. I gave her a pat on the shoulder and promised we'd be back in two hours.

Boulder is an expensive college town nestled up against the base of the Rockies. But for one topless club, there aren't many venues likely to attract bikers. And to convince Bugg that I was earning my money, the posters had to go where Bugg's men were likely to see them. So Scott and I stopped at the topless club to put up a few posters, then drove east to Longmont.

"That's one good-looking therapist," Scott said as we rolled down the highway past snow-covered fields. "I didn't see a wedding ring." I didn't reply. After several minutes he asked, "How's the karate going?"

"I haven't done squat with it since Karlynn and Prince moved in."

"You have to practice every day," he said.

"I understand, Sensei," I said, just a trace of wiseass in my voice. He requires other students to address him that way, but I don't do it outside class. I had been studying karate with Scott for several years, but boxing came more naturally. I had gradually conceded, though, that karate is more useful in street situations, if only because it does not limit you to using only your fists.

Traffic slowed as we came into Longmont. It is an agricultural town on the fertile plains of eastern Boulder County and hosts more than its fair share of biker bars. Not to mention cowboy bars and Mexican bars. "Tell me again," Scott said, "why we're putting up posters asking people to call us with information about a missing woman when, in fact, the missing woman is with us, and the people most likely to see the posters want to find the woman and kill her." I said nothing. He knew why we were doing it and was just remarking on the humorous nature of the whole affair.

At two o'clock on a Tuesday afternoon I wasn't worried about running into Anvil at a biker bar in Longmont. But of course, that is exactly what happened. As Scott and I were about to enter our fourth Longmont establishment, I looked through the window in the solid-wood door and saw the big man playing pool. I put my arm out to prevent Scott from opening the door. "What's up?" he said.

"See that guy playing pool?" He peered in.

"Yeah."

"That's Anvil."

"The one from the mall?"

"In the flesh," I said.

"Let's just staple one of these to the door and get out of here before he sees you," Scott said.

"Why don't you go in and make his acquaintance," I said. "Be interesting to see how he reacts when he learns you're looking for Karlynn." He looked at me and resigned himself to it. Without responding to me, he pulled open the heavy door and went in.

I saw him approach the bartender, a lanky man in his mid-twenties with a ponytail and one of those thick cowboy mustaches. The bartender pointed to an area of one wall covered with posters and business cards. Scott tacked up one of our posters, then walked over to what was apparently Anvil's table and waited for Anvil to finish his game. When Anvil finally missed a shot and his opponent took over, he sat down and drank from a glass of beer. There was a pitcher on the table, as well as a hardcover book. Scott said something to him and held out one of our posters. Anvil responded and Scott said something back. Then Scott handed him a poster. Anvil studied it, said something to Scott. After a few more exchanges, Anvil shouted to the other player. He walked to the table, still holding his cue, and took the poster from Anvil. He looked at it, then shook his head from side to side. Scott thanked them and headed for the door.

"Well?" I said as we walked toward my F-150.

"They wanted to know why I was interested in Karlynn, and I told them I was working for a private eye Bugg had hired."

"Quite true," I said.

"They knew who she was, but they both claimed they hadn't seen her for a couple of months." I started up the truck and headed back to Boulder on the Diagonal Highway. "Why do you think Anvil would lie about that?" he asked.

"I don't know," I said. "Maybe he wasn't sure Bugg had really hired a private eye. Maybe Bugg hasn't told anyone he hired me."

"Maybe Bugg knows you're the guy Anvil saw with Karlynn, and he's just jerking you around until the time is right to kill you both."

"I didn't get that impression," I said.

"I'll tell you one thing," he said.

"What's that?"

"Anvil is more literate than your average biker."

"Why do you say that?" I asked.

"He's reading Plato's *Republic*."

11

IT WAS nine-thirty on a Thursday night. I had taken Karlynn to therapy sessions for three straight afternoons. The jury was still out on whether it was doing any good. "I guess I have to work on my fucking self-esteem," was all she had said after the first session.

But now she was in the living room, wearing a T-shirt and jeans, continuing work on her list of one hundred things she wanted to do in her life. Prince was dreaming doggie dreams beneath the dining table. I was in my study with Buck and Wheat, drinking herb tea and reviewing my file on my cousin's death.

It would not be accurate to say Hal's death had haunted me. We just hadn't been that close after grade school. On the other hand, I had never completely let go of it either. The event was usually hidden in the back of my mind, but never quite gone. But something Karlynn had told the FBI during her interview Tuesday had slowly been pushing the incident back to the forefront of my consciousness.

So for the past two hours, after finishing a pizza we had ordered, I had been sifting through an accordion file containing old police reports. As I reviewed each document, the details came flying back to me.

My cousin had been working a Rockies game at Coors Field.

He loved working baseball games because he got to see them for free. At 10:04 p.m., just as a game against the Dodgers was winding down, he left the ballpark to prepare for the mass of spectators that would soon flood the streets. He heard screaming and observed two white males beating a black man in front of a warehouse a few blocks to the north. He drew his weapon and ran toward them. His last radio report indicated one of the white men appeared to be beating the black man with the butt of a pistol while the other prodded him with a bat.

By the time other officers arrived, it was all over. Hal lay dead in a pool of his own blood, as did one of the skinheads—the one with the bat. The Nigerian immigrant, though badly beaten, was alive and was transported to Denver General. He never regained consciousness and died a few hours later as a result of brain hemorrhaging.

The cops didn't have much to work with. The Nigerian man had come to the United States to study international relations at the University of Denver. As far as the cops knew, he had no connection to either of his attackers and had simply been the wrong color in the wrong place at the wrong time.

The dead skinhead—the one Hal had killed—had been a punk named Lewis "Lizard" McCoy. A wiry twenty-one-year-old with a history of petty theft and minor drug offenses. Lizard had been part of a loosely knit group of about a dozen young skinheads, but no group member had ever done anything more violent than paint swastikas on a local synagogue. Interviews with members and reports from the police department's gang unit both confirmed that what held the members together was primarily their devotion to "White Power" music—hard-driving rock-and-roll that pounds home a message of bigotry and violence.

Not much was known about the other skinhead—the one that

got away. A man claiming to have seen the event from more than one block away described him as about six feet tall, 180 pounds. Shaved head, or nearly so.

One possible clue to the unknown skinhead's identity was the tape of the call made to a local radio station the day after the incident. The man had claimed responsibility for the killings and said Hal's death should serve as a warning to white cops that protect niggers and faggots. The call could have come from a wacko who'd had nothing to do with the killings, but the police nevertheless hauled in dozens of skinheads and neighborhood winos and made them listen to the tape. They even hired a linguistics expert to analyze the voice, but she'd been able to contribute very little. All she could say was that the caller was a white male, age twenty-five to thirty, who had probably grown up in the Midwest.

Based on their interviews with Lizard's known associates, the physical description of the unknown skinhead, and the linguistics expert's opinion as to the age of the man who had called the radio station, investigators were confident the killer had not been a member of Lizard's circle of skinhead friends.

My file included transcripts of interviews with the skinheads and winos brought in to listen to the tape. All but one had denied recognizing the voice on the tape. I was reading the last one when I came across a passage that caught my attention. I found it in a transcript of an interview with one of the skinheads. His name was Paul Krait and he had been only eighteen at the time of the incident. He was not part of Lizard's group but admitted associating with other skinheads and enjoying the lifestyle. Then the cops played the tape for him.

DETECTIVE: Do you recognize that voice, Paul?
WITNESS: I don't think so.

DETECTIVE: What does that mean?

WITNESS: It means I don't recognize the voice.

DETECTIVE: That's not what you said. You said you didn't think you recognized it. So part of you thinks maybe you do recognize it.

WITNESS: No, man, you're twisting my words.

DETECTIVE: You're eighteen now, Paul. With your record, that switchblade we found in your boot tonight could land you thirty days in county.

WITNESS: Thirty days ain't shit.

DETECTIVE: How much do you weigh, Paul? About one-forty? When those big black guys in county see your little skinhead ass, they're gonna fall all over each other to see who can get you first.

WITNESS: It sounds kind of like this guy named Skull.

DETECTIVE: Who's Skull?

WITNESS: I don't know his real name.

DETECTIVE: What do you know?

WITNESS: He's this crazy Aryan Resistance fucker.

DETECTIVE: What does he look like?

WITNESS: I don't know. I've never even seen him.

DETECTIVE: Then how do you know him?

WITNESS: I heard him on a tape.

DETECTIVE: What kind of tape?

WITNESS: It was just some kind of White Power tape somebody gave me to listen to.

DETECTIVE: When was that?

WITNESS: Couple of months ago.

DETECTIVE: Who gave you the tape?

WITNESS: I don't know. These things just kind of float around in the community, you know?

DETECTIVE: Do you still have the tape?

WITNESS: No.

DETECTIVE: Where is it?

WITNESS: I gave it to some guy I met at a concert. I don't even know the guy's name.

DETECTIVE: You're sure the guy on the tape was named Skull.

WITNESS: That's what he called himself.

DETECTIVE: What did he say on the tape?

WITNESS: You know, just the usual stuff about white people having to stand up for their rights.

DETECTIVE: Why did you say he's crazy?

WITNESS: Because, man, he kept talking about some kind of Aryan Resistance training camp—some place up in Idaho where these military guys teach you how to shoot and survive in the woods and shit like that. He said his people could teach you how to be a soldier in the racial holy war so you could kill niggers, fags, and Jews.

The remainder of the interview was unremarkable. I put the transcript down and sipped my tea, which had grown cold. I wished the detective had pressured Krait for more details concerning Skull and the tape, but I realized the reference to Skull was only one lead out of thousands.

I heard the phone ring, but I was absorbed in what I was doing and decided to let it ring. I'm not wild about people calling late at night in any event. It rang only twice, so I figured either the caller had hung up or Karlynn had answered in spite of my warnings. I stayed focused on the task at hand.

As I continued working my way through the file, I realized that those investigating Hal's death had done their best to follow up on the lead Krait had provided. The feds had applied pressure to various White Power groups and made heroic efforts to track down the origin of the tape Krait had described. Local investigators had compiled a list of dozens of criminals and gang members known to have used "Skull" as a nickname or alias, but only a few fit the profile provided by the linguistics expert, and none of those had ties to the White Power movement.

When I finished my review of the file, I sat back and recalled the days following Hal's death. There had been some question as to why Hal shot Lizard—the one with the bat—rather than the one with the pistol. It was impossible to know, but my guess was that the guy with the gun was older and more experienced. He probably took off when he saw Hal. Lizard, caught up in the moment, and perhaps trying to impress the older man, probably tried to get in a few more strikes with the bat, and Hal shot him to protect the black man.

I turned off my desk lamp and walked out to the living room. It was past eleven. Karlynn was still on the couch, and Prince had joined her. "You've done more than half the things on your list," she said.

"Probably the easy ones," I said.

"Swimming a mile in the Arctic Ocean doesn't sound easy," she said.

"I told you, my mom lives in Barrow and there's nothing to do there. It's not the pretty part of Alaska. It's the flattest, whitest, most desolate place on earth. I was bored out of my mind, so I decided to see if I could swim a mile without freezing to death or getting eaten by a polar bear. How's your list coming?"

"I don't even have fifty yet," she said.

"You've been out here nearly two hours."

"I know," she said, "but I started reading that book of yours— the one about Zen and motorcycles."

"What do you think of it?" I asked.

"The guy's all fucked up," she said. "He spends way too much time worrying about his bike. He's always checking the oil and worrying about his damn chain. I mean, Jesus, get a life."

"Interesting to hear a biker's perspective," I said. "Who was on the phone?"

"It was Matt," she said. "After we meet with the feds tomorrow, some guys from the Witness Protection Program are going to tell me all about my new life."

"Big day for you," I said.

"You goin' to bed?" she asked.

"No, I'm kind of hyper tonight. I think I'll see what's on the tube." After several hours revisiting Hal's death, I was unable to sleep. I picked up the TV schedule from Sunday's paper.

"I'm not tired either," she said.

"Hey, look at this," I said. "*Bad Day at Black Rock* is about to start." I love that movie. Especially the part where a one-armed Spencer Tracy uses judo to beat the crap out of a much bigger Ernest Borgnine.

"Never heard of it," she said. I found the remote, clicked on the TV, and surfed until I found the classic movie channel. Then I kicked Prince off the couch, sat down beside Karlynn, and put my feet up on the coffee table.

I must have fallen asleep about midway through the movie. When I awoke, I found a blanket on top of me and a handwritten note in my lap. The note read:

Good movie. I wish I lived in some place
like that where nobody would ever find me.
P.S. Don't worry, we didn't do anything.

12

CLIFF LIVINGSTON AND ADRIENNE VALESKA were waiting for us when we arrived at Fed Central at 9:15 the next morning. "You were supposed to be here at nine," Livingston said. He wore gray slacks, a powder blue shirt, and a maroon tie.

I thought about reminding him that I live nearly an hour from Denver and that we'd had to contend with the morning rush hour. Instead I just said, "I hope the extra fifteen minutes doesn't screw up your case against Bugg." Valeska allowed a barely noticeable smile. She wore a navy skirt from a suit, a white blouse, and navy pumps with short heels.

They offered coffee, which I accepted, and led us to the same interview room we'd been in on Tuesday. Once we were all seated at the rectangular table, Livingston began the questioning.

"All right, Ms. Slade," he said, "today we'd like to talk to you about Edward Rankin. Is that name familiar to you?"

"Yes."

"How do you know that name?"

"He was in the gang," she said.

"The Sons of Satan?"

"Yes."

"When did you first meet him?" Livingston asked.

"Three or four years ago."

"Where did you first meet him?"

"It was at the Black Bear, in Rollinsville. Thad and I were having some beers with some of the guys, and Rankin started playing pool. He was pretty good, so Thad challenged him. They got to talkin' and I guess each of them had been in the Marines and they sort of hit it off. After that, Rankin just started hanging out with us more and more." Livingston handed her an 8½ × 11 black-and-white photo of a man who appeared to be in his early thirties.

"Do you recognize the man in that photo?" Livingston asked.

"Yeah, it's Rankin."

"At some point Rankin became a member of the Sons of Satan, is that correct?"

"Well, yeah, he just started riding with us and he seemed to like it, so Thad gave him this big talk on how the Sons of Satan was the toughest gang around and everyone in it was a member of the one percent club."

"The one percent club?"

"Yeah, Thad said that to a be a member you had to be one of the one percent who had given up on society. You had to be somebody who didn't want to play by society's rules."

"Christ," I said, "if that's all it takes, I'm eligible for membership." They ignored my attempt at humor.

"When did Rankin become a member of the gang?" Livingston continued.

"He was never really a full member," she said. "He was a probationary member. One day Thad just made him a probationary member. I think it was that August. I remember because it was right after my birthday."

"What did he have to do to become a full member?"

"You have to be a probationary member for at least a year," she said. "And if Thad decides you're going to be a full member, he'd put you through some kind of test when you were least expecting it. Like maybe he'd pick ten or twelve guys to stomp you to see if you can take it." Valeska turned to look at Livingston. I got a glimpse of leg and liked what I saw.

"How did Rankin do in the gang?" Livingston asked.

"Fine, as far as I know."

"After Rankin had been with the gang a while, did Bugg say anything to indicate how he felt about Rankin?"

"Not really," she said.

"Do you remember when Rankin was arrested?"

"Yes."

"What do you remember about that?"

"We were at home. It was at night. We were watching TV, and Thad got a call from Rankin."

"How do you know the call was from Rankin?"

"Because we let the phone ring and the answering machine picked up and Rankin started talking, saying he was in some trouble."

"What happened then?"

"Thad picked up the phone and talked to him for a few minutes."

"Do you remember what Thad said?"

"Not all of it," she said. "I remember he said ten thousand dollars was nothing, that he could get that or find a bondsman."

"Did you have any conversation with Bugg about the call from Rankin?"

"Well, I asked what was going on, and he just said that Rankin had gotten busted on some kind of warrant and needed to post bond."

"What did Bugg do after the call from Rankin?"

"He made some phone calls."

"Do you know who he called?"

"No, but one of them had to be long distance, because he asked me to get the address book. I had this address book that we kept with everyone's phone number and stuff." The two agents looked at each other again.

"What do you mean by 'everyone's' phone number?" Livingston asked.

"Well, we had this address book—the kind you buy at Office Depot—and we kept a list of everyone's address and phone number."

"Everyone in the gang, or everyone in the chapter?"

"Everyone. All the other honchos from the other chapters, plus all the other members, the girls that worked for me, and a bunch of other people the gang did business with."

"Did you take the address book when you left Bugg?" Livingston asked.

"No," she replied.

Livingston looked irritated, as if he couldn't believe Karlynn had neglected to take what might be a crucial piece of evidence. He rubbed his meaty hands through his hair. Adrienne Valeska gently placed her palm on Karlynn's arm. "Where does he keep the address book?" she asked.

"It's usually in a drawer in the kitchen," she replied. "Right next to the refrigerator." You didn't have to be a lawyer to know that when the feds drafted an application for a search warrant, Karlynn's statements regarding the existence of the address book would play a prominent role.

"Okay," Livingston said with a sigh, "when Bugg made these phone calls, do you remember what he said?"

"He kept telling the people he was talking to that ten thousand was not enough."

"Did you know what he meant?"

"Well, it sounded like he was surprised that the bond was so low."

"Do you remember anything else that he said when he was on the phone with these other people?"

"No, but when he was done, he told me that instead of posting bond for Rankin he would just pay a bondsman. He was afraid that if we showed up with ten grand to post bond, someone might wonder where we'd gotten the money."

"Okay," Livingston said, "at some point did you become aware of Rankin's death?"

"Yeah, I think it was, like, two days later. Thad hired a bondsman the next day, and then the day after was the day Rankin was killed."

"Did Bugg say anything to you about Rankin's death?"

"Yeah, there was a big story about it in the paper. I saw the story and showed it to Thad. He just glanced at it and said, 'That's life,' or something like that."

"Did you ever ask him whether he'd played a role in Rankin's death?"

"You don't understand our relationship," she said. "I learned not to ask those questions."

The next topic concerned money. They spent an hour questioning her about Bugg's finances and his distrust of banks. She told them he had caches of food, weapons, and money hidden all over the West, but only Thad knew where they were. Then they started asking her about the money she had taken from Bugg.

"Ms. Slade," Livingston began, "we've heard rumors you took a significant amount of money from your husband before leaving him." Karlynn didn't respond.

"Is that true?" Valeska asked.

"I took some money," she said.

"How much?" said Livingston.

"I don't know; I didn't stop to count it. Just enough to get out of town."

"We're hearing close to half a million dollars."

"That's bullshit," Karlynn said. "It was maybe twenty thousand."

"Why would Bugg be telling people you took so much more?" Livingston asked.

"Who knows?" she said. "Maybe it's easier for him to justify killing me if he convinces everyone I stole a bunch of money from him."

"Maybe he's planning on deducting the half million as a business loss," I said. "If she only took twenty thousand, you guys could get him on tax fraud." Neither of the agents appreciated my humor, but I succeeded in steering the conversation in a different direction before Karlynn got caught in one of her own lies.

Now it was nearly one o'clock. Karlynn and I had eaten lunch at a deli on the Sixteenth Street Mall and were walking back to the Federal Building on a sunny but cold and windy day.

The feds had finished interviewing her just before noon. After Livingston had asked everything he could think to ask about Rankin, he had grilled her on the gang's involvement in manufacturing and distributing methamphetamine and other drugs. Karlynn had insisted she'd had nothing to do with those enterprises, and I'd gotten the impression she hadn't told the feds much they hadn't already known in that area.

The one exception was the meth lab in the cabin behind Bugg's house. Livingston and Valeska had been stunned at that revelation. The feds obviously hadn't done any real surveillance of Bugg's home. The antifreeze jugs piled outside the cabin had been a strong indication for me because I know antifreeze is often used to produce meth, but the lanky, ponytailed man who had walked out to the cabin every few hours carrying a machine pistol had been the clincher.

We entered the Federal Building and went through the metal detector—I'd left my Glock in the truck—but instead of taking the elevator to the FBI suite, we stopped on a different floor and walked around until we found the U.S. marshal's office. It didn't take a genius to see that the FBI received more funding. Whereas the Bureau's lobby was carpeted and had dark paneling, the marshal's lobby had plain walls and a tile floor that resembled one I remembered from elementary school.

A counter separated the lobby from the rest of the suite. There were desks and filing cabinets behind the counter, but no people. The place appeared empty. Karlynn and I removed our coats and sat down on some plastic chairs. Matt Simms showed up a few minutes later wearing a gray suit and a tan London Fog trench coat. The wind had not done his hair any favors.

"Anyone here?" he said.

"Not that I can see," I said, "but we've only been here a few minutes."

"Anyone back there?" he yelled.

"Just a minute," said a man from somewhere in the deep caverns of the suite.

"It's always like this," Matt said. "Poor bastards spend most of their time transporting prisoners from one place to another and never have anyone to cover the office."

A man came out from a door and entered the area behind the counter. He was in his mid-twenties and had red hair. About five-ten and 175 pounds. He wore blue polyester slacks, a white shirt, and a gold tie that really didn't go with the outfit. His pistol was housed in a Velcro shoulder holster. "Is this Ms. Slade?" he asked Matt.

"Yes," Matt replied. "I'm Matt Simms, her attorney."

"I'm Jim Davis from the Witness Protection Program," said the man. He and Matt shook hands. "Sorry there was no one here to greet you. The secretary is at lunch, and all the guys who work this office are out earning their meager pay."

"No problem," Matt said.

"I work out of Washington," said the man.

"Fine," Matt said, "let's get started." He gestured to Karlynn to stand up. I could tell he was in a hurry. Probably had another appointment in an hour or two.

"It'll just be me and Miss Slade," Davis said.

"I'm her attorney," Matt said testily.

"I heard you the first time, counselor, but those are the rules. I'll take Ms. Slade back and brief her. Take about a half hour. Everything is in place. She'll need to report back here Monday, no later than noon. We'll accompany her to her destination and help her get set up. If the two of you need to communicate after that, it will have to be set up through me." He handed Matt one of his cards, then looked at Karlynn. "Are you ready, Miss Slade?"

"I guess," she said. She stood up. A portion of the gray counter-top was attached to the rest of the counter by hinges. Davis lifted the movable piece up so she could pass through to the other side. Matt removed his coat and sat down beside me.

"You didn't know you wouldn't be in on the briefing?" I asked.

"Never had a client enter the Witness Protection Program

before," he said. He opened his black briefcase and removed a file. "But I guess it makes sense," he added.

"At least the FBI has some magazines in the lobby," I said. The only reading material the Marshals Service had provided were the wanted posters on the walls. "I think I'll go see if I can find a paper."

"Yeah, fine." He was already immersed in whatever was in his file. He's not happy if he's not doing something he can bill for.

I went into the hallway and took the elevator down to the main floor. I remembered seeing a row of newspaper machines in front of the entrance. I walked out and surveyed my choices. All were empty but one, so I bought *USA Today*, went through the metal detector again, and waited for an elevator. When one finally arrived, I entered and pressed the button for the marshal's floor. The car stopped several times on its way up, and at one stop Adrienne Valeska stepped in. "I'm only going up two floors," she said, "but I'm too lazy to take the stairs."

"Karlynn's being briefed by a man from the Marshals Service," I said. "I'm just riding the elevator up and down, trying to pick up women."

"Any luck?"

"Not yet," I said, "but I just started." The elevator stopped on her floor, and the doors opened.

"Well," she said as she exited the elevator, "I'm sorry your first at bat has to go into the books as a strikeout."

"Lot of innings left," I said.

When I arrived back at the marshal's office, Matt was dictating a letter into a handheld recorder. I sat down beside him and began reading *USA Today*. He looked at me briefly and asked, "Was that all they had?"

"Yeah."

After another twenty minutes Jim Davis and Karlynn reappeared. She seemed subdued. We stood up. "Everything okay?" Matt asked.

"Fine," she said without enthusiasm. Davis held up the countertop again so she could return to our side, then followed her through and stood beside us.

"There's been a slight change in plans," Davis said to Matt. "We won't be able to move her until next Friday."

"Why the change?" Matt asked.

"Just a little misunderstanding," Davis said. "No big deal."

Karlynn looked at me and said, "Think you can stand me for another week?"

"I'll give it a shot," I said. The three of us donned our coats, said good-bye to Deputy U.S. Marshal Davis, and rode the elevator down to the main floor. Matt paused before entering the revolving door that would take us out into the cold. He looked at me.

"Can you bring Karlynn down here next Friday?" he asked.

"Sure," I said. "What about the dog?"

"That's why they can't move me Monday," Karlynn said as she lit up a cigarette. "They weren't going to let me take Prince. I told him they'd damn well better let me take him or the whole deal was off. So he called his boss in Washington, and *he* called *his* boss, and I guess they're gonna let me take him, but they need a few days to work up a cover story and a new identity for him." Matt looked at me and suppressed a smile.

"This is a great country," was all I said.

We left the building and were immediately greeted by a gust of wind. "Cheer up, Karlynn," Matt said as he headed to his BMW. "This will be a new beginning for you."

"I know," she said.

Karlynn and I continued walking until we reached my truck. I started it up and headed west past Coors Field on Twentieth Street. That took us within one block of the spot where an unknown skinhead had killed my cousin. We were both silent, each for his own reasons. As I guided the truck north on I-25 toward the Boulder Turnpike, Karlynn turned to me and said, "Don't you want to know where I'm going?"

"I don't think you're supposed to tell me," I said.

"Iowa fucking City, Iowa," she said. "I'm going to be a receptionist in a company that makes portable toilets for campers."

13

I HAD NOT WORKED out in a week, which was unusual for me because I usually work out at least six days a week, so on Saturday afternoon I took Karlynn with me to my brother's gym.

My brother, Troy, owns a gym in the fashionable Cherry Creek section of Denver. It's a Mecca for serious bodybuilders in Colorado. I have a good gym in my basement, stocked with Troy's discarded equipment, but I hadn't seen him in a while and just needed a break from Karlynn and the constant wind that whips down on Nederland from the Continental Divide between October and May.

The kid at the counter recognized me and handed me a towel. He knew my brother had bestowed on me membership in the elite group of those honored with their own permanent locker. Karlynn scanned the facility and said, "I haven't exercised in ten years."

"Might be good for you to start," I said, "but if you're not up to it, there's a sauna, a steam room, and a Jacuzzi."

I didn't see Troy, so rather than track him down for a free guest pass, I paid ten bucks to purchase a day membership for Karlynn, pointed her in the direction of the women's dressing room, and started toward my locker, which was right next to Troy's locker. I noticed Troy had put a sticker on his locker that read:

Jerry's Dead
Phish Sucks
Get a job.

I got a good laugh out of that, changed into my workout clothes, and walked across the main exercise floor over to what we jokingly called the Ingemar Johansson room—in honor of the last undisputed white heavyweight champion. Troy stands only five-seven, but he has an impressive physique, made more impressive by the fact that he stopped using steroids long ago. He was working the speed bag when I entered.

"You know," I said, "you've got the bad looks and the low intellect to be a fighter, but I just don't think you have the talent."

"A lot of people with no talent achieve success," he said as he continued drumming the bag with his alternating fists. "Look at Congress."

"If you have money, you don't need talent," I said, "but you don't have any money either." He stopped working the bag and stepped to the side so I could take a turn.

"I have one thing you'll never have," he said.

"What's that?" I said as I raised the level of the speed bag.

"Nineteen-inch biceps."

I laughed and started getting into a rhythm on the bag.

"Was that the motorcycle mama I saw you come in with?" he asked.

"Yeah."

"You about done with that gig?"

"One more week," I said.

"Then what?"

"Probably just chill for a few weeks. Go skiing. Kill time until Jayne gets here."

After taking turns on the speed bag and the heavy bag, we decided to fry our legs with ten sets of high-repetition squats. While Troy was doing one of his sets, I scanned the gym floor and saw Karlynn jogging very slowly on a treadmill. To her right a muscleman had loaded a barbell with 315 pounds and was making a big show of getting ready to do bench presses. After swinging his arms in circles, he sat down on the bench, then took a few deep breaths, then lay back, grabbed the bar, took a few more deep breaths, lifted the barbell off the rests and brought it down to his chest, let out a growl like a cougar that had just received a Tabasco enema, then did one repetition and replaced the bar.

"Christ," I said to my brother, "the bonehead puts three hundred and fifteen pounds on the bar and does one rep." My brother finished his set and looked at the guy I was referring to.

"That's a new exercise," my brother said. "It's called the *impress*."

"I ought to go ask him if I can work in."

"Please don't," Troy said. "He pays his bill every month, which is all I care about."

"Oh, look, now he's going to get a drink and talk with the spandex gal next to the water fountain." We watched as he walked toward the fountain, took a few sips, and started talking with the woman just as I had predicted.

"That's another new exercise," my brother said. "It's called jaw cardio."

We finished our squats and I hit the steam room, where I did some stretching. Karlynn must have seen me finish my workout, because she joined me in the steam room shortly after I had entered it.

"How was your jog?" I said.

"I didn't go very fast."

"It's your first day. It'll take a while to work up to a four-minute mile."

After we had showered and said good-bye to my brother, I noticed that someone had delivered the new metro Denver phone books, the white pages and the Yellow Pages, and left one of each on the counter near the entrance. Just for the hell of it I picked up the white pages and turned to the *K*s. There was only one Krait listed, and it wasn't Paul. It was Dorothy. I ripped that page out and headed to my truck with Karlynn.

On Sunday morning I read the paper and did the crossword puzzle while Karlynn worked on her list of one hundred things she wanted to do in her life. We spent the afternoon watching the Broncos humiliate the hated Raiders. The Broncos had been playing well lately, and the entire Rocky Mountain region had playoff fever. After the game I went into my office, sat down at my desk, dialed *67 to block my identity in case she had caller ID, then dialed the number for Dorothy Krait. The phone rang five times before a woman answered.

"Hello?"

"Is Paul there?" I asked.

"He doesn't live here," she said. She sounded as though she was in her mid-forties. Her voice was raspy, and I suspected she'd spent most of her life drinking or smoking or both.

"I'm sorry," I said. "I saw your name in the phone book and assumed you were related."

"I'm his mother," she said. "Who are you?"

"My name is Craig," I said. "I manage Joe's Pawn Shop over on Colfax, and Paul was in here the other—"

"He don't have a phone," she said. "Try him at work."

"Where's that?" I asked.

"Colorado Furniture Warehouse."

"Okay, I appreciate your—" She hung up.

14

I GOT UP EARLY MONDAY morning and practiced kata in the living room, wearing nothing but a T-shirt and some gym shorts. Kata are the formal exercises of karate. Each kata consists of sequences of techniques, both offensive and defensive, against imaginary foes. I hadn't practiced in a while and I felt rusty, but after thirty minutes my techniques were relaxed and fluid.

Prince trotted downstairs, so I let him out and made coffee. I showered and got dressed, then microwaved some instant oatmeal and ate breakfast while I listened to National Public Radio. At 8:15 I telephoned the Colorado Furniture Warehouse, a well-advertised discount outlet in Denver, and asked to speak with Paul Krait. The woman answering the phone transferred me to the warehouse proper, where a man told me Krait wouldn't be in until nine.

Karlynn came downstairs, smoked her customary morning cigarette in the garage, poured some Grape Nuts into a bowl, covered them with milk, then joined me at the dining table. "Feel like taking a drive today?" I asked.

"Sure, where are we going?"

"Just down to Denver. I want to talk to a guy down there."

Forty minutes later we were climbing into my truck for the ride to Denver when Karlynn said, "Damn, I forgot my purse." I gave her my house key while I warmed up the truck. Why she required her purse on this particular day was not a question that occurred to me.

She came back out and we headed down the canyon to Boulder and then Denver. The sky was clear and the temperature was in the high forties. A nice December day in Colorado. Karlynn stared out her window at the river, the trees, and the rock formations.

"How are you doing today?" I asked.

"About the same," she said.

"Iowa City's not a bad place," I said. "There's a big university there; it's like Boulder, but with cornfields instead of mountains."

"It's not the place," she said. "It's the job and the whole eight-to-five thing."

"Everyone has to earn a living," I said. "You'll make friends and after a few months it will seem like home." She didn't reply, just gazed out the window, evidently deep in thought.

The road from Nederland to Boulder runs parallel to Boulder Creek, which is actually a river, at least by my definition. If you can't jump over it, it's a river. The road twists and turns as it descends, and even though this was shaping up to be nice day, I still had to watch for the patches of ice that sometimes appear in places where the road gets little sunlight.

"So who's this guy you're going to see?" she asked.

"Just a man I need to ask some questions," I said. "It won't take long. After that I'll treat you to lunch."

"Okay," she said.

Forty-five minutes after leaving Nederland I pulled into the Colorado Furniture Warehouse parking lot. It was just after ten, but the lot was nearly full. Even in a slow economy people want furniture, and banks and credit card companies are more than happy to accommodate them. No money down, no payments for six months, blah, blah, blah.

I found a space and parked the truck. "This will just take a few minutes," I said. "You wait here. Keep the doors locked and just start honking the horn if there's any trouble."

"Can't I go in and look at furniture or something?"

"That's not a good idea," I said. "You might run into someone you know." Chances of that were slim, but I did not want her with me when I talked with Paul Krait.

"Okay," she sighed.

"Just wait here and think about where you want to go for lunch."

I got out of the car and started walking toward the warehouse entrance. It was downright balmy in Denver, nearly seventy degrees. I wore khaki slacks and a green poplin jacket.

As customers backed their vehicles into the loading area, I opened a metal door and walked inside, where more people were standing around with purchase orders in their hands, waiting for their names to be called over the PA system.

The warehouse itself was gigantic—several football fields long and at least one hundred feet high. There were rows and rows of furniture, and each row was stacked to the ceiling. Young kids maneuvered forklifts back and forth like trained ants. A balding middle-aged man at the desk asked if I'd been helped. I told him I wanted to speak with Paul Krait.

"You a cop?" he asked.

"This is unofficial," I said. "Just need to speak with him for a minute."

"He's over there," said the man. He pointed to a young kid driving one of the forklifts.

"Thanks," I said.

There was a sign indicating no customers were allowed beyond a certain point. I ignored it and started walking deliberately across the concrete floor toward Krait. He was about five-eight and on the thin side. His blond hair was cropped short—still a skinhead. He wore jeans, working boots, and a black sweatshirt. He must have thought I was there for some other purpose, because he paid no mind to me until I was within a few feet of him. "Turn that thing off," I said. "I want to talk with you."

"Hey, man, who the fu—" I grabbed the neck of his sweatshirt and again told him to turn the forklift off. He did. Then I yanked him from his seat and walked him to a spot behind one of the long aisles of furniture stacked to the roof. I pushed him up against a large cardboard box—hard—so that his back was to it, then let go of his sweatshirt.

"A few years back," I said, "the cops made you listen to a tape. You told them the voice on the tape sounded like a guy named Skull. Remember that?"

"Hey, man, what right do—" I placed my right hand around his neck and pinned it to the cardboard box.

"Listen," I said, "I don't like skinheads. I'd just as soon kill your little racist ass, but I have enough problems right now. You answer my questions, we'll be done in three minutes. You don't, you're in for a bad, bad day."

"I'm not a racist," he said. "I'm a member of SHARP." He was thoroughly intimidated at this point—exactly the result I had hoped my forthright approach would produce. I loosened the pressure on his neck slightly.

"What's SHARP?"

"Skinheads Against Racial Prejudice. I'm not into all that hate and violence anymore."

"Good," I said, "then you won't mind answering my questions." I let go of his neck.

"Who are you?" he asked.

"I'm just a guy who wants to find Skull," I said. "You remember that interview with the cops?"

"Yeah."

"Who gave you the tape with Skull's voice on it?"

"Like I told the cops, I don't know." I backhanded him, not hard. "Jesus, man, I don't know. We'd go to these clubs, and people would pass out shit like that all the time."

"Who'd you give the tape to?" I asked.

"I don't know," he said. He waited to see if I intended to strike him again. I didn't.

"You told the cops Skull talked about some kind of camp in Idaho. What do you remember about that?"

"Yeah," he said, "some kind of training camp where they teach you how to shoot and how to survive in the woods and shit like that."

"So you could kill niggers, fags, and Jews," I said.

"Yeah."

"What else do remember about that tape? Think hard." He looked down at the concrete floor as if to think for a moment. "What did the tape look like? Was there an address or phone number on it?"

"There was no label on it," he said.

"How were people supposed to get in touch with Skull if they wanted to visit this camp?"

"I don't know, man; I guess you just had to head up to Idaho and ask around."

"Thanks for your cooperation," I said. "Have a nice day."

I walked back to the warehouse entrance, put a dollar into a vending machine and bought a can of diet Coke, then walked out to the parking lot. When I got to my truck, the doors were locked, but Karlynn Slade and her purse were both gone.

15

AFTER I FINISHED mentally cursing myself for being so stupid, I jogged back to the store and began walking methodically up and down the aisles on the showroom floor. Past recliners, bedroom sets, dining sets, kitchen sets, sofas, coffee tables, office furniture, and home entertainment centers. Then I checked the restrooms, including the women's room, and the warehouse. No sign of her.

I walked back outside, climbed into my truck, and closed my eyes. I had to think. The horn had not sounded; I would have heard it, even in the warehouse. There was no sign of a struggle in or near my truck. The doors to my truck had been locked when I returned from my talk with Krait. If you were going to kidnap a woman from a truck, you probably wouldn't bother to lock the doors after you had pulled her out of there. Suddenly, the purse made sense. Karlynn had ditched me. And by implication she had begun the process of ditching Matt Simms, the FBI, the U.S. Marshals, Thad Bugg, and the Sons of Satan. Not to mention Prince.

I picked up my cell phone and dialed the offices of Keane, Simms & Mercante as my truck idled in the parking lot. The receptionist gave me the standard bit—Matt was in court and could she take a message or put me through to his voice mail.

"Look," I said, "this is Pepper Keane—the man who founded your law firm; my name is on the wall behind your desk. This is important. So if Matt is there, I need to speak with him ASAFP." She put me on hold.

"What's up?" Matt said. "Theresa thinks you're an asshole, by the way."

"Karlynn just flew the coop," I said. "I left her in the truck while I went in to talk with a kid who works at the Colorado Furniture Warehouse. When I came out, she was gone."

"Any chance someone snagged her?"

"No," I said. I explained my answer.

"Think you can find her?"

"It's a long shot."

"She's supposed to report to the U.S. marshal's office on Friday. That gives you four days to find her and talk some sense into her."

"What happens if I don't find her by then?"

"They'll indict her and issue an arrest warrant. She'll be fucked as far as the Witness Protection Program goes. And my credibility will probably be fucked too."

"What if I don't find her until after Friday?"

"That's a tough one," he said. "Congress passed these damn sentencing guidelines, so she'll be looking at some real time if they want to play hardball. The judge has no discretion."

"If I don't turn her in, maybe she disappears and lives happily ever after." I paused. "Or maybe Bugg finds her and kills her."

"Let's revisit the question on Friday," he said.

"I'm sorry about this," I said.

"She fooled me, too," he said. "I thought she was really ready for this."

"Damn it," I said.

"Berating yourself won't help," he said, "even though you're good at it. Let's start working on a plan."

"I've got a plan," I said, "but it's gonna take money." With apologies to George Harrison, it was going to take a whole lot of precious money. Plenty of money.

"We've got nearly three hundred grand in my safe," he said. "Are you still at the warehouse?"

"Yeah."

"That's just a few miles away. Why don't you swing by and pick some up. Having it here makes me nervous."

16

I PUT THE TRUCK IN GEAR and headed downtown to get the cash from Matt. While I was driving, I called Scott on my cell phone and explained what had happened.

"You got a plan?" he asked.

"I'm working on one. Will Bobbi give you a week off?" Bobbi, Scott's longtime girlfriend, is a Boulder realtor. They live in Scott's south Boulder home, but Bobbi still maintains her own condo. This arrangement had worked well and Scott had never seen any reason to superimpose a marriage on it.

"She'll be glad to get rid of me for a week. A woman can only stand so much pleasure."

"Okay, pack whatever you need for a week of driving and eating in truck stops. I'll pick you up in a few hours."

I parked in a lot next to Matt's building. It was one of those lots where you have to slide currency into a slot in a metal box with a number that corresponds to the number of your parking place. I had used my last dollar bill to buy a diet Coke at the furniture place. All I had were twenties, and there was nobody available to make change. For a long time I have kept a phony million-dollar bill in my wallet and offered it now and then to convenience store clerks as a gag. It looked real enough, so I folded it into a rectangle about the size of stick of gum and pushed it into the appropriate slot.

I walked past the receptionist into Matt's office and closed the door. "You going to tell me what the plan is?" he said.

"No time to chat," I said. "I'll call you from my cell phone on my way back to Nederland. Right now I want to make tracks. My guess is, she stuck out her thumb and took the first ride she could get out of Denver. The longer I wait, the greater the distance she may have traveled."

"The money's in that box," he said. He pointed to a cardboard box on the floor—the kind law firms use to store closed files.

"How much is in there?"

"Just about all of it," he said. "I kept twenty thousand to cover her future legal fees. Keep track of how you spend it in case the feds get her first and she happens to tell them she gave me three hundred thousand in drug money. I want to be able to account for it."

I picked up the box. "I'm going to send you an e-mail in about an hour. It would be helpful if you could put a couple of people to work finding a fax number or e-mail address for every truck stop, greasy spoon, and low-rent motel in the mountain time zone. Give priority to places north and west of here."

"May the force be with you," he said.

"McCutcheon will be with me," I said. "That should be good enough."

My F-150 has a shell on the back, so I slid the box as far back into the bed as I could get it, and covered it with an old blanket.

Scott was ready when I arrived at his house, so he loaded a suitcase and backpack into the back of my truck. Then he went back inside and came out with a pistol tucked into his belt, as well as a hunting rifle and two shotguns, which he placed on the floor of the king cab compartment behind the front seats.

We headed up to Nederland so I could pack some things and get my dogs, which evidently now included a bluetick coonhound with excellent tracking skills. "What's the plan?" Scott asked.

"Remember those posters we put up all over the place to make Bugg think I'm actually doing something to earn my money?"

"Yeah. Did anyone ever call you?"

"No, but this time we're going to add our cell phone numbers, my e-mail address, and a big reward, then e-mail it to Big Matt. He can put his minions to work faxing the damn thing all over the western U.S."

"Makes sense."

"Then we're going to head north on I-25." I remembered when it had been known simply as the Valley Highway. Denver is a big city now, with skyscrapers and major league sports teams, but I liked it better when the biggest tourist attraction was the revolving restaurant on top of the Holiday Inn, and the basketball team played with a red, white, and blue ball at the stockyards coliseum.

"Why north?"

"I-25 passes right by the furniture place. The nearest freeway ramp would have been the one for northbound traffic. That's where she would have stuck out her thumb."

"Maybe you're not giving her enough credit," he said. "Maybe she'd had this planned for a while and had someone ready to meet her."

"No way," I said. "She didn't even know I was going to Denver until this morning. And she didn't know I was going to the furniture warehouse until I pulled into the parking lot."

When we got to Nederland, I gassed up the truck at the Sinclair, which had formerly been the Texaco. Next I went to the bank and withdrew twenty thousand dollars I had parked in a savings account just in case all my other investments went to hell some day.

"You've got three hundred grand in the back of your truck," Scott said. "Isn't that enough?"

I explained my logic to him, then drove to Backcountry Pizza to buy a large diet Coke from the fountain. I'm a diet Coke addict. I used to get it at the B&F Mountain Market, but they had switched to Pepsi to cut costs, and the Sinclair/Texaco had always been a Pepsi dealer. With fuel for the truck and a forty-eight-ounce diet Coke for me, I drove to my home.

I put the money I had withdrawn from the bank into a small safe I have that looks identical to a can of Coke, and I put that in the refrigerator. I went to my desk and modified the Karlynn poster on my laptop, then e-mailed it to Matt with instructions on what to do. I tried to call Bugg at his home and on his cell phone, but there was no answer. I guess being the leader of a sadistic biker gang keeps you pretty busy.

"Hey, look at this," Scott said from the kitchen.

I walked into the kitchen and he handed me a yellow legal pad. On it was a note, obviously written by Karlynn: "Prince is yours now. Take good care of him. Thanks for everything. Watch out for Thad—he can hold a grudge for a long time."

"Shit," I said. I could be succinct when I wanted to.

I packed a small suitcase. My backpack is always ready to go, so that was no problem. I loaded both into the back of the truck, along with a five-gallon plastic container of premium duck-and-potatoes dog chow. Wheat has a sensitive stomach and can't eat regular dog food. It has to be duck and potatoes.

I whistled and ushered my three dogs into the back of the

truck. I went back into the house and grabbed my laptop, my medication, my file on Karlynn and Bugg, and Bertrand Russell's *History of Western Philosophy* in case I got any free time. Then it was back down the canyon to Boulder.

There is no cell phone service in the canyon, but as soon as we hit Boulder, I called Nancy at work and asked her for Kendra Carlson's phone number.

"Are you going to ask her out?" Nancy asked.

"Karlynn took off on me," I explained. "I just need to ask Kendra if she has any thoughts on where Karlynn might have gone. They had three sessions last week."

"Kendra won't reveal privileged information," Nancy said.

"I'll take any help she can offer," I said.

"Here's the number," Nancy said. I repeated it as Nancy gave it to me, and Scott wrote it down on the back of a napkin as I repeated it.

I called Kendra right away but was automatically dumped into voice mail. I left a message asking her to call me and said it was important.

I stopped at the Office Depot in Boulder and had them make one thousand copies of the revised Karlynn poster. While I was watching the kid behind the counter to make sure he understood that I wanted the copies immediately, I told Scott to buy two good staplers and a supply of Scotch tape.

It took another thirty minutes to reach I-25 via Highway 52. There is a McDonald's there as well as a few gas stations. I put some posters up at the golden arches while Scott visited the gas stations and handed out posters to truckers.

We headed north on I-25 toward Fort Collins. Scott was looking at a map he had found in my glove compartment. "What are we going to do when we hit Cheyenne?" he asked. I-25 intersects I-80 at Cheyenne, Wyoming. You can go north to Casper, west across Wyoming into Utah, or east to Nebraska.

"Probably go west," I said.

"And you know this because . . . ?"

"Just playing the probabilities," I said. "She's from Nebraska and doesn't have fond memories of it, so I don't think she'd head in that direction. The largest city north of Cheyenne is Casper, which isn't exactly a crossroads of commerce. I figure most of the northbound traffic on 25 out of Denver heads west on I-80 toward Salt Lake, Vegas, and L.A." We were coming up on another truck stop in a place called Johnson's Corner. "Plus, she's thumbing it in December. I'd be wanting to get my ass to a warmer climate."

"It pains me to say this," Scott said, "but everything you just said makes perfect sense. Maybe that year you spent in graduate school did some good." I had spent a year studying philosophy and logic in graduate school early in my legal career, but had quit after one year because practicing law paid more. Also, to be honest, I had already finished my three years as a JAG and wasn't good at taking orders from young graduate assistants who had never set foot off a college campus.

Scott and I did our thing with the Karlynn posters in Johnson's Corner, then got back on the Interstate and headed north. The sun was getting low on the western horizon, and I turned on my headlights. My cell phone rang. Or, more precisely, my cell phone began to sound its digital rendition of the theme song from *Mister Ed*. It was Kendra.

I explained the situation and asked if she had any thoughts on where Karlynn might be headed or what might be going on in her mind now that she was no longer chemically dependent.

"You've put me in a difficult position," she said. "You've given me information that causes me some concern, but I am bound by the doctor-patient privilege, and I take that seriously."

"I know all about the privilege," I said, "but if the feds find her before I do, they'll put her in prison. And if Bugg finds her before I do, he'll kill her. If you know anything that might help me find her, now would be the time to tell me."

"I'm not sure I want you to find her," she said. "Even if you locate her and bring her back against her will, she wants no part of the Witness Protection Program, and I don't think she will testify against her husband. She's just too afraid. It's common with abused women."

"If she doesn't testify, they'll put her in prison," I said.

"That's right."

"Not a pleasant alternative."

"Karlynn would agree with you."

"She doesn't have the skills to disappear on her own," I said.

"Do you have the skills to help her?"

"Maybe." I had about three hundred thousand dollars' worth of skills in the back of my truck.

"I don't know where Karlynn might be headed," she said, "but I'm not surprised she took off. In some ways she's only recently become an adult. She's starting to see how events that took place when she was young skewed her worldview. She's accepting more responsibility for her problems, and she's just now discovering the possibilities that are open to her. She'd love to put her past behind her and start over, and this is her attempt to do that."

"Did she talk about what kind of life she would live if she could start over?"

"You must have made an impression on her," Kendra said. "She was making a list—one like you evidently made—of one hundred things she'd like to do in her life."

"Any idea what was on her list?"

"She didn't show it to me, but she talked about traveling. She wanted to try skydiving; I remember that because it didn't fit with my picture of her. Was that on your list?"

"My brother and I used to skydive," I said, "but we gave it up when he slammed into a cornfield at thirty-five miles per hour."

"Did he survive?"

"Yeah, he owns a gym in Denver."

"Troy Keane, that's your brother?" Everybody in the metro area knows who my brother is because his muscleman photo, complete with computer-enhanced teeth, is on half the buses in Denver.

"Yup, that's my brother. The accident is what started him on his fitness career."

"You took Karlynn to your brother's gym, didn't you?"

"Just once. I was getting cabin fever. I think we went last Saturday. Why? Did she mention it?"

"She said she hated gym class when she was in high school, and skipped class a lot, but going to the gym with you was different because she wasn't competing against anyone and nobody was telling her what to do."

"I thought exercise might be a healthier addiction for her than meth."

"I've worked with many chemically dependent people. I don't think Karlynn will fall back into that."

"What about her dog?" I asked. "She seemed attached to him. I'm surprised she left him." I did not mention that the only reason for my involvement in the whole affair was that one of the best lawyers in Denver, Matt Simms, had hired me to steal Prince from Bugg so Karlynn and Prince could go into the Witness Protection Program together.

"Dogs offer unconditional love," she responded. "Karlynn wasn't getting that from anyone else. She might look for another dog when she gets to wherever she is going."

"Any other insights?" I asked.

"Don't bring her back here," she said. "You'll be sentencing her to prison. She's not going to testify against her husband."

"Thanks," I said. "If you hear from her or have any other thoughts on where she might be headed, please call me. She's out there alone and doesn't have much money."

"She took quite a bit of money from her husband. That's one reason she's so afraid of him."

"She doesn't have the cash on her," I said. I thanked her again, gave her my cell phone number, and said good-bye.

"Does the former Miss North Dakota have anything to offer?" Scott said.

"Yeah, in addition to checking truck stops, we need to be checking health clubs, schools offering instruction in skydiving, and all the animal shelters."

17

Two DAYS LATER, on a Wednesday afternoon, we were still headed west, just passing the Great Salt Lake. We'd had a half-dozen calls since beginning our journey from people who had seen Karlynn or thought they had. Our last confirmed sighting had come yesterday from a truck stop waitress in Rock Springs, Wyoming. She sounded credible. We hadn't found Karlynn yet, but at least we were headed in the right direction.

We were listening to Hank Williams and looking at the lake when the *Mister Ed* theme song sounded. I picked up the cell phone and said, "Pepper Keane."

"Yeah, uh, are you the fella looking for that girl?"

"Yes."

"I seen her 'bout two hours ago."

"Where?"

"What about the reward?"

"Give me your name, address, and phone number. If we find her, we'll take care of you." I motioned for Scott to find a pen and take down the information as I repeated it.

"It was just outside of Twin Falls. Two hours ago."

"Idaho? Was she with anyone?"

"Don't know. She was using the bathroom at a truck stop. I

wasn't paying attention. Didn't see your poster until I stopped at the weigh station just now. She looked okay, though."

I asked a few more questions and assured him we wouldn't forget him if we found Karlynn. I hung up, turned to Scott, and said, "Dig out the map and find the quickest route to Twin Falls." The map was in his lap. He unfolded and studied it.

"Bad news," he said. "We have to backtrack. Gotta head back to Salt Lake City and pick up Interstate Eighty-four. It heads north into Idaho. So much for getting her ass to a warmer climate."

Three hours later we were at the Pride of Idaho truck stop in Twin Falls. We handed out lots of posters and asked lots of questions to lots of people. She was headed north. Wearing black boots, jeans, a white T-shirt (probably one of mine), and a black leather jacket. Possibly with a trucker out of Arkansas. A trucker out of Arkansas—that really narrowed it down.

The temperature dropped when the sun went down. It was dark and cold. We were tired. I felt bad that the dogs had been more or less confined to the back of my truck for three days. We stopped at a motel that looked reasonably clean. We walked into the lobby and took our place in line behind a family that was evidently making a cross-country journey, and a man in a suit who was probably in sales.

The girl behind the counter was in her early twenties and was having a tough time getting people registered because the phone kept ringing. From what I could tell, some callers wanted to make reservations and some were guests needing one thing or another.

She finally got the family registered, but that had taken nearly ten minutes. The phone rang as the salesman had started to say he wanted a room. I rolled my eyes at the salesman and he nodded in agreement. Scott stepped out for a minute. About two minutes later the girl behind the counter was still on the phone. She said, "Hello? Hello?" and then hung up. "The line went dead," she explained.

The salesman got his room and we got ours—a nonsmoking room with two queen beds. On the top floor so we would not have to put up with noise from anyone above us. I registered us as David Hume and Rene DesCartes, paid cash for the room and the pet deposit, parked the truck, and let the dogs run around while Scott carried our gear upstairs.

After the dogs had done their thing, I led them up to our room, where Scott was in a chair, casually cleaning his fingernails with his pocket knife. "Kind of funny how the phone went dead just when we really needed the clerk to focus on getting us a room," I said.

"The Lord works in mysterious ways," he said.

"And sometimes He works through your pocket knife?"

"I'm just His instrument," Scott said with a smile. I sat down on one of the beds and started taking my shoes off.

"Besides," Scott added, "I'm tired of waiting in lines because businesses are too cheap to hire enough help. All I did was shift the cost created by inadequate staffing back to the owner. Instead of us paying the cost by waiting in line, he can pay the cost by having someone come out here and fix his phone line. That's how the free market is supposed to work."

I turned to the three dogs on the floor and said, "There you have it."

18

You might as well come home," Matt said. "The deal is off. The grand jury indicted her for bond jumping. The judge signed the warrant two hours ago. Karlynn is a fugitive, and my credibility with the FBI is shot."

"What did you tell them?"

"I told them the truth. Adrienne Valeska called me after lunch and asked if I had any idea why Karlynn hadn't shown up at the marshal's office. I told her Karlynn had ditched you Monday and you'd been looking for her ever since."

"How did that play?"

"Not well, but what can they do? I had no obligation to tell them Karlynn was missing."

"They know I was babysitting her."

"So what? There was no crime until she failed to appear, and you were working overtime to find her and get her back here on time."

"What did you tell them about my efforts to track her down?"

"Nothing. I told them I hired you on behalf of Karlynn as part of our defense team, and they can't compel you to say a damn thing."

"Is that true?"

"I don't know. I've got a kid researching it."

"They'll be looking for me, hoping I'll lead them to Karlynn."

"Come home. Get back to your life. It's not your problem now. Karlynn screwed herself."

"She left a few things with me," I reminded him.

"Bury it. We'll reassess in five years."

"Let me think on it," I said. "Maybe I can find Karlynn and still make it back to Colorado by the time Jayne returns from China."

"What are you going to do if you find her, make a citizen's arrest?"

"Maybe I can help her disappear."

"That would be a federal crime."

"Only if I get caught."

"Speaking of getting caught," Matt said, "what are you going to tell Bugg?"

"I'll tell him I can't find her. Last time anyone saw her she was in the Greyhound station in Biloxi, Mississippi. The locals think she might have been eaten by a gator."

"Works for me," Matt said.

"Say hi to the guys for me. I'll call you in a few days. You've got my cell phone number if you need it." I ended the call and put the cell phone down on our table.

It was Friday. The day Karlynn was supposed to enter the Witness Protection Program. The day Prince was supposed to enter the Witness Protection Program. It was just past six. We were at a seedy bar and grill outside Boise. It had a good jukebox, a few pool tables, and Sierra Nevada Pale Ale on tap. We had spent two days talking with everyone we could meet between Twin Falls and Boise, but the trail had grown cold.

A waitress in jeans approached our table. Scott ordered a strip steak.

"You want fries with that?" she asked.

"You use Idaho potatoes?" Scott replied.

"I'm sure we do," she said. No sense of humor.

"I'll have the filet," I said. "Make mine rare."

"Fries?"

"No, thanks."

The music stopped, so I walked over to the jukebox and fed it three dollar bills. It was a country kind of place, but that was all right because I love old country music as well as old rock 'n' roll. I don't like the new country sound much, though. It all sounds the same to me. I prefer the old, twangy country. My three dollars would buy us twenty-one songs by artists such as Hank Williams, Johnny Cash, and Merle Haggard. And if that didn't satisfy us, we had more money out in the truck, ably guarded by Buck, Wheat, and Prince.

I walked back to our table. "You want to hit the road tonight?" Scott asked.

"No, I need a good night's sleep."

"I figure we could make Denver in one long day, if the weather's good."

"No use killing ourselves," I said. "We can spend tomorrow night in Rock Springs or Rawlins and drive on into Denver on Sunday."

"I love this music," Scott said. "It's a shame nobody plays it anymore. I've got to think we aren't the only ones who enjoy it."

"I would have loved to be a disc jockey in the forties and fifties," I said. "Just sit around some small-town radio station drinking coffee and playing good music."

"That would've been a good life," Scott agreed.

The steaks took longer than they should have. I decided to call Bugg and give him the bad news. When he answered his phone, he just said, "Bugg."

"Pepper Keane," I said.

"Where are you?" he asked.

"Idaho," I said.

"Any leads?"

On the theory that you should never tell a bigger lie than nec-essary, I decided not to tell him Karlynn had been devoured by an alligator in Mississippi. "We know she passed through here," I said. "She was catching rides with truckers. She told one of them she was headed to Seattle."

"Seattle?"

"Yeah. Any idea why she'd go there?"

"No clue."

"You want me to keep looking?"

"Absolutely," he said. "I don't care what it costs or how long it takes; you find her. And the dog, too."

The steaks arrived. Mine was rare, just the way I like it. I am ambivalent about eating meat, and I struggle with the morality of breeding animals just to kill them, but this wasn't the kind of place where I was going to be able to get a plate of fettuccine Alfredo.

"What happened to being eaten by a gator in Mississippi?" Scott said.

"We're in Idaho. Telling him she was headed to Seattle seemed more believable."

"But there are no gators in Seattle," Scott said. "You blew any chance of us ever using the gator story."

"Could be a stray gator," I said. "Got lost. Made it across the Panama Canal. Didn't like California. Swam up the coast to Port-land, then decided to head up to Seattle to drink coffee and listen to grunge."

"Does Bugg want us to keep looking?" Scott said.

"Absolutely."

After supper we ordered a pitcher of beer, enjoyed the jukebox, and talked about nothing in particular. The crowd got a little rougher as the dinner hour passed and the hardcore drinkers and pool players trickled in.

"So, what's up with you and the therapist?" Scott said.

"Nothing's up," I said.

"Okay."

"She's someone I might be interested in getting to know better if I didn't have Jayne."

"Okay."

"Jayne will be home in a week," I said.

"And when she leaves?"

"C'mon, at least let me enjoy the holidays with her before I start thinking about where the relationship is going and all that."

"Just making conversation," he said.

"What are you and Bobbi doing for Christmas?" I asked.

"Hadn't thought much about it. Probably hit the slopes once or twice. Other than that, I'd be happy to sit around and watch football the whole time, but I'll probably get dragged to the *Nutcracker* ballet somewhere along the way."

The beer remaining in our pitcher was warm, and rather than finish it off, we ordered a new pitcher. Someone else had managed to slip a few bucks into the jukebox when I wasn't looking, and we were now being subjected to some of the new country music.

Four young skinheads wandered in around eight-thirty, wearing mostly black. They snagged an empty table and ordered some beer. At about the same time the members of a band started to appear and set up their equipment behind a small dance floor. "Friday night in Boise," Scott said.

Seeing the skinheads made me start thinking about the death of my cousin Hal. I thought about the anonymous man who had called a radio station the next day proclaiming that Hal's death should serve as a warning to white cops that protect niggers and faggots. Paul Krait had told police the caller sounded like a man named Skull who had narrated a hate-filled audiotape making its rounds in the skinhead community. On the tape Skull had touted an Aryan Resistance camp in Idaho. And I remembered how Krait had answered when I had asked how anyone was supposed to get in touch with Skull: "I don't know, man; I guess you just had to head up to Idaho and ask around."

I was in Idaho. I was a few feet from some skinheads. Why not ask around? I walked over to the skinheads, leaned over their table, and in a real friendly voice said, "You guys are skinheads, right?" I was being a smart aleck, but I figured God wouldn't have given me that talent if He didn't want me to use it.

The biggest of the four, who wasn't that big, said, "What's it to you?" He was the leader.

"I'm trying to find a guy named Skull. He's a skinhead. Heard he was in Idaho. You guys are skinheads. We're in Idaho. Thought you might know where I could find him." I smiled.

"Never heard of him," the big one said. He couldn't have been more than twenty years old.

"He runs some kind of paramilitary camp," I said.

"You're in the wrong part of Idaho," another one said. He had the Nazi SS symbol tattooed on the side of his face. "Those fuck-ers are all up north." The bigger one shot him a look that said "shut the fuck up."

The four sat there, hands folded on the table, looking stoic. The conversation was over unless I wanted to start a brawl.

"Sorry I bothered you," I said to them. "Can I buy you guys an-other pitcher or something?" I walked away from their table, up to the bar, and paid the bartender to have a pitcher delivered to their table.

"What was that all about?" Scott said.

"Let's go," I said. "I'll explain in the truck."

Scott left a few bucks on the table for the waitress and we walked out into the parking lot. It was cold. The moon was out, but the night sky was cloudy, creating rings of light around the moon. Scott started toward the truck, but I began walking around the parking lot. It didn't take long to figure out which vehicle was the skinhead-mobile. It was an old Pontiac sedan. Black. Confederate flag stickers on the rear bumper. I walked back to my truck and climbed in.

Just east of the bar and grill was a small building that housed a sewing machine repair shop on one side and a barber shop on the other. Both were closed. I started the truck and drove over to the barber shop. I parked the truck so we could see the entrance to the bar and grill.

I looked at Scott and said, "I want to talk with those kids again when they come out."

"Why?"

I refreshed his memory concerning the death of my cousin Hal four years ago outside Coors Field in Denver. I told him about Paul Krait and the hate-filled audiotape featuring the voice of a man named Skull.

"Sounds like maybe we won't be heading home tomorrow," Scott said.

"You can catch a flight to Denver tomorrow, if you want. I've got nothing else to do for a week. Can't find Karlynn; maybe I can find Skull."

"I don't mind hanging out for a few extra days. That's one of the advantages of unemployment. It gives me the freedom to be spontaneous." Scott holds an advanced degree in astrophysics, but hasn't held a steady job since leaving the navy umpteen years ago. He earns his living doing computer consulting and advising people on other high-tech projects. He calls himself a self-employed techno geek.

The skinheads emerged from the bar just after midnight. There were too many others in and around the bar to make a scene, so we followed them at a discreet distance. They drove for ten minutes, finally pulling into the driveway of a rundown house in an older part of town. We parked down the block. The two in the backseat exited from the black vehicle and entered the home. The driver began backing the car out of the driveway.

"Go for the two in the house or follow the car?" Scott asked.

"Let's follow the car. Christ only knows what they've got in the house. Shotguns, pit bulls, and who knows what."

We followed the Pontiac another few miles to a nicer house in a better part of town. They parked on the street. I turned off my headlights. They emerged from their car and began walking toward the house. One was the leader and the other was the one with the SS tattoo.

"How do you want to play it?" Scott asked. "If we go straight at these guys, word will get back to Skull pretty damn quick that two guys driving a truck with Colorado plates are looking for him."

"If we don't go straight at them, we could be farting around for weeks waiting for them to lead us to something useful. I've got to pick Jayne up next week."

"I was hoping you'd say that," Scott said.

"Let's do it before they get inside," I said. I turned on my headlights and gunned the F-150, guiding it into their driveway in a big hurry. They turned and started walking toward us.

"What the fuck—?" the one with the SS tattoo started to say. He stopped in midsentence, at about the same time Scott stuck the barrel of his shotgun out the passenger window. I opened my door and climbed out of the truck, my Glock in my right hand.

I walked toward the SS kid and said, "What did you mean when you said I was in the wrong part of Idaho?"

"Don't answer him, Wes," the leader said. "These fuckers got no right—"

Scott opened the truck's passenger door, sighted the shotgun in on the leader, and started walking right at him. When he got close, he looked at me with a grin and said, "Doesn't this guy's head look kind of like a clay pigeon?"

Now I was eight feet from the SS guy. I pointed the automatic at the center of his nose. "What did you mean when you said I was in the wrong part of Idaho?" He looked at his friend, then back at me.

"I don't know no guy named Skull, but those paramilitary types are all up north. Around Coeur d'Alene. There's lots of those camps up there. That's where you need to be looking." I turned to the leader.

"What about you? You know anyone named Skull?"

"Wouldn't tell you if I did," he said.

Scott looked at him and said, "You know what a shotgun does to a clay pigeon at this range?"

The leader just glared at Scott, his eyes full of hate and a determination to violently avenge this humiliating episode as soon as possible.

"Here's the deal," I said. "As of now you two and your two shit-for-brains friends are in charge of finding Skull for us. We know he's a skinhead and we know he's in Idaho, so that should narrow it down for you. We'll check back in a few days to see how you're doing. Don't let us down."

I started backing away, my pistol still out, and Scott did the same. We climbed into the truck and drove off into the Idaho night.

"That should put us on Skull's radar," Scott said.

"Yeah, I guess this raises our threat condition from yellow to orange."

19

WE DROVE TO NORTHERN IDAHO on Saturday and found an off-the-beaten-path summer resort that offered cabins for rent. It being December, the owner gave us a good rate on a cozy cabin with a large stone fireplace and no TV. I registered us as Arthur Schopenhauer and F. Nietzsche just for the hell of it. After checking in on Saturday afternoon, we drove to Coeur d'Alene to buy food and supplies. It was a sunny winter day, and when we had completed our chore at the grocery store, we let the dogs out of the truck and led them across the street to a park, where they could run and play. A police officer drove past, but unlike in Boulder, the cops in northern Idaho didn't give a damn if my dogs were off leash.

We needed exercise and the dogs needed exercise. We ran around and threw sticks for the dogs to fetch. Buck and Wheat enjoy that game, but Prince was a hound and was having none of it. He started sniffing and running, and before I knew it, he was at the far end of the park. He must have come upon an intriguing scent. Then he followed the scent, as hounds are wont to do. I started jogging toward him because I didn't want to lose sight of him. He trotted toward a trio of scruffy biker types just coming out of a burger joint across from the park. He approached them with curiosity and caution. One of them knelt down and held out a palm in an attempt to make friends.

"C'mon Prince," I said as I crossed the street and approached them. He turned toward me and I attached his leash to his collar. "Sorry," I said to them. "He's got a mind of his own."

"Nice-looking dog," one of them said. "That's a bluetick, right?"

"He's got some bluetick in him," I said. "I'm really sorry he bothered you."

"No problem, man," the biker said.

I walked Prince back to the park and eventually back to Scott, Buck, and Wheat. I thought nothing more of Prince's encounter with the three bikers.

We drove back to the cabin. I made spaghetti, salad, and cheese bread while Scott built a fire in the massive fireplace. After supper I read a few chapters of Bertrand Russell's book and Scott did some meditation. The conflict between empiricism—the belief that human knowledge comes from our senses—and rationalism—the belief that human knowledge comes from reason—has always fascinated me, and I enjoyed reading about the history of the debate. I tried to get Scott to discuss it, but he just said it was a false dilemma and went back to meditating.

After a while I concluded I was not going to solve an epistemological problem that had raged for centuries, so I did what perplexed philosophers have been doing since ancient Greece. I went to bed. Actually, I did some stretching, took my meds, and then went to bed.

We slept well. Would have slept past dawn, but the *Mister Ed* theme song sounded at six in the morning.

"Hi, sweetie," Jayne said.

"Hi," I said.

"Did I wake you up?"

"You woke me up. You woke Scott up. You woke Buck, Wheat, and Prince up. What time is it in Beijing?"

"I'm sorry. I should have waited until later to call. I just wanted to hear your voice. Where are you?"

"In a cabin outside of Coeur d'Alene, Idaho."

"Is the biker girl with you? What's her name, Caitlin?"

"Karlynn."

"Is she with you?"

"Not to worry," I said. "She took off on Monday and we've been looking for her ever since. The trail went cold somewhere near Boise."

"And you're still looking for her?"

"Yeah." There was no point in mentioning Skull or the fact that a lot of White Power morons would be looking for us real soon.

"She should be easy to find, what with her humps and all."

"That's what I thought, but it's turning out to be more difficult than we had anticipated."

"Will you be able to pick me up or will you still be searching for Karlynn?"

"I'll pick you up."

"Let me give you my flight information," she said. I got out of bed, found a pencil, and took down the information. "Will you meet me at the gate?" she asked.

"I'll meet you at the baggage claim," I said. "They won't let me go to the gate."

"I forgot," she said. There was a brief pause as we contemplated how militant Islam had changed the world. Jayne understood it better than most; her parents had died more than fifteen years ago when a bomb planted by Libyan terrorists exploded on a jetliner over Scotland. Then the pause was over and Jayne said, "Try not to dwell on the problems of man."

"Ignoring them doesn't make them go away."

"Obsessing about them doesn't make them go away, either." She knew I got depressed when I spent too much time thinking about such things.

"I know," I said.

"Focus on something else," she said. Now she was back to her normal perky self. "Think about how much fun we two infidels can have during my visit."

"That's a good idea," I said. "We can drink. Listen to loud rock-and-roll. You can wear skimpy clothes. Anything we can do to piss off Allah."

"That's the Pepper Keane I know and love," she said.

We traded I-love-yous, then said good-bye.

"If you really want to piss off Allah," Scott said, "you should adopt a pig. Allah doesn't like pork."

"Have to be one motherfuckin' charmin' pig," I said. "Have to be ten times more charming than that Arnold on *Green Acres*." That was a line from *Pulp Fiction*, which both Scott and I agreed was the best "guy movie" of all time. Maybe the second best. *Kelly's Heroes* was good, too.

I let the dogs out briefly, made coffee, started a fire in the fireplace, let the dogs back in, then climbed back into bed, content to know the cabin would be warm and the coffee would be hot when I woke up in a few hours.

A few hours later I awoke again and made blueberry pancakes from a "just add water" mix.

"What's the plan today?" Scott asked.

"I thought we might go to church." It was, after all, a Sunday.

"Seriously," Scott said.

"I am serious. A lot of these White Power nuts take their Bible seriously. Some have formed their own churches."

"I have trouble picturing skinheads going to church."

"The skinheads probably don't, but there are other White Power types who do. What else are we going to do on a Sunday?"

"How do we know what church to go to?" Scott asked.

"We can rule out the Catholics," I said. "We can rule out the Presbyterians and the other established denominations. We'll just drive around until we see one that looks right."

We left Buck and Wheat in the cabin, but took Prince with us because he had a propensity to howl when left without human companionship. We stopped at a convenience store so I could buy a diet Coke, and started driving around the outskirts of Coeur d'Alene. We saw plenty of churches, but all were affiliated with mainstream groups such as the Baptists, the Methodists, and so on.

"Check this out," Scott said as we approached a county road that crossed the main highway. A sign informed us that the Church of Jesus the Almighty was one mile east on the county road. I turned down the county road.

The Church of Jesus the Almighty looked much like any other church. The building was old, white, and made of wood. It had a steeple with a cross atop it. The sign in front did not indicate affiliation with any denomination. There were maybe two dozen cars and trucks in the dirt parking lot, but no people. The service had already begun.

"What's our cover story?" Scott asked.

"How about this? We're bounty hunters. We're looking for a guy—a black guy—who jumped bail on a rape charge."

"Rape of a white woman," Scott added.

"Yeah, and he's real dangerous. We think he's in this area, but we might need some extra manpower to take him down."

"Why do we think he's up here?"

"Our sources told us he came up here to take out a skinhead named Skull. They have a history."

"That's good," Scott said. "What's our guy's name? What does he look like?"

"Jackson. Bobby Jackson. He's six-three and weighs about two hundred pounds."

"We using our real names?" Scott asked.

"Might as well. Got my real license plates on the truck. Easy enough to find out who we are from the plates."

We walked up the three steps, opened the door, and quietly took seats in the back pew. People turned back to look us over, but then turned their heads to focus on the pastor. He wasn't wearing a clerical collar, just a white shirt and navy trousers. He appeared to be about fifty.

The sermon was not filled with hate. The pastor talked about what he called the "myth of the separation of church and state." He said the founding fathers had intended for America to be a Christian nation. I had mixed feelings. I knew the founding fathers had overwhelmingly rejected a proposal to make Christianity the official religion of the new republic. Jefferson and Adams had been Unitarians who rejected the holy Trinity. Jefferson had gone so far as to rewrite the Bible and had called his version *The Life and Morals of Jesus*—a sort of atheist's version of the New Testament. On an intellectual level I supported the separation of church and state. At the same time, though, I worried that Americans no longer possessed a collective set of core values that united them. At times I sounded like Pat Buchanan.

We sat through the service and managed not to fall asleep. By the end of the service I knew I had picked the wrong church. These were just regular folks, nothing sinister about them. After the service we mingled. We're good at that. People introduced themselves and most seemed sincere in trying to make us feel welcome.

We repeated the Bobby Jackson story to anyone who would listen. One who listened was a silver-haired man named Frank Prell. "You guys got a picture of this Bobby Jackson?" he asked.

"Not on me," I said.

"What's his beef with Skull?"

I shrugged. "Something that happened in Denver a few years ago. That's all I know."

"And you think if you can find Skull all you'll have to do is keep an eye on him and wait for Jackson to show?"

"We thought we'd give it a try," I said.

"I'd come up with another plan," he said. "Your guy ain't gonna get within five miles of Skull. And neither are you." He pulled his wallet out of his back pocket and handed me his card. He was Coeur d'Alene's chief of police. I showed the card to Scott. "You want to cut the crap and tell me what you're up to?"

"I told you," I said. I handed him one my private investigator cards. "We need to find Jackson and we think he's going to try to get at Skull."

Chief Prell smiled. "Skull lives on a compound about twelve miles east of here," he said. "The land is owned by a fella calls himself 'the Reverend' Howard Biggs. He's an older man. He was a Klansman for many years in a place called Coosa County, Alabama, but moved up here twenty-some years ago to start a church. The Church of the Sacred Covenant. It's a white supremacist group. Plenty of 'em around here, unfortunately. Anyhow, Biggs made a lot of money off the church. He preaches hate and solicits money all over the country so he can fight the racial holy war when it finally comes. He has used the money to buy thousands of acres of virgin timber. That's where the compound is. There's only one road in, and it's well guarded. Ain't nobody gonna get in there unless Biggs wants 'em to."

"You know Skull?" I asked.

"We've met. His real name is Anders Riddell. He's never been convicted of anything serious, but he's a sociopath. He's like a son to Biggs."

"What does he look like?"

"Six feet tall, about one-eighty. Shaved head."

"What goes on at this compound?"

"War games. Hate rallies. Arms deals. They publish a lot of racist crap and work real hard at getting people stirred up. They even have a Web site."

"Anybody doing anything about it?" I asked.

"Wouldn't break my heart to see every building out there burn to the ground, but except for the arms deals, they're not violating any laws. They don't make or sell drugs, because they believe white people must keep their bodies pure. Anyhow, it's out of my jurisdiction. The compound isn't within the city limits. The sheriff's a good man, but he can't enforce federal laws and wouldn't have the manpower even if he had the authority. All he can do is keep an eye on all these crazy groups and make sure they don't harm anyone else."

"What about the feds?"

"The feds don't tell us much," he said. "They think some of our rank and file might be sympathetic to the White Power cause, so they don't trust us. And these days their focus is on foreign terrorism. The last time I had any contact with anyone from the federal government, it was a woman from the Federal Communications

Commission. Biggs has an illegal FM transmitter out there, but he claims the laws of the Zionist government don't apply to him, and the FCC doesn't want any bloodshed over it."

"How many people out there?" Scott asked.

The chief shrugged. "Probably less than a dozen on most days," he said. "Only time he'd have more than that would be when he hosts a rally, a church service, or something like that. Then he might have hundreds of people out there."

I looked at Scott and said, "Church is probably over by now."

"It ain't the kind of church you can just walk into," Prell said. "Strangers are definitely not welcome. Most of his so-called services are at night, anyhow."

I exchanged glances with Scott. We both knew we'd be heading out to the compound right after lunch.

"Where you two staying?" the chief asked. "Maybe I can swing by and get a picture of this Bobby Jackson from you."

I told him where we were staying and said, "We just have the one picture right now. We can make a copy for you and drop it off at your office tomorrow."

"Fair enough," he said. He shook our hands, walked out with us, and followed us all the way to my truck. Prince started barking as we approached, and the chief peered into the back of my truck. "Bluetick coonhound," he said. "Don't see many of those up here."

20

After church we drove back to Coeur d'Alene and found a sporting-goods store. We purchased some topographical maps of the area in which Chief Prell said Biggs had his compound. We studied them while we ate lunch at a McDonald's. Even though I sometimes flirt with vegetarianism, I like McDonald's. You can't beat their diet Coke. It's much better than what you can get in a can or bottle. I give it five stars.

"The compound is probably here," Scott said, using a straw to point to a location on one of the maps. "It's a level plateau, it's protected by mountains on all sides, and a river runs through it. Nice little lake, too."

"Look at the slope of those mountains," I said. "I wouldn't want to hike those in the summer, much less in the middle of winter."

"Let's drive out there," Scott said, "and see how far up that road we can get before someone stops us. That will tell us something about their level of security."

I refilled my diet Coke and we climbed into the truck. It took less than twenty minutes to reach the area where Biggs had his land. The land adjacent to the highway was covered in tall pines as well as some spruce. The trees were close together, and the floor of the forest contained a formidable amount of undergrowth and fallen trees.

"There's the road to the compound," Scott said. I slowed the truck and we rolled to a stop at the dirt road that was evidently the only road to the Biggs compound. Access to it was blocked by an unlocked gate. A sign on the gate read, WHITES ONLY.

"We white," Scott said.

I held my palms up to my face and said, "Yup."

I put the truck in park and got out to open the gate. There was a spring on it designed to make sure it would return to a closed position, but after opening it I placed a rock the size of a basketball up against it so it would remain open. As I returned to the truck, I noticed a surveillance camera mounted on a tall wooden pole off to one side of the gate. It could have been one of those phony security cameras that don't really work, but I figured Biggs had enough money to buy a real one. Somebody was probably watching us.

I climbed back into the truck and pointed to the camera for Scott. He had a shotgun and a rifle upright between his knees, and an automatic pistol on his lap. I reached under the seat and put my Glock on my lap. Then I put the truck in gear.

The road was narrow. Vehicles traveling in opposite directions could not pass each other unless at least one driver was willing to drive over the rocks and seedlings that lined the edges of the road. It had a gentle upward slope. We were not a mile up it when Scott said, "Here comes trouble." A silver Dodge pickup was heading our way.

"Put the guns away," I said. "We'll just play dumb." He put the rifle and shotgun up against the passenger door but kept his pistol just to his right under a map.

The Dodge pulled up to us so that we could not go around it. I stopped my truck. Their truck had two German shepherds in the back. I got the feeling those two animals took pride in their German heritage.

A twenty-something bodybuilder with a crew cut got out of the driver's side of the Dodge and approached my window. Another man, very tall, exited from the passenger side of the Dodge and started peering into the back of my truck. Both had machine pistols. I rolled my window down. No, I touched a button to lower it. I don't think they make cars with windows that can be rolled down by hand anymore.

"You guys are on private property," the beefy man said.

"We want to do some ice fishing," I said. "Noticed a small lake on the map."

"Are you fucking deaf?" he said. "It's private property."

"We were hoping the owner might let us do some fishing, maybe camp a night or two," I said.

"We always ask permission before hunting or fishing on private property," Scott added with a straight face. "It's the polite thing to do."

"You two turn your fucking truck around and git out of here," he said. "And don't come back."

"Sure thing," I said. "We don't want any trouble."

"Hey, Tommie," the tall man yelled from behind my truck, "I think these are the fuckers that were asking about Skull down in Boise."

The bodybuilder looked confused for a fraction of a second, then started to raise his weapon. I didn't wait to see what would happen next. I slammed the truck into reverse and said to Scott, "You best lay some lead on these boneheads."

I backed up as fast as I could on the narrow road, using my rearview mirror to see where I was going. Scott started firing at them with his rifle. I heard the fire of their automatic weapons, and I know at least one round hit my truck. In the mirror I saw a clearing where I might be able to back up over some young trees and turn the truck around. I backed right over them and turned so that the truck was headed downhill. I punched the gas and guided the truck as best I could as we bounced along the road at what I had to assume was a record speed for it. The gate came into view. I didn't stop when we reached it. I turned right and shifted into overdrive.

"Are they on us?" I asked.

"Not that I can see. I'm pretty sure I hit the tall guy in the leg."

"I guess we're going to threat condition red," I said.

"That's the last time I ask permission," Scott said. "From now on I hunt or fish wherever I goddamn please." I allowed a nervous laugh as I glanced at the speedometer. One hundred and two miles per hour in an aging F-150 isn't bad.

That night at the cabin we dined on beef stroganoff and discussed the big picture as the dogs slept in front of the fireplace. "Okay," Scott said, "I figure Skull knows we're here. He knows we're looking for him, but he doesn't know why. He knows what we're driving. It's a safe bet we're not camping out in the middle of December, so he knows we're staying with someone or in a place like this. What are we going to do when he finds us?"

"Prell's description of him is identical to the description the Denver cops got four years ago. All we have to do is get his voice on tape. Then the cops can do a voiceprint analysis to compare our tape to the recording of the guy that called the radio station after Hal was killed."

"Even if this is the guy that called the radio station, it doesn't prove he killed your cousin."

"Yeah, but it makes him a pretty good suspect. It gives the cops someone to focus on."

"So we have to have an encounter with Skull and get his voice on tape."

"Yeah."

"Shouldn't be too hard," Scott said. "We'll just park your truck in downtown Coeur d'Alene and wait for Skull to try to kill us."

"That's not a bad idea," I said.

21

WE ATE BREAKFAST MONDAY at the International House of Pancakes. We ate lunch at the International Houses of Pancakes. My truck was on the street, the Colorado plates and the bullet hole clearly visible.

We didn't have to worry about eating dinner at the International House of Pancakes, because Skull walked in just after one and headed straight for our table. He had the build of a light heavyweight fighter, the eyes of a rattlesnake, and the words WHITE POWER tattooed across his knuckles. He wore tight jeans, black combat boots, and a jean jacket with lots of Aryan Resistance crap on it. He had recently shaved the blond hair from his head. He had two skinhead buddies with him, and both looked formidable. These guys weren't like the jokers we had encountered in Boise. These guys were the real deal.

"You two looking for me?" he said.

"You Skull?" I asked.

"I know you?"

"I think you knew my cousin," I said. "He used to be a cop in Denver."

"I've never been to Denver."

"I've never been to Spain," I said, "but I kind of like the music."

He was too young to know it was a line from a song written by Hoyt Axton and made famous by Three Dog Night.

"You two know what's best for you, you'll get in your truck right now and head on back to Colorado. You're not welcome here. You don't know what you're getting into."

"We go wherever we want to," Scott said, not realizing he had just uttered the first line of the Monkees' theme.

"Can't travel tonight, Anders," I said. "The Broncos are on *Monday Night Football*. Against the Chiefs. At home."

"Mile High Stadium," Scott said. Though the new stadium is officially known as Invesco Field at Mile High, we hadn't been allowed to vote on it and didn't view the decision as binding on us. To us and a lot of other folks who had grown up in Colorado, it would always be Mile High Stadium.

"You probably don't like football," I said. "Too many niggers."

"The Broncos got a Jew, too," Scott said. "Don't forget about that."

"You've been warned," Skull said. He turned and started to walk away, but one of his goons made the mistake of spitting on Scott, and the fight was on. It didn't last long. From his seated position, Scott punched the spitter in the groin, and when the spitter bent over Scott executed a palm heel strike to the area between the man's mouth and nose. That was that. I covered Skull and the third skinhead with my Glock to make sure they didn't become involved.

The spitter was on the floor, blood dripping out of his mouth and nose. Skull and the other one helped him up and began to assist him in walking toward the door. "I hope the Aryan Resistance has a good dental plan," Scott said to them.

In between the time the skinheads left and the time the patrol car pulled up, we listened to the incident on tape on my microcassette recorder. "Wish we could have gotten him to talk a little more," I said. "Hope we got enough."

The police officer was in his mid-twenties. We told him the truth, more or less. We had been minding our own business when three skinheads came in and started a fight with us for no reason. Scott defended himself, using no more force than was reasonably necessary under the circumstances, and I pulled my gun to make sure the others didn't join in. The skinheads left. We had no idea who they were. Yes, we had permits for our handguns. After we finished telling all this to the officer, he asked each of us to complete a written statement, so we did. Then we headed back to the cabin.

Darkness came and with it came snow. Lots of snow. We couldn't watch the game because we had no TV, but we listened to it on my shortwave radio as we dined on pizza. I drank diet Coke; Scott drank beer. The dogs started barking just before halftime. I looked out the window and saw Chief Prell walking toward our cabin. Buck was already at the door and ready to attack, so I held on to his collar, which gave my lats a good workout, and opened the door to let the chief in, then closed it to keep the cold air out.

"You guys are stirring up a shitpot of trouble," he said.

"It's one of our few skills," I said.

"One of Biggs' men showed up at the hospital yesterday afternoon with a gunshot wound in his leg. Said it was an accident."

"That's why firearms safety training should be mandatory," Scott said. "Ever since Nixon ended the draft, nobody in this goddamned country knows how to handle a weapon."

"What are you two up to?" the chief asked. "There's no Bobby Jackson wanted in Colorado on any rape charge. Not that I ever believed a rape suspect would be free on bond."

"You want a diet Coke?" I said. Buck had calmed down, so I let go of his collar, guided him up onto one of the beds, and gave him the hand signal to stay there.

"No," he said. "I like mine with good-old fashioned corn syrup in it." I took his jacket and he sat down on one of the old wooden chairs near the fireplace. He reached down and rubbed little Wheat's belly. "Interesting assortment of dogs," he said.

"Buck is our muscle, and Prince over there is a tracking dog, but Wheat's the brains of the operation."

"Why do you call him Wheat?" the chief asked. "He's as black as the ace of spades."

"Buckwheat," I explained.

"I don't get it."

"I had a dog named Buck, so I named this one Wheat." He stared at me as if I were out of my mind. "Don't you remember Buckwheat from the old Little Rascals movies?"

"I remember," he said. "I don't like thinking about it because it just reminds me of how damn old I am."

I sat down on a chair across from the chief, but still close enough to enjoy some of the heat from the fire.

"You guys show up on Saturday," the chief said. "Yesterday morning you're in church asking about Skull and I tell you that you can find him out at Biggs' place. Yesterday afternoon one of Biggs' men shows up at the hospital with a single bullet in his thigh. He says it was an accident, but I don't believe him."

"Why not?" Scott asked.

"Because he and all his moron friends out there prefer automatic weapons. If he had shot himself with one of those things, he'd have taken his leg clean off." Scott nodded to show he followed the chief's logic. "No," the chief continued, "the ER doc says he took one bullet from a twenty-two-caliber rifle fired at some distance. Probably a rifle similar to that one you got over there." He pointed to a semiautomatic rifle propped up in one corner of the cabin. Propped up right next to Scott's shotgun.

"I can live with that," the chief said. "The guy that got shot is an ex-con and probably deserved a bullet in the leg just on general principles. But then today, in the middle of the day, right downtown, Chuck Norris over there"—he gestured toward Scott—"takes out one of Skull's pals in front of a bunch of old people at the International House of Pancakes. And that makes me kind of nervous because Skull isn't the kind of man who is just gonna let that slide.

"So I figure maybe I should find out who the two of you are." He looked at me. "I run your plate, get your name, and find out you're a private eye with a law degree. Marine officer. Former federal prosecutor. No criminal history other than a manslaughter charge that resulted in an acquittal. I do a little more digging and find out your friend"—he gestured again toward Scott—"was a Navy SEAL and holds a master's degree in astrophysics. In short, you two ain't your typical bounty hunters and probably aren't bounty hunters at all. And to top it all off"—he looked at me—"the FBI lists you as a 'person of interest' in the disappearance of a federal witness. You gonna tell me why you're up here and what your beef with Skull is?"

Scott and I exchanged glances. I retrieved another diet Coke from the refrigerator and told the chief about my cousin Hal and my belief that Skull was the man who had killed him. I also told him we had given up finding Karlynn. "The feds can follow us until the cows come home," I said, "but we're not going to lead them to Karlynn, because we're not looking for her."

"Why didn't you ask me to get Skull on tape?" the chief asked.

"You're a police officer," I said. "You have to deal with legalities such as search warrants and Miranda rights. We don't."

"Well, now that you've got his voice on tape," the chief said, "I reckon there's no reason for you to remain in Coeur d'Alene. Why don't you do yourselves and me a favor and head on back to Denver tomorrow. Skull won't wait long to come after you." He stood up and headed for the door.

"We can take a hint," I said.

"Good," the chief said. "I won't call the feds for a day or two."

22

THE BRONCOS PLAYED POORLY but beat the Chiefs 20–17. I woke before sunrise, let the dogs out, and started loading our gear into my truck. The owner was already up, so I paid him. Scott was still half asleep, so I scooped up some of the powdered snow that had accumulated in a drift outside our cabin overnight and sprinkled it over his head as I began to sing "Santa Claus Is Coming to Town." He pulled the blanket up over his head. Not sure if that was because of the snow or my singing.

"Let's go," I said. "We're loaded up and ready."

"You make coffee?" he asked.

"We'll get some in town." He sat up.

"I was having a strange dream," he said. "I had to make an important phone call, but every pay phone I went to was out of order."

"It means you're gay," I joked. "Let's get out of here before Skull and his Aryan friends find us."

We bought some coffee and doughnuts in Coeur d'Alene, then started south toward Boise. Buck and Prince rode in the back, but little Wheat rode up front with us. The state highway had been plowed, but patches of snow and ice remained. We listened to *Bob Dylan's Greatest Hits* and rolled along at fifty miles per hour.

We'd been on the road twenty minutes when Scott said, "We've got company." I checked my mirrors. A rust-colored Chevy pickup was coming hard at us. There were three men in the front seat.

"Doesn't look like Skull's crowd," I said. "These guys look pretty shaggy."

"Who else could it be?" Scott asked.

"I don't know. Maybe just some drunk rednecks who want to pass us. Don't jump to conclusions." Scott studied the passenger side mirror as the vehicle closed in on us.

"They've got guns and they're on our ass," he said. "As an empiricist, that's good enough for me." He started grabbing and checking the various firearms we had stored behind the front seats.

Now the truck was right behind us, a rifle barrel sticking out of the passenger's side window. I punched the gas, but the other truck kept pace. I was driving dangerously fast given the road conditions. A skid or spinout would have hurled us off the road and into one or more of the massive trees that lined the highway.

"This is nuts," I said. "I'm going to stop. If they stop behind me, I'll slam it into reverse and ram 'em. That should give us a couple of seconds to get out of the truck."

I started braking and our truck began to slow. They tried to pass on my left and ram us, but I wouldn't let them. I let my truck come to a stop. The other driver pulled up close to my truck and stopped within a few feet of it. Just as the men in it were about to open the doors to their truck, I shifted into reverse and hit the gas. I hit them hard and drove their truck back at least five yards; then I put it in park and rolled out my side of the truck with my Glock as Scott dove out of his side with a rifle and a handgun. I landed behind a bank of snow created by the snowplow. I couldn't see Scott, but I knew he was probably behind a similar bank on the other side of the two-lane highway.

A burly man exited from the Chevy's passenger side with a pump-action shotgun. He wasn't a skinhead and didn't look like the men we had encountered at the Biggs compound. But he looked familiar.

I heard two men exit from the driver's side of the Chevy. I crawled on my belly, behind the snowbank, hoping to get behind the Chevy and behind the man on my side of it. "Y'all might as well come out!" one of the other men yelled. "You ain't a-goin' nowhere." Later I got a laugh out of the fact that we'd been listening to Bob Dylan just seconds earlier, but at the time it didn't seem funny.

I heard one shot from the other side of the highway, then heard glass shatter. The three men turned in Scott's direction, and I took that opportunity to scamper up into the trees. I found a spot behind a boulder, hidden by spruce trees. I caught my breath and thought for a minute. I knew Scott's purpose had been to divert their attention and give me time to get into the trees, but I wondered why he had shot a window rather than a tire. Then I realized he didn't want to disable their vehicle—he wanted them to get in it and drive the hell away. I aimed my Glock at the passenger window on my side of the Chevy and fired one round. I put a nice hole in it. I hoped my shot had given Scott a similar opportunity to find better cover.

I was higher now and could see all three men. They all looked familiar. They were the three bikers Prince and I had encountered across from the park as they were leaving a burger joint in Coeur d'Alene on Saturday. One of them had specifically asked if Prince was a bluetick. Were they members of the Sons of Satan?

The three were perplexed. We had them sandwiched. We could see them, but they couldn't see us. We could have easily killed all three, but we kept still, remained silent, and watched.

Finally, one of them took charge. "All right," he said, "I'll watch this side. Mike, you watch the other side. Pete, see what's in their truck."

"I'll tell you what's in their truck," Pete said. "Three loud fucking dogs. Can't you hear 'em?"

"See if one is a bluetick," the leader said.

Pete peered into the back window of the shell on my truck and jumped back when Buck's muzzle banged against the inside of it with a ferocious growl. "Jesus, fuck!" Pete said. "One of 'em is a bluetick."

"I knew it," the leader said. "That's Bugg's dog. These are the guys that took Bugg's dog and helped his old lady disappear. Bugg will pay top dollar if we pop these two." I hadn't helped Karlynn to disappear, but I had protected her, and it sounded as though Bugg was onto me.

"Get the hound out of there," the leader said.

"You get him," Pete said. "There's another dog in there the size of a lion."

The leader stepped closer to the back of my pickup. Very quickly I had to engage in a form of moral calculus. Was I willing to kill these men to protect Prince and my dogs? Was I willing to kill them to protect the three hundred thousand dollars in the back of my truck? And, most important, if I did kill them, could I do it without going to prison? I had just about answered these three questions in the affirmative when Scott fired three rounds over their heads. Instinctively they hit the pavement and crawled under the two trucks.

They spoke softly to each other, and I had difficulty hearing them. After several minutes the one named Pete crawled out from under their truck, got into the cab, and started the truck. The other two crawled out and entered from the passenger side. They drove around my truck and continued down the highway. A solid wood bumper protected the front of their truck, so I hadn't done much damage to it when I had rammed it.

When they were out of sight, I stood and walked back to my F-150. Scott did the same. The back of my truck didn't look so good. There were large dents in the tailgate, and significant damage to the shell on the back.

"Sounds like Bugg's onto you," Scott said.

"He is," I said. "Remember when we were in the park on Saturday and I had to chase Prince? Those three guys were coming out of a burger joint across the street, and one of them specifically asked if Prince was a bluetick coonhound."

"Every biker in the mountain time zone is going to be looking for this truck," Scott said. I nodded.

"Let's get it off the road," I said. "We'll hide it in the trees. You stay here to protect the dogs and the money; I'll thumb my way back to Coeur d'Alene and buy a new truck."

"Sounds like a plan," Scott said.

I started my truck and turned down the first dirt road I could find. It was a Forest Service road that probably saw plenty of action in the summer but not much in the winter. A few hundred yards up it, I noticed a spot where I could park it in the trees so it wouldn't be visible from the highway.

Because of the damage to the back of the truck, I couldn't get the window on the back of the shell to open properly. I had to pry it open with the claw end of a hammer. Then I let the dogs out to run around. They seemed okay.

I reached into the back of the truck and pulled the box with the cash toward me. I counted out twenty thousand dollars and stuffed the bills in the inside pocket of my coat. I donned my Broncos hat and some warm gloves, then started walking down to the highway.

23

Five hours later I was driving a "pre-owned" F-150 up the Forest Service road. It was just like my old truck, only much newer. It had less then ten thousand miles on it. It was gold, not green, and had a matching shell on the back. It had the king cab, which is essential if you're going to spend any time in a pickup. It had four-wheel drive and a V-8, which are essential if you live in the Colorado mountains. It had a high quality CD player, which is essential if you know who Jack Guthrie was. It even had a CB radio, which, due to the invention of cell phones, is only essential if you are a fan of C. W. McCall. I happen to be one.

"It was time for a new truck anyhow," Scott said as I stepped out of the new vehicle. "I didn't want to have to tell you, but that truck never really loved you."

"Thanks," I said. The dogs were still running loose, enjoying the chance to frolic in the snow. I started removing all our belongings from the old truck and putting them into the new truck.

"What do we do with the old truck?" Scott asked.

"Ideally, we'd push it off a cliff and it would explode in a ball of fire, but since there are no cliffs to be seen, I guess we leave it here."

"The cops will find it sooner or later."

"Who cares?" I said. "They'll tow it and send me a bill for the towing and storage. I'll come up when things settle down, get it fixed, and sell it."

Scott followed my lead and began loading his guns and cold-weather gear into the new truck. I called the dogs and loaded them into the new truck, with Wheat up front and Buck and Prince in the back. When it appeared that we had transferred everything, I took one last look at the old truck and said, "We'll always have Paris."

I started up the truck and unfolded the Idaho map so that both Scott and I could see it. "Looks like we can take the state high-ways back to Boise and pick up the interstate or head east into Montana and drop down into Wyoming."

"I think we've worn out our welcome in Idaho," Scott said.

It was already early afternoon. "All right," I said, "we'll see if we can make Bozeman or Billings tonight."

I guided the truck back down to the highway, then headed east across northern Idaho. It was beautiful country, and aside from the fact that too many neo-Nazis and white supremacists had chosen to call it home, my only complaint about the area was that just about everything was named after Lewis and Clark. Bridges, schools, parks—they were all named after the two men Jefferson had dispatched to explore the American West two centuries ago. There was even a Lewis and Clark Laundromat in one town.

"That must have been some trip," I said. "Imagine seeing all this in its natural state."

"Imagine paddling a canoe all day, eating an elk steak cooked over an open fire, then crawling into the tent with Sacagawea. I wonder how two junior officers managed that assignment."

"Clark was already out of the army when they began their jour-ney," I said. "Lewis asked him to tag along because he wanted company and needed someone to handle the paperwork. Sort of like my relationship with you."

Scott smiled and we continued east. After a while I picked up my Lewis and Clark cell phone and dialed the number for the gas station in Blanca, Colorado.

"Who you calling?" Scott said.

"Uncle Ray," I said.

"Crazy Uncle Ray?"

"Yeah. I figure it might be wise to have a little extra firepower while Jayne is visiting."

"I'll stay with you," he said.

"I thought of that," I said, "but then Jayne would know this is serious, and I don't want her worrying about me."

A woman at the gas station answered, and I asked her to take a message for Ray and give it to him if he happened to pass through town. My mother's youngest brother lives in a plywood shack on five acres of cactus-covered land outside Blanca. A former merchant seaman, Ray was a drunk for much of his life, but he found Jesus several years ago at age fifty-six and now lives in an impressive eight-by-twelve shack that he built in southern Colorado. He has no phone, no electricity, and no running water, but he's happy. And he's good with a rifle. My mom grew up dirt poor in rural Alabama, and everyone in her family is good with a rifle, including my mom.

Next I called the Nederland Police Department. Phyllis answered on the first ring. "Hi, Phyllis," I said, "this is Pepper Keane. Is Glen in? I really need to speak with him."

"Just a sec," she said. She put me on hold. Glen is Nederland's chief of police. He runs the four-man department. The lanky runner had been a cop in Houston for thirty years before taking the job in Nederland a few years back. Though he is soft-spoken, he's been a controversial figure because he actually enforces the drug laws. Well, most of them. Some of the hippies in Nederland don't like him, but the town seems to have reached a homeostasis in which everyone understands that the discreet use of marijuana by adults is acceptable, but other drugs won't be tolerated.

Glen's voice came on the line. "Pepper," he said, "I've been hearing rumors about you."

"Is one of them that Thad Bugg wants me dead?"

"Yeah, that's one. Another one is that the feds think you helped Bugg's girlfriend disappear."

"That one is bullshit," I said. "Hell, I was trying to find her and convince her that the Witness Protection Program was a good deal. We tracked her to Boise, but then the trail went cold and we got involved in some other things."

"What can I do for you?"

"I'd sure appreciate it if you guys could keep a close eye on my house. Jayne's coming home this week, and it would be nice if my house is still standing when she arrives. I'm afraid Bugg will try to torch it."

"We'll keep an eye on it."

"Thanks."

"Why on Earth did you steal Bugg's dog?" Glen asked.

"Why climb the highest mountain? Why fly the Atlantic? Why does Rice play Texas?"

"I remember that speech," he said. "I was in Houston when Kennedy gave it. It was nineteen sixty-two. You would have been four or five years old."

"Then let me finish," I said. "I chose to steal that dog. I chose to steal that dog in this decade, not because it was easy, but because it was hard. Because the goal of screwing with Bugg will serve to organize and measure the best of my energies and skills, but that challenge is one I am willing to accept, one I am unwilling to postpone, and one which I intend to win."

He laughed a little. "Let me know when you get back into town," he said.

"I will," I said. "By the way, I invited my uncle Ray to come visit until this thing with Bugg plays itself out. He'll be driving an old pickup with a big camper on the back."

"I think I met him once. He's the guy who thinks everyone is either a devil worshipper or a drug dealer, right?"

"In a nutshell," I said.

"He may be onto something," Glen said.

The sun went down, darkness came, and we found a nice restaurant in Bozeman. While we were waiting for the waitress to take our order, I looked across at Scott and said, "This has to rank right up there with the worst days of my life. We got the skinheads after us. We've got the Sons of Satan after us. The feds think we helped a critical witness disappear. We've been shot at and we've shot at people. I had to hitchhike to Coeur d'Alene in the snow. I spent twenty thousand dollars in drug money that isn't even mine on a new truck. And I just invited Uncle Ray to my house for the holidays. It's hard to imagine how it could get much worse."

The waitress arrived and asked if we wanted drinks. Scott ordered a cold beer. I asked for a diet Coke.

"Is Pepsi okay?" the waitress asked.

24

JAYNE'S FLIGHT ARRIVED at Denver International Airport just after nine on Saturday morning. I met her in the baggage claim. Even after a twelve-hour flight she looked beautiful and refreshed. We embraced and she gave me a luscious kiss. She's not much for makeup, but she almost always wears pink lipstick. Her brand has a wonderfully erotic scent.

"It's not fair for you to look so damn good right at the airport," I said. "I don't know if I can keep my hands off you during the drive back to Ned."

"I didn't ask you to," she said.

Luggage began to appear on the conveyor belt and to drop down onto the carousel. She pointed out her two bags and I snagged them. "Do you have a coat in one of these?" I asked. "You're going to need it."

She found a coat in one of her bags and put it on. I started to carry her bags, but she pointed out that both of them had wheels, and suggested that we each pull one. Then we walked out into the cold and onto the fifth and top level of the parking garage. Because it is the top level, there is no roof above it. Most people avoid it for that reason, but I favor it because I know it is directly across from the baggage claim and won't require me to wait for an elevator.

The dogs started barking as we approached my truck. "You bought a new truck?" she said.

"Figured it was time," I said.

I opened the door on the back of the shell and placed her bags in the back of the truck. Buck stuck his head through and she caressed his massive face. "I missed you, big fella," she said. His tail was wagging in overdrive.

"That's Prince," I said, though it was rather obvious. She motioned for him to come, but he backed up, raised his muzzle, and let out a loud, melodic howl.

"He's handsome," she said.

I opened the passenger door, and little Wheat poked his black head out. She let him kiss her, then squeezed in beside him.

"You guys are my family," she said as I started the truck. "I'm so lucky."

"I'm the lucky one," I said. I squeezed her hand.

I paid the parking attendant and aimed the truck in the direction of the airport exit. "I might as well tell you now," I said. "My uncle Ray is going to be staying with us for a few days."

"Oh, I've always wanted to meet him," she said. "He sounds like a real character."

"He's all that and more," I said. "The good news is, he'll probably spend most of his time in his camper, so he'll be more or less invisible."

Jayne fell asleep on the drive back to Nederland. I was glad to have her home, but I had a lot of other things on my mind—Karlynn, Bugg, and Skull to name just a few.

I had provided the recording of Skull's voice to a female detective at the Denver Police Department as soon as Scott and I had returned, but I hadn't heard back from her yet. Her name was Michelle Simmons. In the course of our conversation we discovered we had attended the same suburban high school and graduated together. But I had been a jock and she had been active in the theater, so we had never gotten to know each other.

"I think we had a Latin class together," she said.

"I took Latin because it was an easy A," I said.

"Me too," she said. "The only Latin phrase I use in my work is 'rigor mortis.'"

"I took three years of Latin and the only thing I remember is *Quantum materiae materietur marmota monax si marmota monax materiam possit materiari?*"

"Translation?"

"It's Latin for 'How much wood would a woodchuck chuck if a woodchuck could chuck wood?'"

As Jayne and I continued toward Nederland, I was amused that I had remembered that completely useless Latin phrase for close to thirty years.

Uncle Ray was waiting for us when Jayne and I arrived, and he had a roaring fire going. I introduced them to each other. They were quite a contrast. Jayne is five-ten and always looks like a model in an L.L. Bean catalog. Ray is five-six and usually has a week's worth of gray stubble on his face. "My, you sho' are a pretty one," he said to her.

The three of us sat at the dining table for a while and talked. I had been back for several days, and during that time Ray and Prince had become good friends. We were doing our best to keep Prince indoors on the theory that the sighting of a bluetick coonhound on my property would eliminate any doubt Bugg might have concerning my role in the theft of Prince and in Karlynn's disappearance.

Ray stood and stretched his arms. "Well," he said, "I think I'll head on out to my truck and take a nap. C'mon, Prince, let's you and me take a nap."

Once Ray and Prince had departed, Jayne said, "I think my flight is catching up with me. I think I'll take a nap too."

"Get as much sleep as you can," I said. "You'll need your energy tonight."

Not having a real job, I wasn't quite sure what to do with myself. I read some philosophy for a while, then changed into my workout clothes and went downstairs to lift weights and hit the heavy bag. Between Karlynn and our trip to Idaho, I hadn't been able to stick with my regular exercise routine, and I felt guilty about it.

Jayne woke up around three, and after discussing it, we decided neither of us really wanted to go out to eat, so we drove to the B&F to buy some groceries, then walked across to the liquor store and bought six bottles of red wine—cabernets, merlots, and an Australian shiraz. On the way home I stopped at the post office to get Saturday's mail. I left Jayne in the truck. Most of my mail was junk, but there was a postcard from my brother. The front of the card featured a gorilla from the Denver Zoo; on the back my brother had written:

I benched 445 today. You're a puss.

I found a black marker at the counter and wrote "Return to Sender" across the back of the card, then dropped it into the slot for outgoing mail.

25

WE MADE LOVE THAT NIGHT and fell asleep in each other's arms under a layer of cozy quilts my grandmother had made many years ago. The wind, always present between October and May, picked up after midnight. It comes right down off the Continental Divide, sometimes reaching speeds exceeding one hundred miles per hour. I always laugh when people refer to Chicago as "the Windy City."

An incredibly loud bang woke me from a sound sleep just after one. I reached into the top drawer of the table on my side of the bed, grabbed my Glock, and looked out the window. The only thing I saw was the plastic lid to a garbage container, skimming along the ground like a flying saucer. I was sure it belonged to my neighbors, Luther and Missy, and that the wind had sucked it up at their place and slammed it into the side of my house. I put the Glock away and climbed back beneath the covers. Jayne was half awake.

"What was it?" she said.

"Just a lid from a garbage can," I said. "Probably one of Luther's."

"When did you start sleeping with a gun next to you?" she asked.

"When I started babysitting Karlynn."

"But you're done with that, aren't you? You said there's a warrant out for her arrest."

I had concealed the truth from Jayne once early in our relationship, and it had taken a long time to win her back. I didn't want to lie to her. Not about this. She had a right to know.

"Bugg may be onto me," I said.

"How did he find out?"

"Some members of his gang saw me with Prince up in Idaho and I guess they put two and two together."

"He'll come after you."

"I'll deal with it."

"How?"

"I have some ideas."

"Want to share them me? I'm scared."

"He won't come after me here," I said. "We've got Uncle Ray out front, and the PD and the sheriff are driving past here every half hour. Bugg's not that stupid. And even if he was, Scott installed motion detectors and floodlights on all four corners of the house." This did not seem to lessen her concern. "He offered to build a tactical nuclear weapon for me," I added, "but I told him it wasn't necessary." She laughed—a little.

"I just want to enjoy our time together," she said.

"We don't have to stay here. We can go to your place, take a trip, anything you want to do."

"I rented my place to some students, remember?"

"We'll take a trip, then. Where do you want to go? Aspen?"

"How about Vegas?"

"Vegas?"

"Yeah, a woman I met in China has a brother who manages Treasure Island. She said she could get us a luxury suite at a great rate. Maybe Scott and Bobbi could go with us. It would be fun."

"Okay," I said. "We'll call them in the morning, but I don't know about Treasure Island. I think I'd prefer Bellagio or the Venetian—someplace with fewer kids."

"But a suite will cost a fortune at those places."

"We can afford it," I said.

I managed to sleep past eight, and I have to say that sharing my bed with Buck, Wheat, and Jayne was an improvement over Buck, Wheat, and Prince. When I came downstairs, Uncle Ray had already made coffee and put wood on the fire. He was seated at the kitchen table reading the Sunday paper, and Prince was at his feet.

"I think Jayne and I are going to go to Vegas for a few days," I said as I poured some fresh coffee into my Scooby-Doo mug. "Do you mind staying here a few days with the dogs and keeping an eye on the place?"

"Don't mind a'tall," he said. "This here is livin' high on the hog for your ole uncle Ray."

I found the sports section and sat down across from Ray. One of the problems with having Ray as a houseguest is that he can talk your ear off. I hadn't completed the first paragraph of the first article when he said, "Ya know, I had me a dog like dis here Prince when I was a boy growing up in Alabama. Name was Chester, and he was a fine tracking dog. Yessuh, I think Prince here might be a pretty good tracking dog himself." I didn't say anything, just kept reading, but Ray went on to explain how to choose a tracking dog, how to train a tracking dog, and he even talked a bit about the history of the breed. "Yessuh," he continued, "they used to use these blueticks as guard dogs at some of the prisons, don't you know. Their sense of smell is almost as good as that of a blood-hound, but they don't slobber near as much and they easier to train. You see, a bloodhound can be tracking a man's scent, but they can be downright stubborn . . ."

Jayne came down in a terry-cloth bathrobe just as I was finishing the sports section. "Did you call Scott and Bobbi yet?" she asked.

"I'll do it right now." I picked up the kitchen phone and depressed the speaker button so I could pour more coffee while I spoke. Scott answered. "You and Bobbi want to go to Vegas?" I said. "Jayne's worried about the Bugg situation."

"I can get a luxury suite at Treasure Island for next to nothing," Jayne added.

"It's damn cold out," Scott said. "Vegas is looking pretty good right now, but we can do better than Treasure Island. Too many kids."

26

WE LANDED IN VEGAS late that afternoon and found a suite at the Venetian with a fake fireplace, purple carpeting, and two bedrooms connected by a spacious living area. It cost a small fortune, but what Jayne didn't know is that Scott and I had been permanently banned from Treasure Island a few years back because Scott had consumed a fair amount of alcohol and had politely asked two-fifths of the offensive line of the New Orleans Saints to put their fucking cigarettes out. A scuffle had ensued, and we held our own, but the security people got on top of everyone pretty quick, and nobody was arrested or seriously injured.

Scott and Bobbi went to see a show, but Jayne had her heart set on a night of blackjack. With her IQ, memory, and mathematical ability, Jayne knows how to beat the casinos, and she loves doing it. I think she also gets a kick out of the fact that people underestimate her because she's a woman. I watched her for a while, then wandered around until I found the nickel slots and played them for a while. It struck me that a Vegas casino is the only place in the world where you can see a person on oxygen smoking a cigarette.

Jayne was up about a thousand dollars when I made my way back to her. She was having fun, but she saw me and finished her game, cashed in her chips, and then we went outside to walk the Strip. It was a mild night, about sixty-five degrees. Balmy by

Nederland's standards. We held hands, stopping to look in store windows and at anything else that interested us.

We walked back to the Venetian, but Scott and Bobbi had not yet returned, so we had room service send up a bottle of cabernet and locked ourselves in our bedroom. We watched *The Big Chill* on cable for a while, got ready for bed, looked out at all the lights in what had once been uninhabited desert, and climbed into bed. She put her head on my chest, and we lay quietly for a while.

"What are you thinking about?" we said simultaneously.

"Two, four, six, eight, jinx," I said. "You owe me a diet Coke."

"I don't have any soft drinks with me," she said. "Is there something else I can give you?"

"We can probably work something out," I said.

Later we again found ourselves lying in bed with her head on my chest. Out of the blue she asked, "What do you think about our relationship?"

"I like it," I said.

"I know that. Do you ever wonder where it's going?"

"Do you worry about that?"

"I don't worry about it, but I ponder it more than I used to."

"'Ponder' is a good word," I said. "People don't ponder enough these days. They get their opinions from sound bites."

"Answer the question," she said.

"I don't think about it much," I said. "I'm glad I have you. I hope I'll have you for a long time."

"Do you think about marriage?"

"You've always said it's not important to you."

"I know, but do you think about it?"

"I guess I feel like we are married. We just haven't formalized it."

"Why do you think that is?"

"Why haven't I asked you to marry me?"

"Yeah." I thought about it.

"I guess deep down there's a part of me that thinks you can do better. I mean, I think too much, I don't have a real job, I'm on the wrong side of forty, and you're probably twenty points ahead of me on the IQ scale. And as my puss brother pointed out just yesterday, my maximum bench press is one hundred pounds less than his."

"Who says my IQ is higher than yours?"

"You earned a doctorate in mathematics at Harvard."

"Does it bother you?"

"I'm a man," I said. "Nothing about you bothers me as long as we have sex regularly."

"I want to adopt a child," she said.

"The kind you have to feed and care for?" She ignored my attempt at humor.

"A little girl from China," she said. "There are thousands of them in orphanages over there because their families abandoned them."

"I know."

"I've thought about this a lot. It feels right."

"So your question about marriage was really a question about getting married and adopting a child?"

"Yes."

"I'd be honored to have you as my wife, but I don't know about a child. I'm kind of old to be starting a family."

"I think it might help you find some meaning in your life."

"I think it might mean getting a real job."

"I'm not asking you to give up what you do. I'm not asking you to give up how you live. I'm not asking you to go back to practicing law."

"Someone has to care for the child," I said. "Are you willing to give up teaching?"

"Yes."

"I mean, you can't just put the kid in day care and continue your career as if nothing had happened."

"I'm aware of that."

"How are you going to feel the first time I come home and say, 'Hi, honey, Scott and I are gonna head up to Idaho and search for some fucker named Skull this weekend'?"

"I imagine that you and Scott will head up to Idaho and find the fucker named Skull."

"Yeah, but how are you going to *feel* about it? You're a successful professional woman. I think you're going to resent being a stay-at-home mom and having a husband who lets you do the bulk of the child rearing."

"Don't try to read my mind. You don't know how I will feel. I'm not the same person I was when we met. And neither are you. I love you, and I think you'd make a great father."

"Why don't you just raise her for the first fifteen years, and then when she gets old enough to have a boyfriend I'll take a more active role. I'd be real good at intimidating the boyfriends."

"I need to do this," she said. Then she gave me a peck on the cheek.

"I'm going to need some time on this one," I said.

I slept for a few hours but woke up around two in the morning and couldn't get back to sleep. I wandered out into the common area to get a cold beer from the refrigerator and watch TV. Scott was on the couch in his underwear, drinking a beer and watching a program on an educational channel. I sat down in a recliner beside the couch.

"Can't sleep," I explained. No response. "What are you watching?"

"It's about these codes that a bunch of rabbis and statisticians say are hidden within the Hebrew text of the Old Testament. I don't usually buy into this shit, but these guys make a compelling case."

"Who put the codes there?" I asked.

"God put them there when he dictated the Old Testament to Moses letter by letter. Why can't you sleep?"

"Jayne wants to get married and adopt a little girl from China."

"And you don't want to?"

"I'd love to marry Jayne, but having children isn't something I had on my list of things of do."

"Why not?"

"Humanity is rolling downhill like a snowball headed for hell. We're going to be the first generation in history to leave our children a lower standard of living than we had. Who in their right mind would bring a child into this world?"

"As I understand Jayne's proposal," he said, "the child has already been brought into the world, so you can't use that argument."

We continued watching TV, listening to proponents and skeptics debate the existence of the Bible codes. Some proponents claim a fiery war between Islam and the West will soon destroy the world. Others claim a comet will slam into Earth and end life as we know it in 2012.

"That's a cheerful set of alternatives," I said.

"Relax," Scott said. "The comet is going to miss by about two miles. I ran the numbers. We'll put some beers on ice and watch it from your deck."

"What about the battle between Islam and the West?"

"As soon as a terrorist sets off a nuclear device in the United States, whoever happens to be the rich guy sitting in the White House will retaliate by launching nuclear strikes on Damascus,

Tehran, and Baghdad. Game, set, and match. It's a shame hundreds of millions of innocent people will die, but that's life."

By this time we were both laughing at our own dark humor. When the laughter died down, Scott said, "I think you should do it."

"Marry Jayne and adopt a child?"

"Yeah."

"Why?"

"I just have a good feeling about it."

"I thought you were an empiricist."

"Look, I've known you for more than forty years, and the time you seemed happiest was when you were living with Joy and you had that big white dog that you got from the pound and used to bring to class every day. What was that dog's name?"

"Cochise."

"Yeah, Cochise. You know, it still amazes me that you brought that dog to every class through three years of law school and nobody ever said a word."

"Everyone thought it was funny," I said. "He was our class mascot."

"I'll bet there were a few who didn't appreciate it. Nobody said anything, because they didn't want to take a chance that you were having a bad day. Then you met Joy and she brought out the best in you. Jayne has the same effect on you, and it took you more than twenty years to find her. If all she wants in return for hanging out with your sorry ass is to adopt a child, you'd be a fool not to do it."

"If you're so high on the concept, why aren't you and Bobbi raising up a bunch of little McCutcheons on a peach farm out in the country?"

"Here's the thing," Scott said. "You and I are a lot alike. We both believe this world is full of stupidity and misery. We both doubt the existence of God. We both suspect that life is meaningless. But here's the difference: I'm okay with all that, and you're not. I see life as a hilarious cosmic riddle, and if a comet smashed into Earth tomorrow, I'd die laughing. But deep down you're an idealist. You want the world to be free of suffering; you want there to be a God; you want life to have meaning. Jayne's giving you a chance to reduce suffering, to give meaning to your life, and maybe even to find a way to believe in God."

"This might be the deepest conversation we've ever had," I said.

"Well, fuck, we're in Vegas in a room two hundred feet above the desert with a fireplace and purple carpeting, it's three in the morning, and I've had a lot of beer. What do you expect?"

27

We flew back to Denver two days before Christmas and made it back to Nederland before noon. I was pleased to see that my home was still standing. I was not pleased to learn that Special Agents Valeska and Livingston had visited while I was gone. "They wanted to ask y'all some questions," Ray said.

I phoned Matt and explained the situation. "Do I have to talk with them?" I asked.

"I think you should," he replied. "You don't have to share confidential information you received from Karlynn or me, because that's protected by the attorney-client privilege, but I think they can ask you about your efforts to track her down. Might as well do it without making them drag you in front of a grand jury."

"Tell you what," I said. "I want to finish up my Christmas shopping today and tomorrow. See if you can set something up with them tomorrow morning. I'll meet you at your office before I meet with them."

"You want me to sit in on the interview with you?"

"Yeah, and I also want the whole thing on tape or there's no deal."

"They won't agree to that," he said. "That's FBI policy."

"They'll agree to it if they really want to talk with me," I said. "Trust me, I used to do this for a living."

I volunteered to make dinner that night because I had a yen for grilled salmon. Jayne wanted to help and turned on the oven to preheat it. "We won't need the oven," I said. "I'm going to grill it."

"It's twenty degrees out," she said.

"I know, but I don't want baked salmon. I want grilled salmon." I went out on the deck wearing my flip-flops and lit the gas grill.

After dinner Ray and Prince went back to Ray's camper. Jayne and I stayed up and watched *Casablanca*. We both love that movie. Her favorite scene is when Ingrid Bergman tells Sam to play "As Time Goes By." My favorite scene is when Humphrey Bogart shoots the Nazi officer, Major Strasser, and walks off into the distance with Claude Rains. But then, I always was a romantic.

"What about the money?" I asked.

"If they ask about that, I'll advise you not to answer. All you're going to talk about is your efforts to track her down." We were in Matt's office. We had spent the past hour preparing for my interview with the feds.

"Works for me."

"Where is the money, by the way?"

"It's in a safe place."

"Can you account for what you spent, if it ever comes to that?"

"Down to the penny."

We walked over to the Federal Building. Before we arrived, I stopped at a downtown convenience store to buy a forty-four-ounce diet Coke.

Valeska and Livingston greeted us and led us into a nondescript interview room. We took off our coats, and Matt set his digital microrecorder down on the table.

"No tapes," Livingston said.

"We're going to record it," Matt said. "That's the deal."

"We take good notes," Livingston said.

"I don't want there to be any disagreement about what was said," Matt explained.

"The Bureau's policy is—"

"Take a good look at me," Matt said. "Do I look like I give a shit about the Bureau's policy?"

Valeska and Livingston exchanged glances.

"Fine," Livingston said, "record the goddamned thing if it makes you happy."

"Now that we have the testosterone issues settled," Valeska said, "can we get on with the interview?"

Matt started the recorder and made a statement about the date, time, location, and who was present.

I told them about picking up Karlynn at Matt's office and taking care of her up until she ditched me.

"What were you doing at the furniture warehouse?" Livingston asked.

"I had to talk with a kid who works there."

"About what?"

"Nothing that has anything to do with Karlynn or the Sons of Satan."

"You left her in your truck?" His tone suggested he could not believe I had been so stupid.

"Yes."

"And she was gone when you came out?"

"Yes."

"What did you do then?"

"I called Mr. Simms, explained the situation, and asked if he wanted me to try to track her down."

"What did he say?"

"Don't answer that," Matt said. "It was a conversation between you and me in a matter pertaining to a client, and it is absolutely privileged."

I looked at Matt and said, "He told me that if I didn't find her he would personally bury me up to my neck in a giant anthill and smear my ears with jam." Valeska allowed a modest smile. She looked nice. A lot of women look nice. In the brief silence that followed my smart-aleck answer, the question I found myself asking was, how do you decide which one to marry?

"Were those his exact words?" Livingston asked sarcastically.

"No, but the gist of the conversation was that I should try to find Karlynn and convince her that it was in her own best interest to return."

Then I went into a detailed explanation of the efforts Scott and I had made to locate her. I told them about the posters we had put up, the phone calls we had received, and the sighting of her at a truck stop in Twin Falls.

"And that's where the trail went cold?" Livingston asked.

"Yes."

"So then you returned to Colorado?"

"No, we continued north into Boise and ultimately up into northern Idaho. But we never got another lead."

"I hear you had a run-in with some of Bugg's friends while you were up there."

"We had a little skirmish."

"Why do you think Bugg's men would try to kill you?"

"Jealous of my good looks and quick wit," I said. "It happens a lot." Livingston just tapped his pencil. "Look," I said, "it all goes back to the dog."

"What dog?"

"The champion bluetick coonhound I liberated from Bugg in

order to convince Karlynn to cooperate with you guys in the first place."

"You think Bugg tried to have you killed because you stole his dog?"

"Yeah."

"How would Bugg know you stole his dog?"

"I think some of his guys saw me with the dog up in Idaho."

"Were you aware of the fact that Karlynn took nearly half a million dollars in cash from Bugg before she disappeared on him?"

"Don't answer that," Matt instructed.

"She never said anything about it to me," I said.

"You bought a new truck while you were in Idaho?" Livingston said.

"What has that go to do with the price of tea in China?" Matt said.

"It was a pre-owned truck," I said. Matt looked at me, concerned about where this was headed. "There wasn't much left of my old truck after Bugg's guys attacked us. We figured it was best to get rid of it and buy something that wasn't the same color."

"Paid cash?" Livingston said.

"Yes."

"Where did you get the cash?"

"Don't answer that," Matt said. Now he was pissed. And worried.

"I withdrew twenty thousand dollars from a savings account on the day Karlynn disappeared. Check my bank records."

"Do you always withdraw large sums of cash before you set out on these types of trips?"

"No, but in this case I knew I would need money to pay people for information they provided to us, and I was in a hurry to get on the road." Matt relaxed, leaned back, and betrayed what might be called a barely noticeable Zen smile.

The interview reached its natural conclusion before lunch. "Mr. Keane," Valeska said, "as a former federal prosecutor I'm sure you know that aiding in the disappearance of a fugitive and making false statements to federal agents are serious offenses. In the event of a conviction, they carry severe penalties. If you have been less than completely candid with us, now is the time—"

"I didn't help her disappear. I tried to track her down and convince her to return. The last sighting of her was in Twin Falls. And the only false statement I made today was when I told you my attorney had threatened to bury me in an anthill and smear my ears with jam."

I stood. Matt stood. They stood. They thanked me for my cooperation, and we all stood. In the elevator on the way down, Matt looked at me and said, "I am humbled by your very presence."

I did some Christmas shopping while I was downtown, then drove to my brother's gym. He was at the front counter when he saw me. He looked at me and said, "Of all the gym joints in all the towns in all the world, he walks into mine."

28

ON CHRISTMAS MORNING Jayne and I drove to Boulder to open presents with Nancy and Jimmie. It was just the four of us; my brother and family were spending the day with his wife's parents, and Uncle Ray had opted to stay in Nederland with the dogs.

We did not talk as much as we normally do when we are alone in my truck. She was hoping I would say something about the adoption issue, and I didn't know what to say. We listened to José Feliciano sing Christmas songs.

Nancy and Jimmie had erected an environmentally friendly imitation Christmas tree and decorated it with tinsel, ornaments, and, for reasons I am not exactly clear on, a number of Jimmie's baseball caps. We opened presents one by one. I can't recall all the gifts, but I know I gave Jimmie a telescope Scott had helped me select, as well as a new football. Jayne gave me two expensive regimental ties—she knows I love stripes—and several books I had wanted, including a handsome hardcover book about former heavyweight champ Jack Dempsey. I gave her a pair of sapphire earrings and a number of books she had wanted. Buck, Wheat, and Prince also gave Jayne a gift—a gift certificate to use at Victoria's Secret. Who can doubt that a dog is a man's best friend?

* * *

A few days later I drove Jayne to the airport. We arrived early, checked her bags, then bought coffee at Starbucks and sat across from each other, separated by a round table that was much too small. Once she went through the security checkpoint, I would not see her again for several months, maybe not even until the end of the school year.

"I hate saying good-bye," she said.

"Me too."

"I particularly dislike it when I am not sure whether I am saying good-bye for a few months or whether I am witnessing the end of a relationship that means a great deal to me."

"Me too."

"You're afraid," she said. "Afraid you won't live up to your own ideas of what constitutes being a good husband, what constitutes being a good father. Afraid you won't be perfect."

"My brain is telling me that starting a family at this age is not a good idea."

"That logical mind of yours has served you well over the years. It has helped you survive hardship and accomplish great things. But it hasn't brought much happiness, has it?"

I said nothing. She looked at her watch and said, "Well, I guess I should head to the gate."

I walked her over to the line of people waiting to get inspected, detected, and rejected before being allowed to proceed to the concourses. I put my arms around her and said, "I love you."

"I love you, too," she said. "Work on listening with your heart."

I watched as she went through the X-ray machine and stepped onto the escalator down to the trains. She blew me a kiss just before her head disappeared.

Back in Nederland I gave Uncle Ray his present, a brand-new Bellini shotgun. He inspected it and said, "Well, this here sho' looks to be a fine shotgun, son. I tell ya, your ole uncle Ray is gonna do just fine with this beauty."

To say I was depressed would be an understatement. But after forty-plus years of stoicism, I lacked the ability to cry. I watched a meaningless football game on TV, drank some red wine, and started reading about Jack Dempsey, one of my all-time heroes. Any man who would walk thirty miles across a desert to fight another man in a saloon for twenty bucks has a quality not many men possess these days.

I fell asleep in my recliner, and when I woke up, Ray had built a nice fire in the fireplace and was heating two chicken pot pies in the oven. "So what we gonna do 'bout this Bugg fella?" he said.

"I have to make peace with him or wait for him to come after me and kill him."

"Why wait for him to come for you? Just kill him and claim self-defense. Ain't nobody gonna take the word of a dead drug dealer over yours. Hey, did I ever tell ya 'bout the time I spent six months on an attempted murder charge 'cause the police thought I had tried to kill your ole uncle Jake? See, what happened was, Jake's first wife got hopping mad at him one night and gutshot him, but when the sheriff came, she flashed her pretty little eyes and blamed it on me. Took me six months to clear my name. Jake did three tours in Vietnam and never got a scratch, then come home and got gutshot by ole Lucy."

While Ray was recounting the story of his six months in jail— which I had heard many times—I thought about my options with regard to Bugg. Ray was probably right; I could probably kill Bugg, claim self-defense, and walk. There were only two problems with that plan. First, I did not believe myself to be capable of killing another man in cold blood. Second, "probably" wasn't good enough. Some years ago a biker named Melvin Dawson had attacked me with a knife, and I had deflected the knife into his abdomen. Melvin bled to death. Because I had been a vocal critic of the DA, I suddenly found myself charged with manslaughter. The jury acquitted me, but I feared I'd used up my one free shot at the self-defense argument; it seldom works twice for the same man.

"There might be another way out," I said to Ray.

"What's that?"

"The only evidence he has against me is the fact that his guys saw me with his dog up in Idaho. I'll call him, tell him I have good news. I tracked Karlynn down to a place in Idaho. She heard I was in town, and took off before I could get to her, but I recovered the dog and lots of Bugg's cash. I give him the money and the dog; he thanks me for my services; the end."

"Don't hardly seem fair to ole Prince," Ray said. I nodded.

"Okay, I tell him Karlynn and the dog got away, but I recovered most of his money. I give him two hundred grand, he thanks me, and I can stop looking over my shoulder."

"Won't work," Ray said. "His buddies up there saw you with the dog. You gotta be able to explain that."

"Try this," I said. "I recovered the cash and the dog, but some drunk rednecks attacked us and Prince was badly injured by a stray bullet. I put a bullet in his head to end his misery." Just then, as if on cue, Prince raised his head and looked up at me with his big brown eyes.

"The first time Bugg sees you running around town with ole Prince, he'll kill you."

"You take Prince back to Blanca with you," I said. "A dog like that needs lots of space anyhow."

"You're forgetting about dis Anvil fella. What if he finally got around to telling Bugg 'bout seeing you and the chickadee enjoying some of that food court cuisine?"

"Then as soon as I give Bugg the cash, he'll kill me."

"That about sizes it up," Ray said.

"But Anvil saw me when I had my stripe. Bugg's never seen me with my stripe. If we make sure Anvil isn't around when I meet with Bugg, it might work."

"I think I'll check on them pot pies," Ray said.

29

Bugg," he said.

"Pepper Keane," I said. It was early Tuesday morning.

"Ain't heard from you in a while," he said. "You got me on a speaker phone?"

"I've got good news," I said.

"What's that?"

"I found your wife. I tracked her down to a place up in Idaho. She was living in a trailer. She made tracks when she heard I was in town, but I found a shitload of cash in her trailer."

"You got the money?"

"Right here."

"What about the dog? Did she have the dog with her?"

"The dog's dead," I said.

"You sure?"

"I was there when it happened. He's dead."

"How'd he die?"

"Some assholes attacked us. There was a gunfight. The dog got hit by a stray bullet." There was a brief pause.

"How long you been back in town?" he asked.

"I don't know, a few days."

"How come you didn't call sooner?"

"I had a lady friend visiting. You want me to bring the money over? Having this much cash around makes me nervous."

"Sure, bring it over."

"I need directions," I lied.

When Bugg finished telling me how to get to his home, I dialed Scott's cell phone. "What's Anvil up to?" I said.

"Just playing pool."

"I'm getting ready to head over to Bugg's house. Should take me a half hour to get there. Maybe another half hour or hour to conduct business, depending on how talkative Bugg is. You need to make sure Anvil doesn't head up this way in the next hour."

"I know."

I kept about a hundred thousand dollars and put the rest in a brown paper sack from the B&F. Bugg would still get close to two hundred grand.

"You want me to go with you?" Ray asked.

"No, it can't look like I'm scared. I did exactly what he asked me to, so I have no reason to be afraid of him and no reason to take backup." I reached into the grocery sack, grabbed a wad of cash, and handed it to Ray. "For dog food and vet bills," I said.

"Reckon me and Prince will stay here till you get back, then head on home."

"If I'm not back in two hours, call Glen—the chief of police. Tell him there's a meth lab in the cabin beside Bugg's house. Tell him to take some sheriff's deputies with him; everybody up there carries machine pistols."

I tucked my Glock into my shoulder holster, put my jacket on over it, climbed into my truck, and set out for the tiny town of Ward. I kept looking at myself in the rearview mirror to make sure the black hair dye had done its job.

There were a few small pickup trucks and some motorcycles parked on the gravel at the end of the long dirt road leading to Bugg's home. I carried the sack of cash up the steps to the front of the house.

Bugg met me at the door, but a couple of his goons stepped out ahead of him. We were standing on the front deck. "Gotta frisk you," one of them said to me. It was the man who looked like Jerry Garcia, the one I had run off the road the night I stole Prince. He started to move toward me to pat me down. I struck his chest with the heel of my palm so hard and so fast that he would have fallen on his ass if the exterior wall of the log home hadn't been there to stop him.

"Nobody takes my weapon," I said.

Jerry got up and was getting ready to charge. "Whoa," Bugg said to him with something resembling a hearty laugh, "this here is my man. He's a private dick. Of course he's gonna carry a weapon."

I handed the paper sack full of cash to Bugg and would have been happy to leave, but he said, "C'mon in. I want to hear how you found that bitch." Bugg led me to his living room, which had a rustic Western look punctuated by the fierce heads of a mountain lion and a black bear and the not so fierce head of a mountain goat. I took a chair against a wall that would enable me to see people coming into the room from any direction. Bugg sat down in the middle of an expensive leather-covered sofa and set the grocery sack down beside him. One of the goons sat down in a chair beside the sofa, and the other goon walked into some other part of the home.

"Want a beer?" Bugg asked.

"No, thanks."

"So how'd you find her?" he said. I almost slipped. I almost told him she had ditched me at the furniture store. I almost told him that any woman looking for a ride at that location would've stuck out her thumb on the northbound side of the freeway.

"You told me she wouldn't go back to Nebraska," I said.

"Yeah."

"And from what you said, most of her contacts are here in the Rockies, so I plastered posters all over the West and waited for the phone to ring."

"Keep going."

"Most of the calls were worthless, but we got a call from a trucker who said he thought he'd seen her thumbing for a ride on Interstate Eighty westbound just west of Laramie, so we—"

"Who's 'we'?"

"I've got a partner I work with sometimes. So we headed up to Laramie and just keep putting up posters and taking phone calls from people. Next thing you know we're in Coeur d'Alene, Idaho. So we start asking questions up there and find out she's working as a waitress in some bar. The people at the bar tell us she's living in a trailer. So we find her trailer, but when we get there she is gone. She left in hurry. Somebody at the bar probably told her we were in town asking about her. Anyhow, we—"

"How do you know she left in a hurry?"

"Neighbors told us," I said. He said nothing, so I pressed on. "So we get into her trailer, we find the dog on the bed, then we find a ton of cash—get this—inside the freezer."

"In the freezer?"

"Yeah. Now at that point I figure we've got the dog and the cash, and who knows where your wife took off to? So we decided to head home."

"You remember the name of the trailer park?"

"Lewis and Clark Trailer Park."

"So tell me about these guys that attacked you."

"All right, we've got the dog and the money and we're heading east out of Coeur d'Alene, thinking maybe we'll take a different route home, when three rednecks in a pickup start coming up on us from behind, pointing rifles at us, and trying to run us off the road. The road is covered with ice and it's too dangerous to try to outrun them, so I start slowing down and then come to a stop. As soon as they stop behind me, I shove it into reverse and ram them. I dive out my side and run into the woods, and my buddy rolls out his side and ducks behind a snowbank on the other side of the road. Suddenly they're shooting at us, so we shoot back. When they realize we have them sandwiched, they get back into their truck and take off. When they're gone we go back to my truck, which is damaged from me backing into them and is full of bullet holes, and that's when I see that the hound is bleeding from the throat. He wasn't going to make it, so we carried him into the woods and I shot him. Then we buried him."

"You have any other dogs with you?" he asked.

"Sure. I always take my dogs with me."

"They hurt?"

"Just banged up from me ramming my truck into the other truck."

"Any damage to your truck?"

"Plenty. The whole back end is crushed because these guys had a big wooden bumper on the front of their truck. Some of the windows are shattered and the thing is full of bullet holes."

"Your truck looks to be in pretty good shape now," he said. "How'd you get it fixed so fast?"

"That truck outside?"

"Yeah. You own any other truck?"

"That's a new truck," I said. "There was no way I was going to try to bring all that cash back to Colorado in a truck filled with bullet holes. That would've been stupid. We left my truck in the woods, and I bought a new truck."

"With my money?"

"I didn't have time to shop for a loan," I said.

He peered into the grocery sack and looked at the cash. "How do I know this is all the cash you found in her trailer? Maybe you decided to pay yourself a commission."

"I'm not that dumb," I said.

"What I don't get is why three guys would attack you like that."

"Who knows? Maybe they were drunk. Didn't like our looks. Mistook us for someone else. With all that cash on us, it wasn't like we could go to the police."

"So what do I owe you?" he asked.

"Nothing," I said. "Just let me keep the truck, and we're even."

He looked at the cash again and said, "Well, I figure you earned it." I started to stand up. "Hey, before you leave. Did you learn anything about why she left or where she might be headed?"

"I've got some thoughts on that," I said. "You mind if I get a glass of water?"

"Help yourself," he said.

I walked into the kitchen, found a plastic cup in one of the cabinets, and filled it with chilled water from the refrigerator. I heard Bugg tell the goon to go check on things outside; then I heard him get up and go the bathroom. I looked around to make sure nobody else was watching, and quietly slid open the drawer to the right of the refrigerator. I removed the address book and slid it into a pocket inside my jacket. Then I gently removed the gold pen from my shirt pocket and placed it on the floor by the refrigerator.

I took my cup of water back into the living room and resumed my seat. Bugg returned and plopped back down into the sofa.

"Here's the deal," I said. "This is just a guess, but I think the feds backed your wife into a corner—testify against you or go to jail."

"Why do you say that?"

"Think about it," I said. "She's got all this money she took from you, but instead of renting a car or buying a plane ticket, she's catching rides with truckers. She doesn't want to leave a paper trail, because she doesn't want the feds to find her."

Bugg rolled his head a few times. "Why didn't she take the dog when she left me?"

"I don't know. But at some point she decided she wanted to take the dog with her, so she hired someone to steal him from you."

"I'd sure like to get my hands on that bastard," he said.

"Almost impossible to track him down," I said. "Would cost you more than it would be worth."

He sighed. "Okay, any idea where my wife is headed?"

"Only thing we know for sure is, she was headed north and west. She have any friends up there?"

"Not that I know of."

"Coeur d'Alene is pretty close to the Canadian border," I said.

"Canada?"

"Might be harder for the feds to find her if she's living up there."

"Yeah."

I stood. He stood. We shook hands. "Sorry about your dog," I said.

"You did a good job. If I can send you any business, I will."

I climbed into my truck and headed back to Nederland. "Great," I said to myself, "I'm the staff investigator for the Sons of Satan."

30

I KNEW THERE WOULD BE no photocopier in Ward, so I drove like a bat out of hell to Nederland, parked in front of the business supply store, made a copy of every page in Bugg's address book, bought a diet Coke at Backcountry Pizza, and drove like a bat out of hell back to Bugg's house. The whole trip took less than forty minutes.

Jerry Garcia was standing on the front deck with a machine pistol when I parked my truck. He saw me heading for the front door and said, "Forget something?" I didn't see Bugg around, and I was worried that fat Jerry might want a little payback.

"Yeah, I did. My gold pen. It must've fallen out of my pocket. You guys find one?"

"Not that I know of. But come on in and look around if you like. I don't guess Bugg would care."

I followed him in and then made a show of searching all around the area in the living room where I had been sitting. "Shit," I said, "it has to be here somewhere. Where else did I go? Maybe I lost it in the kitchen."

I walked into the kitchen. Jerry didn't follow me, but he could still see me. I stopped by the refrigerator. "Here it is," I said. "What an idiot I am." I bent down, picked up the pen, and put it in my shirt pocket. But how was I going to put the address book back in the drawer without Jerry seeing me do it? "Hey," I said, "mind if I help myself to some water?"

"Go ahead," he said.

I found a clean glass and filled it with chilled water from the refrigerator. Then I pushed my glass up against the device that is supposed to dispense ice cubes, but I jammed the ice up in there with my palm so it wouldn't come out and I held it that way for a few seconds so that the grinding sound of the jammed ice dispenser was obvious. Then, pretending to be frustrated because of the jammed ice dispenser, I opened the freezer door to grab some ice from the ice holder. Using the open freezer door to shield myself from view, I used my right hand to open the top drawer nearest to the refrigerator and I slipped the address book into it.

I walked back out to the living room, carrying my glass of water, and there he was in all his splendor. Anvil.

I set my water down on an antique hutch and slowly started raising my right hand to reach inside my jacket for my Glock. Anvil looked at me, then looked at Jerry and said, "Who's this guy?"

"He's a private eye Bugg hired to find Karlynn. Take your coat off; I'll tell you all about it. I guess we don't have to worry about that bitch anymore."

31

LATER THAT MORNING I said good-bye to crazy Uncle Ray and Prince. As long as Ray didn't start drinking again, Prince would be in good hands. He'd eat what Ray ate, sleep when Ray slept, and always have a roof over his head. And he'd have miles and miles of land in southern Colorado to call his own.

Feeling lonely and more than a little lucky, I drove down to Wanda's bakery.

"Where did your stripe go?" Wanda said.

"Long story," I said.

I gave Wanda's black Lab, Zeke, a pat on the head, then bought a few donuts and some coffee. A tradition at Wanda's is that each customer supplies his own special coffee mug. She washes them each night and hangs each one on a peg until that customer comes in again. Sadly, the Foghorn Leghorn mug I had used for years had broken recently, so I had replaced it with a mug featuring the face of Mr. T and the words "Don't Be a Fool; Stay in School."

Mr. T, for those who don't know, played the role of B. A. Baracus in a TV show called *The A-Team*, which was popular in the 1980s. I'm an educated man, but I am not ashamed to say that I believe *The A-Team* was one of the greatest television programs ever. The good guys always won, the bad guys always got what was coming to them, nobody ever got seriously hurt, and the four members of the A-Team always accomplished their mission with pizzazz. At the end of each episode, the A-Team's leader, Colonel "Hannibal" Smith, played by George Peppard, would light a cigar, flash a big grin, and say, "I love it when a plan comes together."

My heart was still beating faster than it should have been. I needed to put Anvil out of my mind for a few minutes, so I started reading the paper. I was pleased to see that mine was not one of the names on the obituary page.

Scott walked in and sat down across from me. It was the first time I had seen him since our return from Vegas. Immediately upon saying good-bye to Uncle Ray and Prince I had phoned Scott and asked him to meet me at Wanda's.

"What's up?" he said.

I told him the whole story, starting with the tale I had told Bugg about tracking Karlynn down to the Lewis and Clark Trailer Park and how we had just missed nabbing her. I told him about my having to put a bullet into Prince's head and how we had conducted a nice Protestant ceremony for him in the Idaho pines. I told him that I kept about a hundred thousand dollars and gave the rest back to Bugg.

"Sounds like everything went well," he said. "Bugg thinks you're a hero and you're a hundred thousand dollars ahead."

"That's not the end of the story," I said.

"I'd better get some coffee," he said. Scott does not maintain a special mug at Wanda's, so he had his coffee in a Styrofoam cup.

I told him about stealing Bugg's address book, speeding down to Nederland to copy it, then hightailing it back to Bugg's place to return it under the pretense of searching for my gold pen.

"Jesus H. W. Christ," Scott said. "What are you going to do with it?"

"I don't know. Put that out of your mind for a minute, because here's where the story gets interesting." He just looked at me. "As I am coming back into the living room from the kitchen, getting ready to get the hell out of there, who do you think walks in?"

"Karylnn?"

"Anvil."

"Anvil? I did what you told me to. I kept an eye on him for two hours. How was I supposed to know you were going to steal Bugg's address book and go back to his house a second time?"

"I'm not mad at you," I said. "You did your job."

"What happened?"

"Anvil and I make eye contact, and I'm getting ready to shoot both him and the other goon before I make a beeline for my truck, but Anvil just looks at the goon and asks who I am. The goon tells him I'm a private eye Bugg hired. I say adios and walk briskly to my truck."

"Anvil didn't recognize you?"

"I don't know. The only other time he ever saw me was when I had my stripe."

"What's your gut?"

"He recognized me. He was within two feet of me at the food court. How could he not recognize me?"

"Why didn't he take you out or say something to the other goon?"

"I don't know. That's why I wanted to brainstorm with you."

"Maybe he wanted direction from Bugg before doing anything. Some organizations are managed from the top down. Maybe the Sons of Satan is one of them."

"There's been a bounty on my head since I took the dog. Anvil saw me with Karlynn, so he should've known I took the dog. He doesn't need Bugg's permission to take me out."

"Maybe he figured Bugg wants you alive so you can explain what you and Karlynn were doing together and where the rest of his money is."

"I don't think Anvil ever told Bugg about seeing Karlynn with me. If he had, Bugg would have shared that with me to help in my search for Karlynn. Bugg never mentioned it."

"Maybe Bugg's been onto you since he first hired you, and he's just waiting for the right moment."

"Maybe Anvil isn't Anvil."

"What do you mean?"

"What if Anvil is undercover? That would explain why he didn't push things too far when he saw me with Karlynn."

"He was just maintaining his cover for Karlynn's benefit?"

"Yeah. And he never told Bugg about seeing Karlynn with me, because he doesn't give a shit about what Karlynn did to Bugg."

"When I talked with him in that bar in Longmont, he said he hadn't seen Karlynn for a couple of months, and we know that's a lie because he had just seen you and Karlynn at the mall."

"He doesn't want Bugg to kill me. Or Karlynn."

"Okay," said Scott. "If Anvil's undercover, why does the FBI need Karlynn's help in the first damned place? Anvil has been with Bugg for a few years; he knows the operation inside and out. You put him in front of a grand jury, and it's 'so long, Sons of Satan.'"

"That's a good point," I said. "I thought about it. The only answer I can come up with is that maybe it's one of those situations where the left hand doesn't know what the right hand is doing."

"Anvil's working for some other agency?"

"It's happened before," I said.

"What other agency would be interested in Bugg?"

"DEA, ATF—who knows? Could be the Forest Service for all we know."

Scott shook his head from side to side. "We're getting ahead of ourselves here. We don't even know if Anvil recognized you."

"I'm not willing to gamble," I said. "The safe approach is to assume that he did."

"You want me to stay up here until the situation resolves itself?"

"Would you mind? I sent Uncle Ray and Prince home this morning, and I can't ask my brother to stay away from his gym that long."

"No problem," Scott said. "I just need to call Bobbi and make her think that she's giving me permission."

32

Bobbi MAY HAVE GIVEN Scott permission to stay with me for a while, but Scott was smart enough to know that he couldn't leave her by herself in Boulder on New Year's Eve, so we invited her up to my house. It was Friday evening.

After a brief discussion we decided to eat at the Black Forest in Nederland. We chose the Black Forest for three reasons. First, the food is good. Second, the atmosphere is outstanding; the view of the mountains is panoramic and the indoor waterfall provides nice background noise. Third, it wasn't the kind of place where you were likely to run into anyone associated with the Sons of Satan. I didn't tell Scott or Bobbi, but I actually had a fourth reason—the Black Forest serves only Coca-Cola products. No Pepsi whatsoever.

We went back to my house and I built a fire. We drank some red wine and talked while Buck and Wheat curled up near the fireplace.

"Did Jayne make it back to China?" Bobbi asked.

"What you're really asking is, where do I stand on the adoption issue?"

"Yes."

"I don't know. It's not like there haven't been other things going on in my life lately. Her timing sucks."

"Maybe you should talk with someone," Bobbi suggested.

"Yeah," Scott said with just a hint of mischief in his voice. "Maybe a good therapist is just what you need."

"I think I'll just flow with the great Tao for a while and see what happens."

Bobbi stayed the entire weekend. Scott and I worked out in my basement gym on Saturday and Sunday. He told me to relax more when performing my kata. We watched a lot of football on Sunday, and when I wasn't working out or watching football, I continued to read about Jack Dempsey. I imagined what it would have been like to ride the rails in the early part of the twentieth century at the age of nineteen. I think I would have preferred that over what kids do today—hang out at the mall.

On Monday morning, shortly after Bobbi drove back down to Boulder, I sat down at my dining table and really studied the photocopy of Bugg's address book for the first time. It contained no names or addresses, just initials and numbers. I wasn't really sure why I had even taken the risk involved in taking the address book and copying it. *Why climb the highest mountain? Why fly the Atlantic? Why does Rice play Texas?* I was really starting to like that as a potential response to any "why" question.

Scott had just finished taking a shower and walked into the kitchen for some coffee. "Is that the address book?" he said.

"Yeah."

"Anything interesting?"

"Not so far. It's just initials and phone numbers. I'm sure the feds would love to have it."

"You going to give it to them?"

"I don't know. If I give it to them, sooner or later they'll indict Bugg, and when that happens, they'll have to give a copy to his lawyer and reveal how they obtained it in the first place. And then I'll be back to looking over my shoulder for the rest of my life."

"You could send it to them anonymously."

"Yeah, but I'd still be pretty high on Bugg's list of suspects. The only person higher than me on that list would be Karlynn, and I've got Bugg convinced she moved to Canada and isn't a threat. As long as I don't give it to the feds, this thing is an insurance policy for me. It gives me something to bargain with if Bugg ever comes after me. Matter of fact, I ought to make a copy for you just in case I ever turn up dead."

The phone rang. I walked over to the counter and picked up the receiver. "Mr. Keane?" It was a female voice.

"Yeah."

"This is Detective Simmons from the Denver Police Department."

"Michelle, hi, how are you?"

"I'm fine," she said. "Listen, I've got good news and bad news."

"The yin and the yang," I said. "You can't have one without the other."

"The voice of the man on the tape you gave me is the voice of the man that called the radio station after your cousin was killed."

"I assume that's the good news."

"It is. The bad news is, Skull won't talk with us. I flew up there with another detective to interview him—we thought it would be best not to give him any advance notice—but we couldn't get near him. He lives on some sort of heavily guarded compound."

"Yeah, I know."

"When we got back to our motel, we had a message from an attorney in Spokane."

"He lawyered up?"

"Yeah. I told the lawyer about the voiceprint match and she basically told me to pound sand."

"Great."

"I did obtain a photo of him from the local sheriff up there, and I showed it to the witness that gave us a description of him the night your cousin was killed, but he was just too far away to get a good look at the guy's face. The DA doesn't think we have enough to charge him."

"This guy killed my cousin, a police officer, calls a radio station and claims responsibility for it, and there's nothing we can do?"

"We don't have any other evidence. You're a lawyer. You know how it works. Assuming our voiceprint expert can't be discredited, Skull will admit calling the radio station but deny being involved in the killing. There are plenty of nut cases out there who make a habit of claiming responsibility for crimes they didn't commit. That will be his defense. He'll probably even come up with some alibi witnesses to say he was a thousand miles away at the time of the murders."

"Thanks for trying," I said.

"Are you okay?"

"No, but it's not your fault."

"The file is still open," she said. "We just need some corroboration. I'll spend all my spare time on it."

"Thanks."

I gave Scott the bad news.

"What about that ATF agent that got killed up in Wyoming?" Scott said. "What was his name?"

"Lowell."

"You said Karlynn told the feds a guy named Skull might have been involved in that. If they can't get him for killing your cousin, maybe they can get him on that."

"Might not be the same Skull," I said. "We've got no way to

connect our Skull in Idaho to Lowell's death. Hell, we don't even have Karlynn to testify that Mongoose told Bugg Skull had done a good job taking care of Lowell."

"Anything in the address book that might be the initials for Skull or Mongoose?" I thumbed through my copy of the address book.

"I don't know Mongoose's real name, but I don't see any *M* or *MG* with a Wyoming area code."

"What about Skull?"

"His real name is Anders Riddell." I flipped through my copy of the address book again. "No *S* or *SK* or *AR*."

Scott walked around me and into the kitchen, where he put two pieces of raisin bread into my toaster. When they popped up, he covered them with raspberry jam.

"Maybe we're done," Scott said. "Karlynn's gone, Skull's untouchable, and if Bugg doesn't kill you in the next few weeks, it's probably safe to assume he doesn't know you stole his dog and helped protect Karlynn."

33

Two weeks later I sent Scott home. Bugg hadn't come after me, and neither had Anvil. That didn't necessarily mean I was safe, but I couldn't keep Scott in Nederland indefinitely.

I worked hard at getting back into a daily routine. Shower, meditate, stretch, eat, feed the dogs, read the paper, work at my desk, check the mail, eat, exercise, work some more, eat, feed the dogs, read, watch TV, go to bed.

The trouble was, I didn't have much work to do. I had a few small projects for Matt or one of the other attorneys at Keane, Simms & Mercante. Some involved computerized research. Some involved telephone interviews. Once in a while I had to get in my truck and track down someone who didn't want to be tracked down and obtain a statement from them.

In addition to doing private eye work I sometimes worked as a ghostwriter for Matt. He does not like legal writing, he's not good at it, and he knows it. I like writing, I'm good at it, and he knows that. So he pays me seventy-five dollars an hour—in cash—to write briefs for him. Nobody else knows this, not even the other partners. And certainly not the client.

I was in the middle of one such writing project when I noticed some unfamiliar handwriting on one of the yellow legal pads strewn about my desk. It was an early draft of Karlynn's list. I knew this was an early draft because there were only nine items written down. And because I could see that sheets of paper underneath had been torn away from the pad. The list looked like this:

Go skydiving
Get down to 120 lbs
Visit Lyle
Publish a poem
Go to college
Learn to ski
See Alaska
Learn to swim
Balloon ride

Lyle was the brother serving twenty to life at the Nebraska State Penitentiary. With a federal warrant out for her arrest, Karlynn wasn't going anywhere near there. The only other physical location on her list was Alaska. My stories of Alaska had captivated her. And Alaska offered what she wanted most right now—a chance to be left alone. I'm no expert in geography, but I know enough to know that if you draw a line from Denver to Alaska, that line is going to pass through Idaho. Or at least pretty damned close to Idaho.

My excitement was short-lived. Alaska is a big place. Other than my mother, I knew nobody in Alaska. Alaska is even colder than Nederland. How would I find her? Why would I want to find her? If she had succeeded in making her way to Alaska and starting over, what right did I have to intrude?

Because my mom lives in Barrow, I knew that the area code for Alaska was 907. I looked through my copy of Bugg's address book to see if any of the phone numbers in it contained a 907 area code, but none did.

At noon I decided I had to get some exercise, so I donned my high-tech long underwear, my high-tech running suit, my high-tech running shoes, and my low-tech wool cap. I put Buck's leash on him, left little Wheat at the house, and started jogging toward Caribou Road. I hate running in the cold and I hate having to wear three or four layers of clothing when I do. I made a mental note to see if I could get my brother to sell me one of his treadmills. There are people who choose to live in Nederland because they like winter activities such as cross-country skiing and snowshoeing. I am not one of them.

Later that night I was watching an episode of *Dragnet* when the phone rang.

"Hi, sweetie," she said.

"Hi," I said.

"What are you doing?" she asked.

"Just another manic Monday," I said.

"I said *what* are you doing, not *how* are you doing."

"Oh. Watching *Dragnet*."

"No *Monday Night Football*?"

"It's January; there is no *Monday Night Football*. I might as well hibernate until September. How are things in Beijing?"

"It's cold here," she said. "I didn't know it would be so cold. I should've chosen a university in the southern part of China. Is Uncle Ray still with you?"

We had not talked since she had returned to China, so I brought her up to date on the Bugg situation. I told her about Karlynn and the Lewis and Clark Trailer Park, about putting a bullet into Prince's head, and my newfound status as staff investigator for the Sons of Satan.

"I'm still worried about you," she said.

"Don't be. It's over. Bugg thinks I did what he hired me to

do, so he's happy. If Anvil recognized me, he's not saying any-thing."

"Are you doing okay?" she said.

"Sure."

"You don't sound convincing."

"It's been a rough couple of months," I said. "Eight weeks ago I didn't know who Karlynn Slade was. I've been through a lot lately. I'm just tired."

"Maybe you should take a vacation."

"We just went to Vegas a few weeks ago."

"I don't think that was much of a vacation for you. You went there to make me happy. You were thinking about Bugg the whole time." Actually, I had been thinking a lot about Skull, too, but I hadn't told her about any of that.

"It was good to experience some warm weather for a few days," I said.

"I shouldn't have brought up the adoption issue when you had so much on your mind," she said. "I'm sorry."

"You have a right to say what's on your mind. How can a rela-tionship work if you don't feel free to say what's on your mind?"

"Have you given any more thought to it?"

"I just got rid of Scott today."

"Will you think about it?"

"Hard not to," I said.

I finished talking with Jayne, watched more of *Dragnet*, let Buck and Wheat out one last time, then went upstairs to go to bed.

I was still tossing and turning an hour later, so I went down-stairs, made some ramen noodles, and watched ESPN. I took something to help me sleep. Then I got my suitcase out of the closet and started packing.

34

THIS IS THE CITY. Anchorage, Alaska. A sprawling metropolis of 260,000 people and a like number of sled dogs. It was Wednesday and I was working the day watch in the Nothing Else to Do Unit. My name's Pepper. I carry a Glock. And some business cards.

I landed in Anchorage in the afternoon, after a long flight from San Francisco. I had dropped the dogs at my brother's house on Tuesday and flown to San Fran that evening. There are a lot of Chinese people in San Francisco, and that got me thinking about Jayne. And fatherhood. And sweet-and-sour shrimp. That's what I had for dinner in San Fran.

I had never been to Alaska during the winter. It was dark. And it looked cold. I retrieved my bag from the baggage claim and secured it in a locker. I bought a cup of coffee and started walking around the airport with a photograph of Karlynn.

None of the people at the car rental places recognized her. None of the clerks in any of the stores recognized her. None of the workers at the airline ticket counters recognized her. A cashier at the restaurant recognized her. "I remember her," the young man said. "She wasn't dressed for Alaska. I told her where she could buy some warm clothes."

"She say where she was going?"

"Are you a cop?" he asked.

"No, just a friend. Did she say where she was going?"

"Not really. Just said she had always wanted to visit Alaska. I guess nobody told her it's better in the summertime."

"What's the name of the store you sent her to?" I asked. He wrote it down for me. I retrieved my suitcase from the locker, removed the Glock from it, and hailed a cab.

It was an outdoor-sports store located in a large one-story building in the central part of Anchorage. When I walked in, the man behind the counter was swapping moose-hunting tales with a customer. I assume they were swapping moose-hunting tales, because the man behind the counter was holding a rifle and using terms of the trade such as "big fuckin' moose."

"Can I help you?" said the man behind the counter. He was my age and wore a red flannel shirt over a gray sweatshirt.

I showed him Karlynn's picture. "I'm trying to find her," I said. "I think she might have been in here a few weeks ago to buy clothing." He studied the picture.

"Oh yeah," he said, "she's a hard one to forget. Wouldn't have lasted a day with the clothes she had on. No insulation, no ventilation, no hat."

"Any idea where she might be staying?"

"Not a clue," he said. He handed the photo to the customer.

"Not bad-looking," the customer said. "She won't be lonely up here." The customer was a bit younger, maybe thirty-five.

"I take it she bought some clothes," I said to the store employee. Maybe he was the owner.

"You bet. We covered her from head to toe. If she freezes up here, it ain't gonna be our fault."

"How did she pay for it?" I asked.

"Paid cash, I think. Yeah, she did. Seemed like she had a lot of cash on her."

"Thanks," I said. "I appreciate your help."

"You bet," he said.

I looked around the store and decided there were some items I probably needed to buy for myself, so I started browsing. "If you need any help, just holler," said the man behind the counter.

Living in Nederland, I have a good collection of winter gear, but if I was going to have to go door-to-door in Alaska showing everyone my photo of Karlynn, I wanted to be warm. So I purchased a top-of-the-line parka, insulated face mask, and goose-down mittens. I also bought a very powerful and rugged flashlight, the kind powered by six "D" cell batteries.

I placed my items on the counter and opened my wallet. The total came to nearly five hundred dollars. I paid cash.

"Can one of you recommend a motel?" I said to the two men.

"How long you going to be staying?" the customer asked.

"No clue," I said.

"You won't have any trouble getting a room this time of year," he said. "You want big and fancy or small and rustic?"

"Small, rustic, and warm."

"C'mon," he said, "I know just the place. My name's Chris."

About five minutes later Chris guided his big Bronco into the parking lot of a long building with a log exterior. He left it running, and we walked into the lobby. There was a wood stove putting out some good heat in the lobby, but nobody was visible. "Hey Fred," Chris yelled, "I've got a guest for you."

Fred turned out to be his stocky brother-in-law. He lived in a suite of rooms behind the front desk. "How long will you be staying?" Fred asked.

"Don't know."

"You here on business or pleasure?"

"Business," I said.

"Lighten up, Hoss. It's a joke. Nobody comes here for pleasure in January."

"Sorry," I said.

"That's okay. I'll just have you fill out the registration form, and we'll take good care of you. What's your name, by the way?" He slid a registration form across the counter to me.

"Pepper," I said. I extended my hand and we shook hands. Then I opened my wallet and handed him five hundred-dollar bills. "I'll be paying cash," I said. "I'd kind of like to avoid leaving a paper trail." He and Chris eyed each other; then he slid the registration form away from me.

I thanked Chris for his hospitality, and Fred led me down the hall to room 1, which was the room closest to the front desk. Fred turned on the lights, then found the thermostat and turned it up.

"It'll heat up pretty quick," he said. "Meanwhile, there's a space heater over there that you can use. Let me know if you need anything. I'll have coffee for you in the morning."

"Thanks," I said.

It was a nice room. Spacious. Beautiful log furniture. Expensive television set. I turned the space heater on and looked at my watch. It was four-thirty in the afternoon. I peeled the curtain back and looked out the window. It was darker than a CEO's heart.

Fred let me borrow his Jeep to drive around town and look for a place to eat. As I was leaving, he said, "Pick up some beer on your way back, will ya?"

I found a decent-looking restaurant and ordered king crab and diet Coke. I stopped at a liquor store on the way back and purchased a case of very good beer.

Fred was nowhere to be found when I returned, so I left his keys and twenty-two bottles of beer on the front counter. I took two beers to my room. The room was starting to warm up. I sat down on one of the chairs but left several layers of clothing on. I opened a bottle of beer and considered my next move.

Karlynn was probably still in Alaska. Even if she had a passport, she couldn't use it without alerting the feds to her whereabouts. Where in Alaska? I would've chosen Anchorage. Anchorage has shops, supermarkets, taxicabs, electricity, indoor plumbing, and other things we take for granted in the lower forty-eight. But if I worked on the premise that Karlynn was in Anchorage, that meant I would have to drive from one motel to the next showing my photo of her. And she might not even be staying at a motel. Maybe she had made friends with someone or found a situation where she could trade her labor for room and board.

What would be the most productive use of my time? I could check the bars, place an ad in the paper, maybe even tap into whatever criminal/biker community there might be in Anchorage, but that sounded like a lot of work.

How was she getting around? She couldn't have rented a car; that would have required a credit card, and the feds could trace credit cards. For that matter, how did she get to Alaska? I knew she had been at the airport, but if she had taken a commercial flight, she would have had to present a driver's license or some other form of identification, and she was smart enough to know that. It seemed reasonable to assume she had flown in on a private plane. That was a manageable project. If I could find out how she had gotten to Anchorage, I might find out what she had planned to do when she arrived.

I looked at my watch. It was 7:45. I drank the second beer, then climbed under the covers and went to sleep.

35

It was dark when I awoke, but the digital clock told me it was eight-thirty. I enjoyed a hot shower, then walked out into the lobby. Fred was gone, but there was a fortyish blonde in a sweatshirt sitting next to the wood stove, drinking coffee and reading the morning paper.

"Morning," I said.

"Good morning," she said. "Want some coffee?"

"Sure."

"Help yourself."

I poured some coffee into a mug, with a little cream, and sat down in the chair beside her.

"Are you Fred's wife?" I said.

"Sister," she said. "My name's Renee. I live here too."

"My name's Pepper."

"What brings you to Alaska?" she said.

"I always wanted to freeze my ass off in total darkness, and I had a little free time this week, so I figured what the heck."

"A sense of humor. I like that in a man."

"Yeah, sometimes I laugh my ass off at myself."

"We are intrigued by the fact that you paid cash and didn't want to fill out a registration form."

"Don't be. I'm just looking for a friend who might be in some trouble. If anyone else is looking for her, I don't want to be the one that leads them to her."

"Your girlfriend?"

"No, she's too low-maintenance for me."

"Usually men complain about women who are high-maintenance."

"There's got to be a happy medium," I said. "What do you do?"

"I'm a bush pilot, but I don't get much business this time of year, so I help keep Fred in line and I read a lot. What do you do?"

"I'm a freelance investigator," I said. "I used to practice law, but I decided there had to be an easier way to make money."

"Do you want to go out to dinner tonight?" she said. I guess she wasn't big on segues.

"I'm sort of involved with someone," I said.

"Just dinner," she said.

"Sure. Why not?"

"Okay, let me know when you're ready. Ring the bell if nobody is here."

I filled my coffee mug again and started heading for my room. "Come to think of it," I said, "you might be able to help me. I think the person I am looking for flew into Anchorage on a private plane. I'd like to find the pilot. He or she might know what my friend planned to do in Alaska. Do you have any suggestions on how I might go about it?"

"Have you got a picture of your friend?"

"Yes."

"Go get it. I'll scan it in and we'll send it out on the pilots' Listserv. That covers just about everyone with a pilot's license in Alaska."

"You just saved me a lot of phone calls," I said.

While my photo of Karlynn was circulating in cyberspace, I wasn't sure what to do with myself. I had my copy of Bugg's address book with me, and it suddenly dawned on me that I could use the computer shared by Fred and Renee to seek information about the name and address associated with each number in the book.

One by one I conducted a Google search on each phone number in Bugg's book. Some queries produced no results, but others did. Within a few hours I had names and addresses to associate with many of the phone numbers. I didn't know what I would do with them, but part of being a good investigator is getting as much information as you can. Some may turn out to be irrelevant, but some may be highly relevant. You never know.

It took several hours to check every number in Bugg's book, and in the process I determined that not all the numbers in the book were phone numbers. Telephone numbers in the United States consist of seven digits or ten digits. But some of the numbers in the back of Bugg's book consisted of eight or nine digits, and those had no initials. What was up with that?

Fred's sister checked her e-mail around noon, but so far nobody responding to the message she had sent out on the pilots' Listserv had seen or heard of Karlynn.

With nothing else to do, I took an afternoon nap—a treat we rarely get to indulge these days. It wasn't hard to fall asleep. It was already dark.

Renee was one of the few people in Anchorage not driving an SUV or a big truck. She drove a small truck. But it ran and it got us to the restaurant she had selected just fine. It was a steak house, much like a steak house in any other American city, but more expensive and less formal. A steak house with a dart board.

A waitress in jeans came to our table. Renee ordered beer, so I did too. Renee had replaced her sweatshirt with a red flannel shirt and had traded her jeans for tan corduroy slacks. It looked as if that was as dressed up as anyone in Anchorage was going to get.

"What made you decide to be a pilot?" I asked.

"My dad was a bush pilot," she said. "I've never imagined doing anything else. Fred has a pilot's license, too."

"You said you don't get much business in the winter?"

"Not too much. A friend of mine flies for an air ambulance service. Sometimes I fill in for him."

"A jet?"

"A Learjet Thirty-five. Ever flown in a private jet?"

"Yeah. A friend of mine in Denver runs a charter service. He makes a lot of money flying corporate executives around. His name is Jeff Smart."

The waitress arrived with our beers. No glasses, just two cold bottles of beer. She asked if we wanted to order dinner. Renee suggested the elk steak, so that's what I ordered.

"Do you have children?" Renee asked.

"Two dogs," I said. "Do you?"

"Two boys. One lives in Seward with his dad; one lives in Juneau. So tell me about this woman you're sort of involved with."

"She's a math professor. She's teaching in China for a year."

"How's that working out?"

"It was working pretty well until she went to China."

"Long-distance relationships are hard," she said.

"We spent some time together at Christmas, and that was nice. But she wants to adopt a little girl from China and I'm not sure that's what I want."

"You don't like kids?"

"It's more complicated than that," I said.

"Want to talk about it?"

"Not really. I'm still trying to sort it all out."

"I married young," she said, "but my children were a blessing. I wouldn't trade them for anything. Were you ever married?"

"Came close once."

"Want to throw some darts?" she said. Renee knew how to change topics in a hurry.

"Sure," I said. She led me to a little corner near the bar, where there was a dartboard set up. We each asked the bartender for another beer.

"I should tell you that I'm really good," she said.

"We'll see," I said.

She was really good. "If it makes you feel any better," she said, "you throw harder than anyone I've ever seen. Did you see the way the bartender was looking at you?"

"I don't know why," I said, "but that does make me feel better."

My elk steak was medium-rare and covered with sautéed mushrooms and some kind of mushroom sauce. It was delicious.

By the time we finished dinner we had each consumed three beers, and that's a lot for me. I was feeling good. Renee drove us back to the motel. Fred was there watching a bass-fishing program, which struck me as odd because the nearest bass was probably two thousand miles south of Anchorage. Renee walked behind the counter, disappeared from sight for a few seconds, and came back out with two more bottles of beer.

"Let's go down to your room," she said.

"Not a good idea," I said.

"Afraid I'll get you drunk and take advantage of you?"

"I'm afraid I would enjoy it," I said. "But I don't think I'd feel too good about myself in the morning." She stood there for a few seconds, still holding the two bottles of beer.

"I'll see you in the morning," she said. Then she turned and walked behind the counter.

It's a good thing I had the self-discipline to say, "Just walk away, Renee," because Jayne called me on my cell phone a half hour later. I told her I was in Alaska and what I was doing there. She brought me up to date on her experiences in China. Eventually we got around to talking about our relationship.

"I love you," she said, "but I am serious about this adoption. I want to do this. And I'm not going to wait forever."

"How long are you going to wait?" I said.

"I don't know. How long are you going to continue to think about it? At some point you have to make a decision."

36

I HEARD SEVERAL LOUD KNOCKS on my door. "Wake up, Clark Kent," said Renee. "We've got a lead on your friend."

I hopped out of bed in my boxer shorts to open the door. She handed me an e-mail she had printed. I read it:

Renee:

I flew this woman from Juneau to Anchorage a few days ago. She told me she had taken the ferry from Bellingham. Hope this helps. Don't know if I can provide much more info, but give me a call if you want to talk.

Dan Montgomery
Juneau Air Charter Service

I glanced at the digital clock. It was seven-thirty. I looked at Renee and said, "It's morning, right?"

"It's morning," she affirmed. I handed the e-mail back to her.

"Do you know this guy?" I said.

"Sure. Diving Dan has been around a long time."

"Diving Dan?"

"He's not a believer in gradual descents. He flew A-tens in the air force. That's what they use to attack tanks and—"

"I know what an A-ten is." Every Marine knows what an A-10 is—even the lawyers. "Do you think he'd be up now?"

"He'll be up," she said.

I showered, got dressed, and called Diving Dan from the phone in my room.

"How did she pay?" I asked.

"Cash. Didn't seem like she was hurting for it." Maybe she really had taken half a million dollars from Bugg, as Livingston had suggested, then given roughly three hundred thousand to Matt for safekeeping and kept the rest.

"How did you hook up with her?" I asked. "Why didn't she take the ferry all the way to Anchorage?"

"All I know is, she was in Juneau when I found her. She was at a McDonald's and had a map of Alaska spread out in front of her. She looked out of place, so I asked her if I could help. Next thing I know, she's my copilot."

"Did she say anything about where she was going?"

"Is she in some kind of trouble?"

"She's going through some hard times," I said. "Did she say anything at all about where she was going or why she was in Alaska?"

"She was pretty tight-lipped about that," he said. "I got the impression she'd been around the block once or twice and just didn't trust people."

"You guys must've talked about something," I said.

"She had plenty of questions about Alaska. What are the best jobs, where are the best places to live, stuff like that. She even asked me if motorcycles were big up here and were there any outlaw gangs."

"What did you tell her?"

"I told her lots of people in Anchorage and the coastal areas like motorcycles in the summer. No outlaw gangs that I know of, maybe some wannabees. 'Course, there are some places up here, like Barrow, where are there damn few motorcycles because you can't drive there. And even if you could, only an idiot would ride a motorcycle in Barrow. Even in the summer it doesn't get above forty degrees there."

"You told her that?"

"What?"

"There are no motorcycles in Barrow."

"Something like that. I don't remember my exact words."

In sharing my Alaskan adventures with Karlynn, I had described Barrow as the "flattest, whitest, most desolate place on earth."

It made sense.

The fact that Karlynn might be in Barrow was not good news. It wasn't good news, because I knew it would be thirty degrees below zero and windy as hell. And it wasn't good news, because my mother lives there.

I asked Renee to fly me there, but she said I'd be better off taking a commercial jet. They do better in the cold and wind, and on a jet I could get there in about three hours.

The flight on the 737 wasn't bad until we started to descend; then the wind just buffeted the hell out of the aircraft. It felt as if God were playing air hockey and the jet was the puck. I don't remember what time we landed. I had more or less lost track of time. It was dark, cold, and forty-four feet above sea level. That was all I needed to know.

I took a taxi to the government-built housing my mother lives in. The taxi was a big Chevy Suburban. My mom works as a nurse for the U.S. Public Health Service. Why the U.S. government built a hospital three hundred miles above the Arctic Circle is best left to historians, though I suspect it had something to do with white guilt. The locals were doing just fine until the white man showed up.

My mom's apartment building sits on concrete pillars because it was built on tundra. If you are going to erect a building in Barrow, you are pretty much stuck with tundra. The tundra softens up during the summer, but the pillars allow the building to sink a little during the thaw without turning your first floor into a basement. They also serve another purpose—they prevent the polar bears from climbing in through your bedroom window and eating you.

Mom was waiting for me when I knocked on her door, as was Scamp, her nuclear powered Jack Russell terrier. I had called from Anchorage to give her the good news about my visit. She gave me a hug, offered to cook me something, and did all the things mothers do. I removed my parka, hat, and gloves and stared out the window. Her apartment had a great view of the ocean, except that the ocean was frozen solid and it was pitch black outside.

I took a diet Coke from the refrigerator and sat down on the couch. My mom sat in a recliner. "You're not eating enough," she said. "You're thin as a rail."

"Mom, I'm weighing in at about two-twenty these days."

"How's Jayne?" she said.

"Fine," I said.

She started talking about the latest political turmoil at the hospital in Barrow and asked whether she could be sued if one of the government doctors malpracticed on one of the natives. She doesn't like it when the doctors disagree with her. She has been a nurse for fifty years. She thinks they're all incompetent.

Eventually she got around to asking me what I was doing in

Barrow, and I explained that I was just trying to find a young woman who needed some help. I didn't tell her about Bugg, or the Sons of Satan, or Skull. Or Anvil or the FBI or the drug money.

I updated her on Uncle Ray and told her I'd probably be heading back to Anchorage in a day or two. There are only four thousand people in Barrow, and I could exclude all the men as well as all Eskimo women. It wouldn't take long to find Karlynn. She would stick out like a sore thumb.

37

I FOUND HER THE NEXT DAY. I use the term "day" in the broader sense; I don't mean to imply that there was the slightest hint of sunshine or any other kind of natural light. It was a Saturday, which for many people meant it was shopping day.

There is really only one store in Barrow. Sure, there are restaurants, liquor stores, and even some motels, but if you are looking for groceries or hardware, there is really only one store. I stood just inside the entrance and showed Karlynn's picture to anyone who entered. A number of people recognized her, but some were natives and didn't speak English. My Inupiat was rusty, but eventually an Eskimo kid who spoke English looked at the photo of the dark-haired Karlynn and said, "She has red hair now."

"Yes," I said. He offered to take me to her for twenty bucks. I climbed aboard his snowmobile and away we went.

Within a few minutes we came to a small house made of wood, aluminum, and possibly an old whaling boat. A satellite dish was mounted on one side, just below the roof. There were two huskies out front, each with its own insulated shelter. I knocked on the door, but there was no answer. It was unlocked. I signaled the kid to wait a minute and went inside. Nobody was home, but I recognized the coat she had been wearing when she ditched me in Denver. I went outside, paid the kid, and told him to take off.

I looked at my watch. It was noon. The place wasn't bad on the inside. It had running water and a furnace. I removed my outer clothes, flopped down on the couch, and watched TV for a while. She came in around four, saw me through the holes in her face mask, and said, "Jesus fucking Christ."

"I'm glad to see you, too," I said.

"I'm not going back," she said as she removed her face mask. She was still a redhead, but her hair was much shorter.

"I didn't come to take you back."

"Why are you here?"

"I'm missing some T-shirts," I said. "I thought you might have them." She removed her parka.

"Why are you here?" she repeated.

"To make sure you are okay."

"I'm fine," she said.

"Do you need money? You left about three hundred thousand with Matt. I had to give some of it back to Bugg, but I brought some of it with me."

"You gave it back to him?"

"It's kind of a long story," I said. She offered hot tea and I accepted.

I spent the next hour recounting the tale of the road trip to Idaho, including finding her at the Lewis and Clark Trailer Park, shooting Prince in the head, returning the money to Bugg, running into Anvil again, and tracking her down to Barrow.

"So Prince is okay?" she asked.

"He's fine. He's living with my uncle Ray in southern Colorado. They're a match made in heaven."

"Is Thad still looking for me?"

"I don't know. I don't know if he bought my story. I'm pretty sure Anvil recognized me. Any idea why he didn't just try to kill me on the spot?"

"He knows you carry a gun. Maybe he didn't think the time was right."

"Scott and I discussed the possibility that he might be an undercover agent."

"Anvil?"

"I don't think he ever told Bugg about seeing you and me in the mall. He told Scott he hadn't seen you for two months, and that was shortly after he'd seen us together at the mall. And the other day at Bugg's house he pretended he didn't recognize me."

"Why would the feds need me to testify if Anvil is one of them?"

"I don't know. We thought he might not be with the FBI, that maybe he is with the DEA or some other agency."

"No way is Anvil a cop," she said as she turned her head from side to side. "I've seen him get drunk; I've seen him smoke dope; I've seen him rough people up. I don't buy it."

"Just a theory," I said.

"I'll tell you one thing about Thad. He won't give up. If he finds out what you did, he'll pursue you to your dying day. And me."

"He'll never find you up here," I said. "If I were you, I'd be more worried about the federal arrest warrant. Are you using your real name?"

"No, I bought a new identity in Seattle. Got a new birth certificate and a new Social Security number. My name is Jenny Watson now."

"What about a driver's license and a passport?"

"I don't need those right now, so why take the risk?"

"You never answered my question," I said. "Do you need money?"

"I have enough."

"I still have something like a hundred grand."

"Keep it. Give it to Matt. I don't care. If I spend too much at one time, it will attract more attention than I need."

"Are you working?" I said.

"I'm working the front desk at a motel. Today was my second day."

"How did you get a job so quickly?"

"It's not hard," she said. "Anyone with half a brain and no alcohol issues can get a job here. I'm going to take some classes after I get settled."

"Is there a college here?"

"Ilisagvik College."

"I bet it doesn't attract many nonresident students," I said. Yeah, my kid applied to Harvard, Yale, Princeton, and Ilisagvik.

She made more hot tea and we continued talking. "I want to show you something," I said. I handed her my copy of Bugg's address book.

"How did you get this?" she asked. I told her.

"I've managed to figure out who some of the phone numbers belong to, but maybe you can help me with some of the others."

We went through my copy of the address book page by page, and she was able to provide names for some of the initials associated with some of the numbers. We spent more than an hour on it, and she provided a wealth of information about the Sons of Satan. I took copious notes.

"One thing I noticed," I said as we came to the end of the address book, "is that there are some numbers in the back of the book that aren't phone numbers. Each series has eight or nine digits, and there are no initials next to them." I showed them to her. "Any idea what those are?"

"I never noticed them before," she said. "Thad never said anything about them."

Was there anything else I wanted to ask her? This would probably be my only chance. I turned to the topic of Skull. I had no way of knowing whether the Skull who had killed my cousin was the same Skull who had killed Agent Lowell. Maybe Karlynn could help.

"Karlynn," I said, "when the feds were questioning you about the murder of Agent Lowell, you told them someone named Mongoose had told Bugg that Skull had done a good job. Do you remember that?"

"Yeah."

"Had you ever met Skull?"

"No."

"Had Thad ever met Skull?"

"I don't know. I don't think so. He never mentioned it to me."

"Do you know how Mongoose knew Skull?"

"No."

"Do you remember anything else at all that Mongoose said about Skull?"

"Just that Skull had done a good job."

"Anything else about that conversation that you remember? How did Bugg react when Mongoose told him Skull had done a good job?"

"I think Thad just said 'fuckin' skinheads' or something like that."

"Skull was a skinhead?"

"I guess. Why else would Thad say that?"

At some point I ran out of questions. There was an awkward silence. It was time to leave. I stood and looked at her. "Are you sure you want to stay here?" I asked. "You won't be able to communicate with anyone you used to know. That's how they'll find you."

"I know."

"It will be lonely."

"I'm okay with it. There are worse things than loneliness."

"My mother lives here," I said. "She's a nurse at the hospital. I'll give you her phone number. If you're ever in real trouble, call my mom and have her call me." I removed my pen from my pocket, wrote the number down on a notepad, and handed the piece of paper to her.

"Okay, thanks."

I put my parka and my other winter gear on, then opened the door and was greeted by an assault of cold, wind, and darkness. "You want me to call a taxi?" she asked. "That's how we get around up here."

"Hell, no," I said. "It's a beautiful night for a walk."

"You're funny," she said.

"That's what I keep telling people," I said. I stepped outside, so we had to speak louder because of the wind. The huskies were still there.

"The dogs belong to the man I rent from. They keep the polar bears away. I've tried to make them indoor dogs, but they like the cold. Prince wouldn't be happy here."

"No raccoons," I said.

"I'm worried about you," she said. "Don't underestimate Thad. He plays for keeps."

"Me too," I said. "I'm going to help the feds put him away for good.

"Sooner or later I'll have to come up to visit my mom. I'll look you up when I do."

"I'd like that. You'll be my only connection with my past."

"Who knows, I might even bring Prince if I come in the summer."

38

I LANDED IN DENVER on a sunny Tuesday afternoon, having opted to spend a night in San Francisco on that leg of my return trip. I took an airport shuttle to my truck, which I had parked in an outlying lot. It started right up. I headed south to my brother's house to retrieve Buck and Wheat.

Nobody was home, so I loaded the dogs into my truck, then went back inside to rifle the pantry for any junk food I might be able to consume during the hour-and-a-half drive back to Nederland. The pickings were slim. I had to settle for some beef jerky and a diet Pepsi. I left my brother a note suggesting he show more consideration in the future.

I ended up having to drive through Denver at rush hour. Past tree forts that were now office buildings. Past rope swings that were now fast food joints. Past vast grazing lands that were now municipalities. "All is flux," said Heraclitus.

When I reached Boulder, I decided to swing by Scott's house and tell him about my latest exploits. Bobbi was out showing a home. Scott was reading an astronomy journal and apparently listening to a CD of old Donna Summer tunes.

I opened my jacket to reveal the Glock in my shoulder holster. I tapped the weapon a few times with my right index finger. "If I hear 'MacArthur Park' come out of those speakers," I said, "I'm going to shoot you right here. For the good of the gene pool. I want to be straight with you about that."

"Where've you been?" he said.

"Barrow."

"How's your mom?"

"Almost as crazy as Uncle Ray. There's no doubt they've got some of the same DNA floating around in their systems."

He turned the music down. I took my jacket off, sat down, and told him how I had found Karlynn.

"Why didn't you tell me where you were going?"

"I was just playing a hunch," I said. "Didn't want to drag you along on a wild-goose chase. Figured the time alone would do me good, give me some time to think about my future with Jayne."

"Did you make any decisions?"

"Not about that."

"You made some other decisions?"

"Yeah. I think I'm going to give Bugg's address book to the feds."

"Why?"

"I think Bugg's onto me. I know Anvil recognized me. If I'm right, giving the address book to the feds doesn't put me in any more danger than I'm already in."

"Want me to move back in with you?"

"No, but I wouldn't mind borrowing a shotgun, a rifle, and some ammo. All I've got is the Glock." Scott is not a "gun nut," and he says half the members of the NRA are crackpots, but he grew up hunting and does not think it unusual to have a dozen firearms in his home.

"Sure, take your pick before you leave. Sorry I don't have any rocket-propelled grenades, but the CIA gave its surplus to the Arabs."

I smiled and I handed him my copy of Bugg's address book. "I had plenty of free time in Alaska, so I spent some time online trying to learn what I could about all the phone numbers in Bugg's book. I learned quite a bit, and Karlynn was able to help me fill in some of the gaps. I've got a name and address for most of these phone numbers. And in some cases I've got a lot more than that."

"That's great," he said.

"By the way, the Skull that killed Lowell was a skinhead."

"That's interesting."

"It's very interesting. We've got two different people killed by a skinhead named Skull. We know a skinhead in Idaho named Skull. And we know Mongoose lives in Wyoming and hired a skinhead named Skull to kill Lowell."

"Idaho and Wyoming are right next door to each other."

"Yeah, I had the same thought."

Scott opened the address book and began to thumb through it.

"Look at the back page," I said. "There is a series of numbers there, and each one consists of eight or nine digits. No initials. Any idea what those might be?"

"Not off the top of my head, but I'll copy them down and give it some thought."

"I guess I'd like to know what they are before I decide whether to give this to the feds."

Before I left, Scott led me downstairs to his "war room." This room contains more telescopes, microscopes, radios, computers, maps, and electronic gadgets than any other basement in America. It also contains Scott's two gun cases, so I picked out a shotgun and a .22-caliber semiautomatic rifle with a scope. I loaded both before heading back up to Nederland.

39

I WAS ASLEEP but nevertheless conscious of the fact that I was dreaming about snakes. When I was a kid, I had frequent terrifying nightmares about snakes. Now, in my forties, such dreams are rare.

The dream woke me up and I figured I might as well empty my bladder. Then I heard it. Just as I started to put my feet on the floor—the unmistakable warning of a coiled rattlesnake. I pulled my feet up and stood on the bed. My heart was racing. We'll never know for sure, but I believe that in those few seconds I let loose with one of best examples of spontaneous cursing in the history of the English-speaking peoples.

I stood for a minute so my eyes could adjust to darkness. The dogs, who had both been sleeping beside me on the bed, were alert now. I commanded them to stay, then retrieved a flashlight from the bedside table. I aimed the light beam at the snake, then scanned the room to see if he had brought any friends. I didn't see any. Slowly I began to regain my composure.

It's just one fucking snake, I thought. I can jump toward the bedroom door and get out of the room without ever getting into snake range. Then I'll get a rake or something from the garage and kill the damned thing.

I saw no other snakes on my way to the garage. I would have seen them if there had been any, because I had turned on every light in the house on my way to the garage. I found an iron rake with a long handle. I also found a shovel I could use to chop the snake in half. I had no experience with this, but Dad had always told me the secret to success was to use the right tool for the job. I grabbed Scott's shotgun on the way back up to my bedroom. Now I had three tools.

I flicked on the overhead light in my bedroom. The dogs were on the bed barking. Mr. Snake was still there, quite content to lie coiled on my carpet. The only reason I didn't shred the thing with the shotgun is that I didn't want to have to clean up what would surely be a bloody mess. Carefully I made my way around the snake to one of the bedroom windows. I opened the window as much as it would open.

I began to slide the pronged end of the iron rake toward the snake. He didn't like that and made that clear. I caught part of his underbelly on the prongs of the rake and lifted him up. I walked to the open window and flung him out, down onto the frozen ground below.

I supposed he would die from the cold, and that was okay by me. He shouldn't have been in Nederland in the first fucking place, and he certainly shouldn't have been in my bedroom. But I'm not a herpetologist and I wasn't absolutely sure he would die from the cold. What if it had been a female? Would the land surrounding my home be infested with baby rattlers next spring? I put my flip-flops on, walked downstairs, took the shotgun out on to the back deck, located the rattler on the snow, and fired two shells right at it.

I looked at the clock in the kitchen. Two-seventeen a.m. I

downed a few swigs of Jack Daniel's to calm my nerves and started a methodical check of my house for snakes. When I was satisfied that there were no others, I took the Jack Daniel's and Scott's shotgun to my recliner, then leaned back to think it through.

Contrary to popular belief, rattlesnakes can live at this altitude. But it's extremely rare; you've got a better chance of meeting a Republican at a Planned Parenthood meeting than you have of finding a rattler at 8,236 feet. I had never encountered one above six thousand feet. And they hibernate in the winter. So this was not a case of a confused rattler that just wandered into my expensive mountain home. Someone had put the snake there, either to kill me or to fuck with me. I intended to find out who. Then I would kill him or find a way to fuck back.

The phone rang. It was Glen, Nederland's police chief. "We had a report of gunfire in your area," he said, "and you naturally came to mind. Everything okay?"

"Everything's fine," I said. "You don't need to send anyone."

"Good. There's nobody to send except me. What happened?"

"I took a couple of shots at an animal that got too close to the house, that's all."

"Mountain lion?"

"Rattlesnake."

"In January?"

"In my bedroom."

"You think Bugg had something to do with it?"

"He's the obvious suspect," I said. Bugg, someone associated with Bugg, or perhaps Skull or one of his local contacts.

"This is getting out of hand. You want me to go up and interview him?"

"He's out of your jurisdiction," I said.

"The crime took place in my jurisdiction."

"I appreciate the offer, but don't do anything. Let me think it through."

I said good night to Glen, again assured him that everything was fine, and leaned back in my recliner. Eventually I fell asleep.

I woke up around nine with a mild hangover from the Jack Daniel's. I walked into the kitchen, poured some orange juice, then swallowed four Motrin. I checked all the doors and windows to see if there was any sign of forced entry. Nothing. Whoever did it had a key or was very good with locks.

After I'd had some coffee, I got dressed and walked the few hundred yards over to the home owned by my aging hippie neighbors, Luther and Missy. The dogs came with me.

Missy answered the door wearing something with half moons on it that was either a dress or a nightgown. A dog I failed to recognize was at her side. At any given time Luther and Missy usually have three or four dogs and a couple of houseguests.

"Hi, Pepper," she said. "Come on in. Do you want some herb tea?" I stomped my boots on the steps to get the snow off them, then entered the home, leaving Buck and Wheat to play outside. Then I noticed that another woman, much younger, lay asleep on the sofa. She was covered by quilts, but her feet were sticking out from the covers and I could see she was wearing orange hunting socks. "That's our daughter," Missy explained. "She goes back to college in a few days."

"Luther around?" I asked.

"He's in Rapid City for a week," she said. Luther plays in a rock band named the Stress Monsters, so he's on the road a lot. They're actually damn good, and I don't know why they haven't ever become more than a regional band. I guess there could be worse jobs than touring the American West and playing great music.

I sat down at their kitchen table and Missy handed me a cup of herb tea. Red Zinger, I think. She sat down opposite me. I heard soft flute music in the background.

"Did you hear those gunshots last night?" she asked.

"That was me," I said. I did not elaborate.

"I'm sensing tremendous tension in you," she said. Missy is into a lot of new age mysticism.

"I'm dealing with some bad people," I said. "Did you or Luther see anything unusual at my house recently? I had to go up to Alaska for a few days."

"I can't think of anything."

"I'd appreciate it if you and Luther would let me know if you see anything strange around here during the next few weeks. If anything strikes you as funny or out of place, just pick up the phone. Don't be afraid that you might be making something out of nothing."

"Sure," she said.

"Thanks."

"It's not healthy for you to carry so much tension," she said. "Your aura is the color of mustard. Why don't you let me lead you through a guided visualization to help you relax?" What the hell, I figured. Why live in a hippie town if you can't take advantage of its resources?

She turned up the flute music and lit some jasmine incense and some candles. I closed my eyes and listened as she began to speak in a calm and somewhat monotonous voice. I don't know how long I was "out," but I felt much more relaxed when I left Missy and walked back to my home with Buck and Wheat.

I looked at the dogs and said, "Do you guys notice any difference in the color of my aura?"

*　　*　　*

Later that I night was watching old fights on ESPN Classic. I was watching the first Ali-Spinks fight, one of my favorites. Ali was without question the greatest, but on that night in 1978 the 197-pound Spinks pushed Ali around the ring like an unrelenting bull and pulled off a stunning upset.

I tried calling Jayne when the fight was over, but there was no answer. I thought about calling Kendra Carlson but decided against it. I would have been doing it for all the wrong reasons.

The dogs started barking and I saw Missy walking toward my front door with her daughter. I invited them in.

"This is Allison," Missy said.

I extended my right hand and said, "Pepper Keane." They sat down on my couch. "Can I get you something to drink?" I asked.

"Herb tea," Missy said.

"Beer, if you have any," Allison said.

I made a cup of peppermint tea in the microwave for Missy, then pulled two bottles of Sierra Nevada Pale Ale from the refrigerator, handed one to Allison, and sat down in my recliner.

"You're home from college?" I said to Allison.

"Just for a few more days," she said.

"Where do you go to school?" I asked.

"Cal Tech," she said. You could have knocked me over with a rabbit sneeze. I would have bet money that any child of Missy and Luther attended Berkeley. Or maybe the School of Arts at NYU.

"What are you studying?"

"Nuclear engineering." Another shocker. Luther and Missy take great pride in heating their home entirely with solar panels and a wood stove.

"Top ten percent of her class," Missy added.

"I'm impressed," I said.

"Don't be. I have a photographic memory. It just comes naturally."

"Tell him," Missy said to her daughter.

"Mom says you wanted to know if there had been anything strange at your house in the past few days."

"Yeah."

"A few days ago I went jogging with our dogs and I saw a pickup truck on the road in the front of your house. There were two men unloading something from the back of the truck. One was very big and the other was taller than average height and skinny. It was a black nineteen ninety-four Dodge Ram fifteen hundred with Bridgestone tires and a dual exhaust. It had Wyoming plates."

"Do tell," I said.

"Would you like to know the license plate number?"

"I would like that very much," I said.

40

Many private investigators are former police officers. I had never been one and consequently did not have as many contacts in law enforcement as some others. But I had a few. Glen was the obvious choice, but I didn't want to put him in the position of having to do something illegal. In a town where one-third of the voters have dreadlocks and smoke pot, his job was tenuous enough. He couldn't afford to get caught doing something questionable.

My second choice was a police lieutenant in Walla Walla, Washington. I had met Dick Gilbert a few years back in connection with another case. Like me, he had been a Marine. He was a chain-smoker, but if he hadn't died from lung cancer yet, he would probably run the Wyoming license plate number for me.

"Pepper Keane," he said. "I haven't heard from you in a while. You must want something."

"Just want you to run a license plate number. And maybe a criminal history on whoever owns it."

"Anything else I can do for you today?"

"If you feel like it, you can send me a box of those Walla Walla sweet onions. I love those things."

"Give me the plate number," he said.

It was a beautiful Thursday morning. Unusually warm for January. Warm enough to run in shorts as long as I kept my upper body warm. I put on a T-shirt, then put a sweatshirt over it. The dogs looked at me, each hoping to be the chosen one. Taking both was out of the question—trying to control both took all the enjoyment out of running. Anyhow, since I was going to have to run with the Glock in my hand for the foreseeable future, taking even one dog was not practical.

I headed up to Ridge Road. Once you get there, it offers about two miles of level road and a great view of Barker Reservoir. There is little traffic on it, and since I was carrying a loaded handgun, I figured that was a good thing. I know of at least one runner up here who carries a handgun whenever he goes running, but in his case it's for protection from mountain lions.

The red message light was flashing when I returned home. It was Gilbert, and his message just said, "Call me."

I dialed his direct number. "What are you involved in?" he asked.

"Somebody put a rattlesnake in my bedroom a few nights ago. This license plate number might tell me who did it."

"The truck is registered to a company called Wind River Locksmiths in Lander, Wyoming."

"Yeah."

"I called Lander PD and learned that Wind River Locksmiths is a trade name used by an ex-con named Monte Corliss."

"Let me guess," I said. "Monte is sometimes known by the nickname 'Mongoose.'"

"That's right. And he has a very impressive criminal history. It's so long that I decided to scan it and e-mail it to you. You should have it already."

"Thanks. I owe you."

"Yeah, you do. I don't know what you're into, but this guy looks like bad news. Be careful."

I looked through my copy of Bugg's address book and found a Wyoming phone number with "M.C." written next to it. I dialed the number. The man on the other end of the line just said, "Locksmiths." I told him I had dialed the wrong number, and hung up. Now I could connect Bugg with Mongoose even without Karlynn's testimony.

I checked my e-mail and reviewed Mongoose's criminal history, which included a number of federal firearms convictions. He was thirty-seven years old, six feet tall, and 175 pounds, which was consistent with how Missy's daughter had described him.

I dialed Scott's number. "McCutcheon," he said.

"Moe's Bagels in forty-five minutes?"

"Hey, Bobbi," I heard him shout in a smart-aleck tone. "May I please meet Pepper at Moe's in about forty-five minutes?"

"Yes, you may," I heard her say. "Bring back a half-dozen bagels and some cream cheese."

Forty-five minutes later I guided my truck into the parking lot of the shopping center in Boulder where Moe's Bagels is located. I arrived before Scott, so I ordered a turkey-and-onion with Swiss cheese on a garlic bagel, and a large diet Coke. I was reading the *Rocky Mountain News* when Scott walked in. He ordered some food, as well as the bagels and cream cheese Bobbi had told him to purchase, then sat down across from me.

I told him about the rattlesnake incident and Wind River Locksmiths. I said, "I figure the big guy was Anvil and the other guy was Mongoose. If Anvil was one of them, that pretty much kills our theory that he's an undercover cop."

"Maybe not," Scott said. "An undercover cop might do something like that, if he had to, to maintain his cover. Very few people die from rattlesnake bites, maybe one in one thousand. Maybe Anvil figured he could help Mongoose with the snake job without putting you in any real danger. Realistically, what's the worst that could have happened? You would have had a swollen leg for a few days."

"Now we're going on the theory that Anvil is a humanitarian?"

"The bottom line is, we still don't know who Anvil is, and we still don't know if he told Bugg that he saw you with Karlynn."

"He saw me again at Bugg's house," I said. "I know he recognized me."

"You *think* he recognized you," Scott said. "And even if he did, we don't know whether he told Bugg about that either."

"The snake is pretty strong evidence that he told Bugg."

"We need to be sure," Scott said. "If we go after Anvil and he hasn't told Bugg about you, we could be stirring up a hornets' nest."

"I've got rattlesnakes in my bedroom. I'm not too concerned about stirring up a hornets' nest."

"Let's say we beat Anvil and Mongoose half to death in a few hours. That still doesn't tell us whether Anvil said anything to Bugg about you."

"Why would Bugg want a snake in my room if Anvil hadn't said anything to him? How else would Bugg know about me and Karlynn?"

"Maybe he never bought your story in the first place?"

"All I know is, I can't live like this much longer."

"If Bugg is onto you, you'll be living like this until you kill him or until the feds put him and his entire gang away."

"We need Mongoose to talk," I said. "If he says Bugg gave the order to kill that ATF agent, and he hired Skull to do it, Bugg goes away for life. Maybe even gets the needle."

"S.P.D.," Scott said. "Slow, painful death. Mongoose won't talk."

"Sure he will," I said. "We just have to make sure he fears our version of slow, painful death more than he fears Bugg's version."

I said good-bye to Scott. It was a little after noon. I used my cell phone to call Adrienne Valeska.

"Hi, Adrienne," I said. "Pepper Keane."

"Mr. Keane, what can I do for you?"

"Can I buy you lunch today?"

"I'm already involved with someone," she said.

"It would be a business lunch," I said. "I've got some information you might want as part of your investigation of Bugg and the Sons of Satan."

"Why not call Agent Livingston?"

"You're better-looking," I said. "If I have to have lunch with a federal agent, it might as well be you."

I met her about forty-five minutes later at a little Mexican place in Larimer Square, just a few blocks from Coors Field.

"What's up?" she asked.

I told her about Anvil seeing me with Karlynn in the mall, but that Anvil had denied seeing Karlynn for several months when Scott had questioned him at the bar in Longmont. I did not tell her about running into Anvil at Bugg's house; I did not want her to know I had double-crossed Bugg or that I had a copy of his address book. Not yet. I did not tell her about the snake. As far as she knew, I had never met Bugg, and the closest I had ever come to having contact with him was when I had liberated his prized bluetick coonhound.

"You think Anvil is working for some other agency?" she asked.

"I think it's possible."

"He's been with Bugg for several years."

"I know."

"What do you care?" she asked. "Karlynn's gone. You're out of it."

"I used to be a prosecutor. I thought you might want to check it out. If Anvil's undercover and you guys blow it for him, you could destroy years of his work and your own careers at the same time."

"We'll look into it," she said.

We continued eating. I recognized a few people in the restaurant as lawyers I had known when I had practiced law. I tried to make small talk with Valeska.

"What kind of name is Valeska?" I asked.

"It's Polish. What kind of name is Pepper?"

"Poor white trash. On my mother's side."

"What's your ancestry on your father's side?"

"I don't know. Irish or English, I guess. Someone told me Keane derives from O'Kane, but someone else told me it meant 'keen' or 'sharp' in medieval England."

The waiter brought the check. I snagged it and set my American Express card down beside it.

"I'm not supposed to let you buy lunch," she said. "The Bureau has strict rules about that."

"I'm not good with rules," I said.

"I've heard that," she said. "From a number of sources."

"I'm flattered that you would check up on me. Who did you talk with?"

"Some people in the U.S. attorney's office. A couple of agents who don't work in Denver anymore. Tim Gombold spoke highly of you. He said you're very intelligent, incredibly persistent, and you think you're funnier than you really are." Gombold had been an agent in the Denver office for many years and was now the Bureau's resident agent in Flagstaff. We had been friends a long time.

"I'll thank Tim for that glowing reference. Did you also speak with Mike Polk?"

"He said you're a dick."

I laughed. Polk had been one of my law school classmates and had later been an agent assigned to the Denver office of the FBI. We had never liked each other.

"Is Polk still in Alabama?"

"Mobile," she said.

The waiter reappeared to take the check and my credit card. "There's one other thing I want to tell you," I said.

"What's that?"

"Even though Karlynn's gone, I can help you get a search warrant for Bugg's property."

"How?"

"I scoped his house out three or four times before I stole his dog."

"Tim said you were the consummate professional."

"I can testify he's got a meth lab on his property. Every time I was there I saw empty bottles of antifreeze outside the cabin. Lots of them. Every so often one of Bugg's men would walk out to the cabin with a machine pistol to make sure things were okay."

"Can I list you as a confidential source if we apply for a search warrant?"

"You don't have to keep my name confidential. I'll sign an affidavit, testify to a grand jury, whatever you want."

"It could put your life in jeopardy," she said.

"I could use a little excitement," I said.

41

SATURDAY. THE SUN WAS just coming up. My brother, Scott, and I were rolling along a Wyoming state highway on our way to Lander. We had been on the road for several hours in my brother's Jeep Grand Cherokee. The dogs were with Troy's wife and kids. My truck and Scott's Land Rover were parked in front of my house to make it look as though I were still in Nederland. The lights and the TV were on timers.

Scott and I had spent Friday keeping an eye on traffic to and from Bugg's house. We hadn't seen any black Dodge Rams, so we figured Mongoose had headed home. We had discussed the pros and cons of visiting Mongoose and had decided that the pros outweighed the cons.

My brother was driving and now he was raising some of the same issues Scott and I had struggled with two days ago.

"Even if we get this guy to admit he hired Skull to kill Lowell," Troy said, "he'll deny it later. He'll say he only confessed because we beat it out of him."

"It's not about getting a confession," I said. "Even if we got him to confess on videotape, we couldn't give it to the feds. The judge would throw the confession out because we beat it out of him, and the feds would indict us for violating his civil rights."

"Then, other than retribution for the snake incident," Troy said, "why are we doing this?"

"Retribution for the snake is good enough for me," Scott said. "It's about time our team went on offense."

I explained it to my brother just as I had explained it to Scott. "Maybe he'll tell us something we can give the feds, some little fact, some little thread they can pull on until the whole thing unravels. Maybe he'll help us fill in some of the gaps in Bugg's address book."

"I hope so," Troy said. "This was supposed to be my leg day. I don't like missing leg workouts."

Lander is a town of about seven thousand people near the Wind River Mountains. We arrived in the early afternoon, then drove up into the mountains and found a four-wheel-drive road. About a mile down that road we found a clearing that was free of snow.

"This will do," my brother said.

We set up a big winter tent Scott had provided and moved all our gear into it, including three small camp chairs. Then we took the cross-country skis off the top of the Jeep and laid them up against a tree. The only other people driving on this road would be outdoor enthusiasts in four-wheel-drive vehicles, and they would assume we were just nice Colorado folks taking advantage of the area's winter recreation opportunities.

We gathered firewood and put some rocks in a circle to make a place for our campfire. Someone came by on a snowmobile and waved at us. We waved back.

When we had gathered an adequate supply of firewood, we drove back into town and found Wind River Locksmiths. It was one block off the main street. There was a black Dodge Ram 1500 parked in the alley behind it, and the license plate matched the plate number Missy's daughter had given me. There was also a white van with "Wind River Locksmiths" painted on both sides. There was one entrance from the street and another from the alley. I told Troy to park on the main street.

"Now what?" Scott asked.

"We need to know how many people are in there," I said. "Go in and ask them to make a copy of a key for you." Scott shrugged, got out of the car, and started walking toward the shop.

He returned a few minutes later and climbed into the backseat of the Jeep. "Just two guys," he said. "One guy fits the description of Mongoose perfectly. The other guy was just shooting the bull with him. I don't think he works there. I didn't see any weapons. How do you want to do it?"

"Listen," my brother said. "Here's an idea. We tell him we have another SUV at our campsite and my dumb-ass brother locked the keys in it. We need him to come out to our campsite and get us into the vehicle."

I looked at my watch. It was three-thirty. "That won't work," I said. "He'll want to take his truck, and we can't afford to have it seen anywhere near our campsite."

"It will be dark in a few hours," Scott said. "Why don't you two take a drive? I'll have a cup of coffee in that place across the street and call you on your cell phone as soon as his pal leaves."

"Works for me," I said.

We let Scott out of the Jeep, then drove a few miles out of town and parked. "Have you given any more thought to the Jayne situation?" Troy asked.

"Yeah, I think no child should have to live in a home where rattlesnakes drop in whenever they want to."

"Snake is a delicacy in China," he said. "The finer dining establishments will let you select the one you want for dinner."

"I'll keep that in mind."

"Any other women on your radar?" he asked.

"Too many," I said. "A therapist, a bush pilot, an FBI agent, and a Denver homicide detective that was in my high school Latin class. Where were they when I was twenty-five?"

My cell phone rang. "Now's the time," Scott said. "Pick me up on the main street where we were parked."

"Time to rock-and-roll," I said to Troy.

We drove back into town and found Scott. He climbed into the backseat. "His buddy is gone," Scott said. "I think we should go in through the alley. We're less likely to be seen."

Troy drove around the block and into the alley, stopping his Jeep in front of the back entrance to the shop. The sun had gone down. It was dusk. We put our ski masks on. "Keep her running," I said to Troy. He nodded.

I attempted to quietly open the back door to the shop, but it was locked. I rapped on it a few times with my knuckles. As soon as Mongoose opened the door, Scott zapped him with the taser and down he went. How Scott had acquired a taser, I did not know. He's always liked gadgets.

We carried the stunned locksmith to the Jeep and loaded him into the backseat. Scott climbed in beside him while I took my seat up front. Troy drove out of the alley at a cautious speed, then turned and headed out of town toward our campsite, being careful to obey all traffic laws.

Scott used duct tape to bind Mongoose's arms and legs. He was regaining his senses now. He realized something bad had happened and that his ability to move was restricted.

"I don't know who you guys are," he said, "but you're fuckin' dead."

"If you say one more word," Scott said to him, "I'm going to bash your skull in with this flashlight." He picked up the flashlight I had purchased in Anchorage. It had six fresh "D" cells in it.

By the time we returned to our campsite, it was dark. And with darkness came the cold. "Start a fire," I said to my brother. "We'll deal with him."

Scott and I helped Mongoose into the big canvas tent we had erected earlier. It was the kind hunters use for a base camp, and it was tall enough that we could stand up straight if we were in the center of it.

We were still wearing our ski masks. Scott swept Mongoose's feet out from underneath him, and Mongoose landed on his side. Then Scott kicked him in the ribs. Not hard, just enough to remind him that we were in charge. I didn't feel good about what we were doing, and I wanted to get it over with.

"Okay, Mongoose," I said, "You're miles from town. You're outnumbered. You have no weapons. You're totally dependent on us for food and shelter. You can't even go to the bathroom without asking. Now, as you can see, this is a big tent. We have enough supplies for several weeks. And we're going to stay here until we get the information we want from you."

"What do you want?" he said.

"Let's start with how Bugg told you to kill an ATF agent named Lowell last year and you hired a guy named Skull to do the job."

"I don't know what you're talking about," he said. Scott kicked him in the ribs again and he curled up into a fetal position.

"That was the point after touchdown," Scott said. "The next one is going to be the sixty-three-yard field goal."

"This is illegal," he said. "You'll go to prison for this. Cops always go to prison when they step over the line."

I looked at Scott and said, "He thinks we're cops."

Scott laughed and said, "We ain't cops, Monte. The cops would be satisfied with a conviction and a prison sentence, even if they never got a word out of you. You'd be in a nice warm prison cell, secure in the knowledge that you weren't going to die a horrible death at the hands of Bugg or some of your fellow bikers."

"If we were cops," I said, "you'd have the luxury of being able to remain silent to save your own life. But we're not cops, so if you don't want to die a slow, painful death, tell us what we want to know. Then we'll let you go and you can take your chances with the Sons of Satan."

My brother walked into the tent, still wearing his mask. Mongoose tensed up when he saw my brother's build. "Got a nice fire going," Troy said. "I guess I'll start dinner. If we're going to be up all night torturing this dickhead, I want to make sure I don't get hungry in the middle of the night."

We continued to ask questions about Skull, Lowell, and Bugg, and he continued to refuse to answer. After forty-five minutes or so, my brother carried three aluminum plates into the tent. Each one boasted grilled salmon, garlic bread, fresh corn on the cob, and a tomato-and-mozzarella salad. "Good job," I said to Troy. "Let's blindfold this guy so we don't have to eat with our masks on."

Scott wrapped a kerchief around the man's eyes and secured it with duct tape. Then we removed our masks.

"This is excellent," Scott said. "On a cold night this really hits the spot."

"You won't be eating for a while," I said to Mongoose. "Too bad, because it's supposed to get down into the teens tonight."

When we finished eating, Troy boiled some water on the camp stove and cleaned the dishes. Then the three of us stood around the fire and allowed the heat to radiate through us. Mongoose was in the tent, covered with duct tape. None of us was entirely comfortable with what we were doing, and I suspect we were each silently asking how far we were willing to go with it.

"I gotta take a shit," Mongoose yelled from the tent.

"That was inevitable," Scott said.

"Let him crap in his pants," Troy said.

"Are you kidding? I don't want that smell in our tent."

"I've got an idea," Scott said.

Scott went to the tent and led the blindfolded Mongoose out of it. Then he took a big log from our pile of firewood—it must have weighed fifty pounds—and used duct tape to attach it to Mongoose's leg. When that was done, he cut the tape that secured Mongoose's wrists, then handed him a roll of toilet paper and said, "Walk over there ten or fifteen yards. I don't want you doing it near our tent."

Later that night, when it was time for bed, we unrolled our sleeping bags. "This is going to feel good," Troy said. "I'd forgotten how cold it can be in the mountains at night. I can't wait to get into my sleeping bag."

"Don't get your hopes up, Monte," I said. "You're sleeping outside." His wrists had already been taped together again. I led him out of the tent and told him to lie down near the fire pit. "The fire has died down," I said, "but you might live through the night if you stay close to the coals."

Back in the tent we waited. "We can't let him die," I said.

"We won't," Scott said. "We'll check on him every so often, and put some blankets on top of him if we have to."

He survived through the night, but in spite of the blankets he was shivering the next morning. He was still blindfolded and still had the heavy log attached to his leg. I pulled him away from the fire pit, stirred up the ashes in it, and put more wood in it. I poured Coleman fuel on the logs, then stood back and flicked a match. Instant campfire.

I made coffee and pancakes on the camp stove. "Good pancakes," Troy said.

"You have to eat a lot of carbs in this environment," Scott said.

"They say Lowell died in a place like this," I said. "Alone and afraid."

"What do you guys want?" Mongoose said from his position on the ground. He had lost hope and was on the verge of tears. He looked older than his thirty-seven years and not nearly as tough as he had appeared in the photo the FBI had shown Karlynn. Scott and I looked at each other. The moment had arrived.

"I told you, we want to know about Skull and the ATF agent he killed last year."

"I might as well put a bullet in my head if I talk about that," he said.

"That's the problem with free will," I said. "You must constantly make difficult choices."

"I need water," our prisoner said. Scott looked at me and I nodded. Scott held a bottle of water up to Mongoose's lips and let him drink just a sip.

"That's enough," Scott said. "You can have more when you're done talking."

"Last year we stole some explosives from a ski area in Jackson," he began.

"Why?" I said.

"Bugg had a buyer for them."

"Who?"

"I don't know." I noticed Mongoose inching his way closer to the fire in order to stay warm.

"Go on."

"A few months later this Agent Lowell shows up in Jackson and starts asking questions. We didn't pay much attention, but then he moved into Lander and was causing trouble for us. I drove down to Colorado to talk with Bugg about it. He said Lowell had to go and told me to take care of it."

"So you put Skull on the job?"

"Yeah."

"How did you know him? He's not part of the Sons of Satan."

"I knew his brother in prison."

"What prison? You've been in several."

"Leavenworth. His brother is in for life. They're both big into White Power. His brother leads the Aryan Brotherhood at Leavenworth. Skull lives on some compound up in Idaho with a bunch of other skinheads. I mean, these guys are true believers. They really believe there is going to be a racial holy war and all the niggers and Jews will be killed."

"So you figured Skull would be only too happy to cap a black federal agent?"

"He couldn't wait to do it."

"Had you ever used Skull on a job before?"

"No, I'd only met him a few times. I promised his brother I'd keep in touch with him."

"When did you contact Skull about the Lowell job?" I asked.

"Maybe a month before it happened."

"How did you contact him?" Scott said.

"I called him. He agreed to meet me in Bozeman. I told him what I needed and asked if he was interested. He said he was, so I gave him two thousand dollars and promised another three when the job was done."

"How did he do it?"

"I don't know."

"How did you know he really did it?"

"He stopped by on his way out of town and gave me Lowell's wallet and FBI credentials. I gave him the rest of the money and never saw him again."

"What did you do with the wallet and credentials?"

"Soaked them in gasoline and burned them."

I was still hoping to find a thread that the feds could use, but I wasn't having much luck.

"What did you do with the ashes?" Scott asked.

"I didn't do nothing with them. They're probably still in the bottom of the garbage can at my shop."

"You know anything about the death of a guy named Rankin?" I said.

"I had nothing to do with Rankin."

"What do you know about it?"

"Bugg thought his bond was too low. He figured Rankin had cut a deal in return for the low bond, so he decided to hit Rankin."

"Who did it?"

"I don't know. I hear it was brutal. Bugg wanted to send a message to everyone."

We questioned Mongoose for the next several hours and obtained a wealth of information about the Sons of Satan in Wyoming, crimes he and his men had committed, the names of those who had bought weapons or drugs from them, distribution methods, and so forth.

"Let's go back to Skull," I said. "Did Bugg know Skull?"

"No."

"Bullshit," I said. "You told Bugg that Skull did a good job on Lowell."

"How do you know that?" he said.

Scott kicked him in the ribs—hard—and said, "Don't worry about how we know what we know. Worry about whether you'll be alive in few hours."

"Bugg knew I had hired a skinhead named Skull to do the job. That's all. He didn't want to know more."

"There's no connection between Bugg and Skull?"

"No. Skull doesn't even like bikers. He doesn't think they're dedicated to the racial holy war, and he doesn't like that they sell drugs to white people. He only did the job for me because I knew his brother and it was a chance for him to pop a nigger and get paid."

42

WE MADE IT BACK to Nederland Sunday night. Troy and Scott both opted to spend the night with me rather than drive back to their respective mates. We had left Mongoose blindfolded and tied up off the side of the highway just outside Lander. The log was still attached to his leg when we dumped him.

We ordered a pizza and discussed our weekend. Our mood was subdued. All of us had wanted more from Mongoose. And we wouldn't have been human if we didn't feel some moral uncertainty about what we had done.

"Look," I said, "it's not that bad. We got information that will help the feds. Even if they can't get Mongoose to talk about Lowell, they'll nail Bugg on plenty of other criminal charges."

"We couldn't find a direct link between Bugg and Skull," Scott said. "If Mongoose keeps his mouth shut, Skull just keeps living the good life up in Idaho."

"Fuck that," Troy said. "If that happens, I say we take care of Skull ourselves."

"You haven't seen the compound," I said. "There's only one road in, and it's rough terrain. It's patrolled by some German shepherds that take their jobs seriously. We can't just drive in and grab Skull."

"We could jump in," Scott said facetiously—a clear reference to Troy's skydiving accident.

"That's great," Troy said. "Jump out of a plane over Idaho in the winter. Our corpses would land in Iowa."

"Let's see how it plays out," I said. "I'll meet with the feds this week and give them Bugg's address book. I'll give them some of the information I got from Karlynn and some of the info we got from Mongoose, without telling them how I got it. They ought to be able to take it from there."

I didn't sleep well that night. None of us did.

On Monday I followed Troy to his house to retrieve Buck and Wheat, then followed him back to his gym. We worked out, and the exercise helped me forget the horrible things we had done to Mongoose over the weekend.

Before heading home I decided to call Valeska to see whether she had learned anything about Anvil. She invited me to lunch.

She was waiting outside the Federal Building when I pulled up in front of it. Actually, you can't pull up in front of it, because the security people will assume you are a terrorist. Rather than make them nervous, I parked across the street and waited for her to cross. Sometimes it is better to be prudent than to be a gentleman.

"Where to?" I said.

"Pick a place," she said. "I'm not big on lunch."

"Why did you invite me?"

"Because I think you stumbled onto something."

I pulled into a McDonald's about ten blocks north of downtown Denver, in what is politely called a minority neighborhood. "Come on," I said, "they have good diet Coke here. I'll treat."

Inside we ordered food and found a table. "Anvil is not an

undercover agent," she said. "No other agency is claiming credit for him."

"Who is he?" I said.

"That's where it gets interesting. All his public records refer to him as Robert Alton Pugh, but the real Robert Alton Pugh died three years ago. He was a graduate student at the University of Chicago."

"Anvil assumed his identity and joined the Sons of Satan?"

"Looks that way," she said.

"Any idea who he really is?"

"We're working on it. We have to tread lightly so word doesn't filter back to him that we're onto him."

I sipped my diet Coke. "When are you going to apply for that search warrant?" I asked. The sooner, the better. Until Bugg was in prison, there would be no such thing as "normal" for me.

"We're not ready yet. We have to get all our ducks lined up and strike every chapter at the same time. We're still gathering information and building an organizational chart. That's how we do it. You know that. Karlynn's disappearance really set us back."

"Remember when we had lunch last week?" I said.

"Yes."

"You said you heard I wasn't good with rules."

"I remember."

"How are you with rules?"

"What are we talking about?"

"We're talking about me giving you a lot of information about Bugg and the Sons of Satan."

"How did you obtain it?"

"Some I got firsthand, like the meth lab on Bugg's property. Some I got in other ways. It will save you months of work."

"What do you want in return?"

"When the time is right, after Bugg and his friends are all in prison, I want you to quietly make the warrant for Karlynn disappear and get the indictment dismissed."

"Why don't you ask me to do these things now?"

"Because Bugg's lawyers would have a field day with it. They'd want to know why and you wouldn't have a good answer."

"I could have the U.S. attorney bring you before a grand jury right now," she said.

"You'd get tired of hearing me invoke my rights under the Fifth Amendment. Besides, I think you feel for Karlynn. It's the right thing to do."

I dropped Valeska back at the Federal Building and was headed west on the Boulder Turnpike, back to Nederland, when the *Mister Ed* theme song sounded. I picked up my cell phone and said hello. It was Scott and he was singing.

"I'm a freaking gen-i-us. Doo-dah! Doo-dah! I'm a freaking gen-i-us, oh de doo-dah day."

Not to be outdone, I responded in song. "I win my money on the bobtail nag. Doo-dah! Doo-dah! I keep my money in an old tow-bag, oh de doo-dah day! Goin' to run all night, goin' to run all day; I bet my money on a bob-tail nag, somebody bet on the gray."

"Tell me you don't know all the words to that song," he said.

"'Camptown Races,' by Stephen C. Foster. I know every verse."

"You need a kid," he said. "No creature with any purpose in life has time to memorize that stuff."

"You called me," I said. "What do you want?"

"I figured out those numbers in the back of Bugg's address book."

"What are they?"

"They're locations. They are actually pairs of numbers, and each pair describes a longitude and a latitude."

"Can't be," I said. "There were no degrees, minutes, or seconds."

"That's right. Bugg converted them to decimal form but didn't put the decimal points in. He knew where they belonged, so he didn't need them."

"Have you plotted these on a map?"

"Yeah. Where are you?"

"On the turnpike."

"Meet you at Moe's in a half hour?"

Now we were at Moe's, surrounded by college kids and looking at maps Scott had spread across our table.

"There are eight pairs of numbers," he said.

"Eight locations?"

"Yeah. All in the western U.S. Three in Colorado, two in Utah, one in New Mexico, one in Wyoming, and one in Idaho." He had marked each location on his highway map for that state.

"All in national forests or national parks," I said.

"Any idea what it means?"

I just smiled and said, "Oh de doo-dah day."

43

WE FIGURED IT WOULD be best to split up. That way nobody would be able to say they had seen us together near any of the eight locations. I took southern Colorado, Utah, and New Mexico; Scott took northern Colorado, Wyoming, and Idaho. Four for each of us.

The final place on my list was in the Carson National Forest in north-central New Mexico. One and a half million acres ranging from high desert to peaks more than thirteen thousand feet above sea level. A man could easily get lost in a place like that. Fortunately, I had a Global Positioning System and a U.S. Geological Survey map. I knew exactly where I was going.

It was Groundhog Day and I saw my shadow, as did Buck and Wheat. The sun was out, and if you looked carefully, you could see signs that spring was on its way. I had left my truck at the trailhead and was backpacking on a Forest Service trail. Buck was wearing a doggie backpack that held potatoes and duck dog chow.

The sun made hiking enjoyable, and I even took my jacket off, but I knew that when the sun went down, its warmth would quickly disappear. I pitched my lightweight tent before the sun went down. I fed the dogs and made ramen noodles for myself on my portable backpacking stove. I had purchased the tent and stove at a railroad discount warehouse in Denver thirty years ago when I was home from college. I had a summer job as a bouncer at a place called the Grizzly Bar and was earning more money than I knew what to do with—seven dollars an hour. I bought a lot of camping gear that summer. The warehouse has since been converted into expensive lofts.

There was not a cloud in the sky, so I did not put the rain fly on the tent. I could see the stars through the tent's screen.

I had the dream again. But this time it wasn't Joy walking with me in the extravagant china shop; it was Jayne. She looked at different pieces, selected one, and we drove away in a Ford Taurus.

The next day was easy. I hiked another two miles on the trail until the GPS told me to turn north. The dogs and I then hiked uphill through thick trees for about three-quarters of a mile. I looked at the GPS and said to the dogs, "Boys, we have arrived." I set my backpack down, sipped some water from my canteen, and removed the collapsible camp shovel from my backpack.

Bugg had done a good job of burying his cache of food, weapons, and money. It was at least twenty inches beneath the surface, and in the Rocky Mountains that is twenty inches of hard digging.

This was my fourth site, so I knew what to expect. I found Ziploc bags filled with twenties and fifties, probably about twenty thousand dollars in all, based on what I'd seen at the other three sites. There was a ten-millimeter Colt semiautomatic pistol, a .22-caliber American 180 submachine gun, and plenty of ammo, all wrapped in plastic. There were cans of soup and beans as well as containers full of rice, noodles, and other dry foods.

I put the Colt in my backpack. I unrolled my sleeping bag, then rolled it up again with the 180 inside it so that it was largely hidden. The plastic bags of cash went into my backpack. The food went back in the hole. Then I removed a dollar bill from my wallet and watched it float down into the hole. I replaced dirt and packed it down with the heel of my hiking boot. When I was satisfied, I sprinkled some pine needles over the area where I had dug.

The hike back to my truck was mostly downhill, and I made it back late in the day. Instead of driving back to the interstate, I took side roads and ended up in tiny Manassa, Colorado—the birthplace of Jack Dempsey. The little cabin he had been born in was now a museum, so I stopped in and looked around.

I knew boxing history almost as well as I knew music trivia, so seeing photos and news clippings of Dempsey's fights in the early decades of this century was a thrill. Dempsey is probably most famous for a fight he lost—he lost to Gene Tunney because, after knocking Tunney down, he failed to return to a neutral corner as instructed by the referee. The ref could not start counting Tunney out until Dempsey went to a neutral corner. Thus, the famous "long count," which gave Tunney fourteen seconds instead of ten. Tunney was able to get back up and win the fight by a decision.

But there is another Dempsey story that I find easier to relate to. On July 4, 1919, the 187-pound Dempsey fought 245-pound heavyweight champ Jess Willard for the title. Despite being five inches shorter and fifty-eight pounds lighter than Willard, Dempsey broke Willard's jaw with one of his first punches, a devastating left hook. He knocked Willard down seven times in the first round and walloped him for two more rounds. When Willard didn't come out for the fourth round, he had four teeth missing, his eyes were closed, his nose was smashed, and two ribs were cracked, not to mention the broken jaw. He also suffered permanent hearing damage.

Manassa was not far from Crazy Uncle Ray's shack in the San

Luis Valley, so I decided to swing by on my way back to Neder-land. He was working on his truck, and Prince was just trotting around checking everything out. I ended up spending the night. I claimed the top bunk and Ray claimed the bottom. The three dogs shared the plywood floor.

We talked as we lay in our bunks. I brought him up to date on the Bugg situation, but I did not tell him about the caches of weapons and cash we had looted. Somehow Ray got on the tale of how he'd spent six months in jail for the attempted murder of my uncle Jake after he'd been gutshot by my aunt Lucy. "Yessir," he said, "six months in the Coosa County Jail. That weren't no fun at all."

"Coosa County?"

"That's right."

"That's where you grew up, right?"

"Son, that's where your mama and her whole family grew up," he said.

"The name Howard Biggs mean anything to you?"

"Now, let me think. Howard Biggs. Howard Biggs. Oh, yeah, don't that take me back a lot of years. Biggs must be older than Moses by now, but in his day he was mean as a water moccasin. Was real active with the Klan for a while. Didn't have a decent bone in his body, I tell you. I wonder what ever happened to him. I reckon God will take him when his time finally comes."

44

A week later Scott and I met at my house to tally our haul. The amount of money Bugg had buried at each location had not been consistent, but between the two of us we had taken close to one hundred forty thousand dollars from Bugg's eight caches. We also had an admirable supply of handguns as well as some illegal machine guns.

"I felt sorry for Bugg," I said, "so I left a dollar bill for him in each location."

"I left something for him, too," Scott said, "but it wasn't currency." He sipped from a bottle of beer. "What should we do with these weapons?"

"We can't keep all of them," I said. "Some are illegal and most are probably stolen. There are severe penalties just for possessing them."

"We can't turn them in to the cops unless we want to say how we found them. And we're really not in a position to do that."

"I hate to say it, but the smartest thing we could do would be to rent some welding equipment, buy some hacksaws, and mutilate these things. Dump 'em in the reservoir near the dam."

"You want to keep any of them?" Scott asked.

"I might keep that ten-millimeter Colt," I said. "How about you?"

"I'd love to have that One-eighty. A man needs a good machine gun."

"I hereby convey it to you," I said. "Don't tell anyone where you got it."

"Can I leave it here until I prepare Bobbi for it?"

"Sure."

"What about the cash?" Scott said.

"What about it?"

"What do we do with it? You can't just deposit that kind of money in a bank without being able to explain where it came from."

"That's the thing," I said. "People always dream about finding these large sums of cash, but there really isn't much you can do with it. You can't buy a new Jaguar; you can't suddenly change your lifestyle. If you go six months without writing a check or using a credit card, the IRS might get suspicious. My advice is, keep a few thousand on you at all times, give some to charity, hide the rest. Just spend a few thousand a year; that's the secret."

"Have to spend it all by two thousand twelve," Scott said.

"Why?"

"That's when the comet hits."

45

I was in the Federal Building with Valeska and Livingston. Drinking government coffee at nine a.m. No matter who is in the White House, government coffee always tastes the same. This was worse than the coffee at the Sinclair station in Nederland. Imagine hot water, instant creamer, and brown food coloring, and you've got a good idea of what FBI coffee tastes like.

We were seated around a rectangular table in an interview room. As a defense lawyer I had always insisted that law enforcement record any interview that my client agreed to, but today there was no recorder and I didn't want Matt Simms or any other lawyer. I was there to help them put Bugg and the Sons of Satan away. I began to tell my story.

"You already know that Matt hired me to steal Bugg's dog and then to guard Karlynn while she was waiting to be relocated. What you don't know is that a few days after Karlynn started living with me, Bugg left a message on my machine. He said he wanted to hire me."

I spent the next hour telling them about meeting Bugg at the Pioneer Inn, going through the motions of looking for Karlynn for Bugg, then making a very real effort to find Karlynn for Matt, for the feds and for truth, justice, and the American way.

I told them how I had lied to Bugg about finding Karlynn at the Lewis and Clark Trailer Park and having to put his dog down. I told them I had given Bugg a lot of cash to convince him that I really was on his side.

"Where did you come up with the cash?" Livingston asked.

"Karlynn had it and didn't take it with her when she ditched me. She lied to you when she said she only took twenty thousand from Bugg. She took a lot more than that."

"What else have you got for us?" Valeska asked.

"Your're going to love this," I said. "While I was giving Bugg money and telling him how close we had come to nabbing Karlynn in Idaho, I remembered that Karlynn had told you about an address book Bugg keeps in the drawer beside his refrigerator."

"You stole the book?" Livingston asked.

"Sort of. I stole the book, drove like a madman to Nederland to photocopy it, then drove like a madman back to Bugg's house to put it back." I told them how I had purposely left my gold pen on the floor next to Bugg's refrigerator so I would have an excuse to return.

"So I put the address book back and I'm getting ready to leave when who walks in the door? My old friend, Anvil. Now, Anvil had seen me with Karlynn at the mall, so I figure I'm going to have to try to shoot him and the other guy, then make a run for it, but Anvil just ignores me."

"Did he recognize you?"

"I think he did.

"Here's your copy," I said as I handed Livingston his copy of Bugg's address book. "I also made a second copy for you that has all my notes on it." I handed that to him. "And here's my memo summarizing everything else I was able to learn."

"Why did you do all this?" Valeska asked.

"Self-preservation," I said. "I still don't know whether Bugg knows I double-crossed him, but I think he does. Otherwise, there would have been no reason to put a rattlesnake in my bedroom. The surest way to get my life back to normal is to help put Bugg and his pals away for good."

"Is there anything else you'd like to tell us?" Valeska said.

"Yeah, but one of you has to leave the room."

"Why?" said Valeska.

"I don't want two people to be able to testify as to what I said. I have to be able to deny I ever said it."

"I'll leave," Livingston said. He left a legal pad on the table but picked his long body up and left me alone with Valeska.

"This concerns the ATF agent, Agent Lowell."

"Okay."

"Karlynn told you she heard Mongoose tell Bugg that Skull had done a good job taking care of Lowell."

"Right."

"When Bugg gave Mongoose the order to kill Lowell, Mongoose contacted Skull. Skull's real name is Anders Riddell. Mongoose had been at Leavenworth with Skull's older brother, who happens to lead the Aryan Brotherhood there. Bugg never met Skull; I don't think you'll be able to connect them. Mongoose met Skull in Bozeman to discuss the hit and gave Skull two grand, with the promise of another three grand after the job was done. Skull killed Lowell about a month later. After he did it, he stopped in Lander to see Mongoose. To prove he had really killed Lowell, he gave Mongoose Lowell's FBI credentials. I assume that included a leather wallet, some business cards, and a badge. Mongoose burned those things in a metal can at his locksmith shop. If you happen to search it, you may find evidence of burning in that can. You might even find microscopic particles of Lowell's credentials that you can match to the type of paper and leather used by the Bureau."

"How do you know this?" she said.

"I live in Nederland. We're all big believers in psychic phenomena." She smiled. "I guess that's it," I said. "If I think of anything else, I'll let you know."

"Are you still willing to testify?"

"I'll testify to most of it. I just want one favor."

"What's that?"

"When you arrest Bugg, let me know. I'll sleep easier. Any idea when you might do it?"

"Soon," Valeska said. "Very soon."

46

IT WASN'T SOON ENOUGH. That night, around two in the morning, Buck started barking. Then Wheat started. They know the difference between normal nighttime noises, such as raccoons crawling through trash cans, and man-made noises. Something wasn't right.

I looked out my bedroom window and saw two shadowy figures approach my house from the side, with shotguns. Without turning on any lights, I quietly got dressed and put my shoes on. I closed my bedroom door so the dogs could not get downstairs. Holding the Glock in one hand, with the Colt tucked in behind my back, I started walking downstairs and looked out the dining room window only to see two more shadowy figures. There were at least four of them. I knew they were getting closer, because the motion detectors Scott had installed had automatically turned on the floodlights.

The trick was not to get sandwiched between them. I figured I was in better shape than they were, and if I could get outside, I could run into the trees and they'd never catch me. But how did I know there weren't more of them out there? And what about my dogs?

Glass shattered. The doors from the dining room to the back

deck. At least one of them was in the house now. "C'mon, motherfucker," I heard him say, "now the tiger will show his true spots."

I was crouched down in my dining room and saw him come around the corner holding a shotgun. I shot him three times with the Glock and he fell dead. If a man is worth shooting, he's worth shooting right. Then more glass shattered from a direction I hadn't anticipated. Could there be more than four? I duckwalked over to the dead guy, took his shotgun, and said, "Stripes, motherfucker. Tigers have stripes."

That's when I saw it. Scott had left the machine gun at my house. I didn't need the dead guy's shotgun. The 180 shoots from a flat pan magazine that sits atop it, so it looks as if there were a small Frisbee on top of it. It was loaded. I had 275 rounds and a weapon that could shoot twelve hundred rounds a minute.

Now somebody was trying to get in through the garage. I could go to the concrete basement and try to take them one at a time as they came downstairs. Or I could take the machine gun, leap off the back deck into the snow, and head for the trees. That's what I did.

I made it to the trees without getting shot at. I fired at one with my Glock to let them know I wasn't in the house. "Shit," someone said, "he's out there."

I kept still and tried to see what I was up against. There were four of them, all well armed. As soon as they reached a position where I could fire the 180 without filling my house full of holes, I fired a burst above their heads. I think that's the point at which I gained the psychological advantage.

"What the fuck was that?" one of them said.

"I don't know," another said, "but it trumps what I've got."

They started retreating. I fired another burst just over their heads. I saw them running through the snow toward the road and presumably to their vehicle or vehicles.

Just for the hell of it, I emptied the entire magazine.

As I walked back toward my house, still holding the 180, I saw Luther walking toward me. I was too far away to know whether he was carrying a shotgun or a rifle, but as we both approached the area near my house that was lit by the floodlights, I could see it was a shotgun.

"Pepper," he said, "are you okay?"

"I'm fine," I said.

"I see you've been rethinking your position on assault weapons."

I heard sirens in the distance. "It's a long story," I said.

"I'm thinking maybe I ought to take that back to my house," he said. "As far as I'm concerned, I didn't hear any automatic gunfire. And if I did, it came from the guys you chased off."

"I didn't know you knew anything about firearms," I said.

"Hell, yeah, I was an MP in the army."

"You were in the army?"

"Surprised you, huh?"

"Yeah."

"Nixon gave me no choice."

47

I FELT BAD ABOUT LYING to Glen, but I had no desire to go to prison for possession of an illegal weapon. He probably would have looked the other way, but he would have had to let the ATF check the history of the weapon, and I really didn't want to explain how it had come into my possession.

Later that day, after I had gotten some sleep, I walked over to Luther's house. He was smoking a joint and experimenting with riffs on his guitar. "I owe you big-time," I said.

"Living next to you is an adventure," he said.

"Likewise," I said.

"You want to talk about any of it?"

"Just believe me when I tell you I'm one of the good guys."

"I never doubted it."

"Hey, Luther," I said, "catch." I tossed him a stack of bills, held together by rubber bands. It totaled ten thousand dollars.

48

THE NEXT TUESDAY I drove down to the Federal Building and signed some affidavits that would help the feds obtain search warrants for Bugg's house and plenty of other addresses listed in his address book.

It was Valentine's Day, so I stopped at a downtown flower shop and made arrangements to have two dozen roses delivered to Jayne in Beijing. It wasn't as if I couldn't afford it.

Since I was downtown, I decided to stop in at Keane, Simms & Mercante. I didn't recognize the receptionist. It wasn't the same one I had seen on recent visits. I introduced myself to her and asked if Matt was available. She asked me to have a seat, so I did.

Matt walked out into the waiting area a few minutes later, smoking a cigar, his tie hanging loosely around his neck, his sleeves rolled up. "Long time, no see," he said as he extended his hand.

I followed him back to his office, closed the door behind me, then took a seat across from him.

"This goes way beyond the attorney-client privilege," I said. "This is between you, me, and God. Nobody else."

"Since when do you believe in God?"

"I've survived a lot of shit lately. As much as I'd like to think it was due entirely to my intelligence and skill, I think there might have been some higher power looking out for me."

Matt and I go way back. I told him everything. "I'm sorry I had to give the two hundred grand back to Bugg," I said, "but Scott and I agreed you should get an equal share of the cash we took from Bugg's eight caches." I handed him a box that was wrapped like a birthday present. It was full of cash.

"What about Karlynn?" he said. "Shouldn't she get some of this?"

"Karlynn took more than the three hundred grand she gave to you," I said. "I don't know how much. She might have taken as much as half a million dollars from Bugg."

"Did she tell you that?"

"No, but Bugg was telling people that's how much she took, and people in Alaska say she paid cash for everything."

"How's she doing?" he said.

"She's doing well. I think she might surprise us all."

I worked out with my brother at his gym, then headed home to Nederland. When I got home, I saw Ray's camper parked in front of my house. Ray had never just dropped in without being invited. This was a first.

"How y'all doing?" he said when I entered. He had a fire going and was making spaghetti sauce. Prince was on the floor beside him.

"I'm fine, Ray. What brings you up here?"

"Had me a vision last night," he said. "The Lord was telling me loud and clear to come up here, that I was going to be needed."

"A vision?"

"That's right. I know you don't believe in all that, and you can make fun of your ole uncle if you want, but when a man has a vision like that, it's best not to ignore it."

"I had a vision last night too," I said. "I had a vision that I should make some garlic bread to go with that spaghetti."

We enjoyed dinner and I told Ray about my trip to Alaska. He said one of the funniest things I've ever heard him say. He said, "How's your mama, son? Does she still have that little Jack Daniel's terrier?"

49

The call from Valeska came a few days later, early on a Friday morning. "We hit them this morning," she said. "Bugg got away."

"He got away?"

"It didn't go down well. There was a gunfight. Bugg took off on foot. We'll catch him."

"He knows how to survive. Karlynn said he knows these mountains as well as anyone."

"We've requested a chopper with heat detection equipment, and help from local agencies. We're putting a team together."

"There was some survivalist guy down south that avoided capture for five years."

"That's the exception, not the rule."

"What about dogs?"

"No teams available right now," she said. "The sheriff has the only trained bloodhound in Boulder County, and she's a drug dog, not a tracking dog."

"I've got a tracking dog," I said. "A real good one."

"Are you volunteering?"

"Yeah. It'll take me a few minutes to pack some gear. Are you still at Bugg's house?"

"Yeah."

"I'll be there in forty-five minutes."

I hung up the phone and turned to Uncle Ray. "Ray, your vision was right on target. The feds raided Bugg's house, but he got away. He's on his own in the mountains. Think you and Prince are up to it?"

"I reckon Prince is, but I don't know about your ole uncle. I'm afraid I'm too old to be runnin' up and down God's mountains."

"I don't know how to handle a tracking dog."

"Ain't nothin' to it with a dog like this," he said. "Just let him have a sniff of Bugg's ole underwear or something, give him some words to get him fired up, then just follow him."

I quickly stuffed some gear into a backpack, loaded Prince in the truck, and headed to Bugg's house near Ward. There were numerous federal agents there. Some were carrying boxes of evidence out of Bugg's house and the meth lab beside it. I found Valeska and Livingston talking with some sheriff's deputies and U.S. Marshals. Valeska and Livingston were not dressed for a prolonged journey into the mountains. They introduced me to the others.

"What's the plan?" I said.

"We're going to send several teams after him," a sheriff's lieutenant said. "We're still putting the teams together, waiting on some horses and overnight equipment."

"I've got a dog," I said. "A bluetick coonhound. A champion tracker."

"You know how to handle him?" the lieutenant asked.

"Oh, sure. Been tracking my whole life."

"We're not ready to start yet," he said. "When we go into these mountains, we want to go in as a team."

I said, "The longer we wait, the less chance the dog has of finding him."

"Too dangerous," he said. "We go as a team."

"I'm going to need some of Bugg's clothing for the dog to sniff."

Valeska said, "There's plenty of dirty laundry in there. This guy was a pig. Help yourself."

She accompanied me inside, and in Bugg's room I found a flannel shirt that was in what appeared to be a pile of dirty clothes. I picked it up and walked back outside to my truck. I let Prince out of the truck and he followed me back over to Valeska and the group.

"He's ready to go," I said. "Give me a radio and let me get started."

"No," the lieutenant said, "I can't let a civilian go in by himself."

"I'll go with him," Livingston said.

"You guys don't even have any supplies," said the lieutenant. "No food, no shelter, no sleeping bags."

"I've got a backpack in my truck that's ready to go," I said. "It has everything. If we're not back tonight, we'll use my sleeping bag as a blanket for both of us."

"There's some camping gear in Bugg's house," Valeska said. "I'll go see if I can find another backpack and sleeping bag."

"Get a warm coat, a hat, and some gloves," I told Livingston.

"I've got some in the car," he said.

He trotted over to the big Ford, then returned wearing a parka that had "FBI" emblazoned on the back of it. He also carried a semi-automatic rifle.

Valeska found a backpack in Bugg's house and brought it up front. "I put a few bottles of water in there," she said.

I looked at Livingston and said, "You ready?"

We were six hours into it, and Prince had taken us in a southerly direction, back toward Nederland and Rollinsville. Other teams were now searching the areas north and west of Bugg's home.

The miles of walking up and down hills gave me some time to get to know Livingston. I decided he wasn't such a bad guy. A lot like me in some ways. His undergraduate degree had been in meteorology, of all things, and he had even been a TV weatherman in a small town in Missouri, but he had tired of it and joined the FBI. He had a wife and two small kids. We both liked the Broncos.

"We're awfully far south," Livingston said. "You sure this dog knows what he's doing?"

"He knows what he's doing; the question is whether I know what I'm doing."

"You said you'd been tracking your whole life."

"I exaggerated a little."

"Great."

"I trust the dog," I said. "He's a champion."

I also trusted my sense of logic. I guessed Bugg would head to one of his three caches in Colorado, and I was pretty sure I knew which one. One was in southern Colorado, near Durango, and there was no way he was going to try to cover that distance in February. Another was in western Colorado near Grand Junction. That would be a long hike, too, unless he got brave and tried to thumb a ride on the interstate. The third one wasn't that far from his home. It was near the Winter Park ski area.

Winter Park is south and west of Ward. To get to Winter Park from Ward would take two hours by car. Even though they are probably only twenty-five miles apart as the crow flies, that twenty-five miles includes the Continental Divide. If you were not a crow, you would have to drive thirty-five miles south from Ward, through Black Hawk, then catch the interstate west, then head north on Highway 40.

If Bugg was headed toward Winter Park on foot, he had two

choices. He could get the uphill leg of his journey down first by heading west from his home over the Divide, then south. Or he could do what Prince apparently thought he was doing; head south first, then turn west and uphill.

Why head south first? Why not get the uphill leg out of the way? Why risk being above eleven thousand feet when night falls?

We continued south. Up one ridge, down into the next valley. Livingston monitored his radio to keep track of what the other teams were doing. When we stopped for water, I used my Global Positioning System and USGS map to determine where we were. I showed the map to Livingston and pointed to our location.

"We've come a long way," he said. "We're just a few miles west of Nederland?"

"Yeah."

"I don't get it," Livingston said. "He's staying off the designated trails, but heading toward more populated areas. You think he's trying to get to the interstate?"

"Maybe," I said. "He's a gutsy guy."

"What's this?" Livingston said as he pointed to a place on the map.

"The Moffat Tunnel," I said. "Trains use it to go under the Divide. Saves lots of time."

"Maybe he's hoping to hop a train," Livingston said. "If he gets a train, he's on the other side of the Divide and long gone before we get near him."

"It wouldn't be hard," I said. "Most of the trains carry coal. They're long and they don't carry a big crew. They go pretty slow through here."

"How big is the tunnel? Could he hide in it?"

"It's a little more than six miles long. I don't know how wide it is. Probably wide enough for a man to stand up without getting hit by a train. I'd be a little concerned about ventilation if I went deep into it."

I got Prince fired up again and we continued south. Livingston got Valeska on the radio and told her our theory.

"I'll call the railroads," I heard her say. "We'll stop and search all eastbound and westbound trains."

Within a few more hours Prince had us at the entrance to the east portal of the Moffat Tunnel, a few miles west of Rollinsville. It was dusk now. The tunnel looked to be eighteen or twenty feet wide, wide enough that a man could stand in it without getting hit by a train.

"Maybe he's in the tunnel," Livingston said. "Think we should check it out?"

"No. He could be two or three miles into it. And, like I said, I don't know how good the ventilation is in there. It would be kind of embarrassing for me, you, and the dog to die of suffocation or toxic fumes. Get on the radio. Maybe Adrienne can get the Gilpin County sheriff to send some deputies to keep us company tonight, and get some deputies over in Grand County to watch the west portal."

Forty-five minutes later two SUVs driven by Gilpin County deputies pulled up to our position. They had to stop a few hundred yards east of us because the dirt road does not go all the way to the east portal.

We introduced ourselves, and Livingston briefed them. If Bugg was in the tunnel, it was a waiting game. If Bugg was not in the tunnel, he might be very close to us—waiting to hop the first train that came through. Or Prince might be a tracking school dropout and Bugg might be in Utah by now.

It had been a long day, so I asked one of the deputies if I could take a nap in his SUV. I put the back of the passenger seat down as far as it would go and fell asleep.

By early morning we had more law enforcement and more equipment. Someone's radio crackled at around six and I heard a male on the other end say, "You'll have a westbound coal train stopping just east of the tunnel in about thirty minutes. The engineer has been advised to stop before entering the tunnel."

"We'll have to search every car," Livingston said. "See if he's hiding on top of one or in between two of the cars."

"Could be underneath one of them, too," a deputy said.

An FBI agent I did not know offered me coffee and I gladly accepted. We waited.

I heard the train even before it reached Rollinsville. I looked east every few minutes and eventually the train came into view. Then I heard the squeak of metal on metal as the engineer began braking. It was a long train, maybe a half mile long, and it was powered by four diesel locomotives. The ground vibrated as the train neared us. The engineer brought her to a stop just a hundred yards or so from the east portal, but the diesel engines continued to run and the noise was defening.

Some of the feds started at the Rollinsville end of the train, at the caboose, and began working their way toward us. Livingston and I and the deputies who had arrived last night started at the first engine and worked our way east toward the caboose. Everyone was armed.

One of us had to climb up the ladder on each car to look into the top of it. It dawned on me that Bugg could be buried under a mound of coal and we might not see him.

At some point Prince trotted down a few cars to the east and started barking wildly. Now he was jumping up at one of the railroad cars, howling, and generally going crazy. "I think the dog's got something," I said.

Livingston came up to me and motioned the two deputies to approach the other side of the car.

I saw the head of one of the deputies as he climbed to the top of the car from the ladder on the other side. "There's nobody up here," he said. "Just coal."

Prince was still going nuts. Livingston and I exchanged glances. Then he started climbing the ladder on our side until he could see into the car. Holding on to the ladder with one hand, he set his pistol down on the top of the car and picked up his radio. "The dog is alerting on this car," he said. "We think he might be hiding beneath the coal, but I'm wearing a four-hundred-dollar suit. I'm going to fire some rounds into the car to make sure nobody is hiding. Ignore the gunfire. Repeat, ignore the gunfire."

I thought he was bluffing, but he fired three rounds right into the coal. Suddenly a figure covered in black dust appeared from beneath the coal, jumped to the ground, and sprinted toward the trees. "Go get him, Prince," I said.

It didn't take the eighty-five-pound Prince long to catch the 250-pound Bugg. Prince lunged from behind and took a bite out of Bugg's thigh. Now Bugg was on the ground. Snarling and snapping, Prince was coming at him from all directions. Bugg raised an arm to swat the dog, but Prince sank his teeth into the arm and wouldn't let go. I trotted over to them, aiming my Glock at Bugg with my right hand, and used my left hand to pull Prince off him. Livingston and the deputies joined us. Livingston cuffed him, then got on the radio and shared the good news.

50

Anvil turned out to be a graduate journalism student who had hoped to make it big with a book about his life and times with the Sons of Satan. His real name was Evan Roberts. He had penetrated the gang with good intentions, but got in too deep. I was still pissed about his role in the snake incident, but I realized he had done what he could to protect Karlynn and me from Bugg. Still, he had committed crimes and would be prosecuted.

I talked Matt into defending Anvil. We visited him at the jail where he was awaiting trial. He was less scruffy-looking now. In a small room with no windows Matt explained the criminal justice process and conducted his first interview with his new client. We wanted to see how much he knew and how much help he could give the feds in return for a deal.

Anvil didn't know anything about Rankin's death because that had been before he had joined the Sons of Satan. He could testify that Bugg and Mongoose discussed options with regard to Lowell, but he knew nothing about Skull's involvement. Nevertheless, it didn't take long for us to realize that Anvil knew enough about the gang and its operations to sink Bugg and the Sons of Satan for good. For two years he had been part of Bugg's inner circle. During those two years he had lived alone in a small cabin near

Jamestown, Colorado, and he had kept a daily journal about his life in the gang.

Matt looked at me and said, "What do you think? You were a federal prosecutor."

"They might relocate him if they think he has enough to offer. If not, you can probably still get a pretty good deal. If he has to do time, he can use it to write his book. He might make some money on a book like that."

"I'm going to call it *A Son of Satan,*" he said.

"I've got to ask you one question," I said. "You didn't tell Bugg you saw Karlynn with me. At the bar in Longmont you told my partner you hadn't seen her for months. And you pretended not to recognize me when I saw you at Bugg's house. Bugg tried to kill me three times. Once up in Idaho, once with the snake, and once by sending his army to my house. How did Bugg know what I had done?"

"The guys in Idaho saw that you had Colorado plates and a bluetick coonhound, so they thought you might be the guy that took Bugg's dog. When they described you and your truck to Bugg, he gave them the go-ahead. Then you came back here, gave him the money, and told him that story about Karlynn and his dog. He started having doubts. He thought he had jumped the gun in Idaho. It was hard for him to believe that you were lying, because you had given him so much money. He went back and forth. He did everything he could think of to try to figure out whether you were lying. He even had some guys check to see if there really is a Lewis and Clark Trailer Park in Coeur d'Alene. That's when he decided you had been suckering him all along. That's when he told us to put the snake in your house."

We said good-bye to Anvil, and as we left the building, Matt said, "I've got a better name for his book."

"What's that?"

"I Was a Thirty-Year-Old Dumbshit."

"I've got a name for his book, too," I said.

"Yeah?"

"Bluetick Revenge."

51

DURING THE NEXT FEW MONTHS things began to return to normal. I had coffee with Kendra Carlson a few times. I told her Karlynn was safe and perhaps on her way to the life she wanted. I was honest with her about Jayne. I told her about my dream.

"That's easy," she said. "You're in a china shop. Jayne is in China. She wants to bring something back."

"What about the Ford Taurus?"

"Taurus is the symbol of the bull," she said.

"I don't get it."

"You're the bull."

"I'm the bull?"

"You're the bull in a china shop. You're afraid you'll break something."

Though I enjoyed talking with her, we figured out fairly quickly that we were not a good match. Karlynn was right; Kendra was too high-maintenance for me. She wasn't the kind of woman who was going to allow Buck and Wheat to sleep on her bed.

I spent more time working out and practicing my karate. It was May and I enjoyed taking the dogs on walks. In my spare time I testified in front of a federal grand jury. I told the truth about almost everything.

One day, as I was coming out of the federal courthouse, I walked over to Coors Field to meet Scott so we could spend an evening watching the Rockies lose to the Dodgers. When the game was over, we decided to grab a beer and ended up walking right past the spot where Hal had been murdered. I pointed it out to Scott.

"Do you ever think about Skull?" he asked.

"Every day."

"Me too," he said.

"Even if we could get to him, what would we do with him? Mongoose and Bugg aren't talking about Lowell, and neither is anyone else. Anvil knows nothing about Skull. Nobody has enough evidence to prosecute him."

Scott didn't answer me.

"I don't think I could kill him," I said. "Not unless it was in self-defense."

We continued walking. Scott remained silent for a while, then said, "How would you feel about kidnapping him and burning every building on that compound to the ground?"

"I could live with that," I said.

We found a sports bar and went inside. We ordered two beers and some nachos. Scott likes sour cream and green chilis, so I asked the waiter to make sure that stuff was on the side.

Scott said, "Remember when I told your brother we could jump into the compound, and he made some comment about our corpses landing in Iowa?"

"He has no sense of humor when it comes to skydiving," I said.

"May is the ideal time for skydiving in northern Idaho," he said. "Statistically, Idaho has less wind in May than in any other month."

"I think a small plane flying a few thousand feet over the compound on a sunny day would be pretty obvious," I said. "They'd shoot us before we landed."

"I ain't talking about a small plane," Scott said. "I ain't talking about daytime or a few thousand feet."

52

I HAD BROKEN MY SHARE of rules. But usually they had been silly or unimportant rules. Staying in the girls' dorm after midnight, bringing prescription drugs over the border from Canada, things like that. Now we were considering conspiracy, kidnapping, and arson.

I had been taught that the end never justifies the means, but when I analyzed that statement, I began to question it. Wouldn't you have to weigh the two and decide each case on its own merits? In some cases might the end justify the means? It came down to a choice between an absolute morality, in which certain acts were just wrong, and a utilitarian morality that required weighing competing interests. True, society would deteriorate quickly if we could commit crimes without fear of legal consequences, but were there cases in which it was desirable to teach someone a lesson and destroy his base of operations? If so, who gets to decide?

These were the thoughts going through my mind as we sat in Scott's "war room," finalizing our plan. There were five of us: Scott, Matt, Troy, me, and Troy's friend Jeff Smart. Jeff is a pilot. He owns an air charter service called Smart Charter, though we sometimes call it Get Smart. This was our third and final meeting.

"Now, the trick to making this work," Scott said in conclusion, "is total surprise. We have to get in, do our work, and get out without getting caught.

"Does anyone have any questions or concerns?" Scott asked. No response.

"Does anybody have any second thoughts?" I asked. "If any of us falter, we all go down. So if you're having second thoughts, now is the time to say so. Once Scott and I exit the aircraft, there's no turning back." Again, no response.

"All right," Scott said, "see you in Idaho."

53

I HAD BEEN SKYDIVING BEFORE, a few times in the Marines and a few times just for fun, but all my jumps had been low-altitude static-line jumps, the kind where the parachute opens as soon as you exit from the aircraft. I had never experienced free fall.

Now I was in Jeff's luxury business jet ten thousand feet above Idaho. It was dark, as it usually is at three a.m. Jeff was flying the aircraft. Matt was there to help us with our gear and to close the door once we were out of the aircraft. It might look funny if Jeff landed with the door wide open.

Scott and I were going to do a tandem dive because he felt that if we jumped separately we might land too far apart on the ground and screw up the whole plan. My aura must have been the color of Grey Poupon.

We had done our homework. We had hiked four miles to the compound over pretty rough terrain to get an idea of the layout of the buildings, the number of people around, and so forth. We had found a rock formation overlooking the compound about a half mile from it. Using one of Scott's telescopes, we had observed the compound and its inhabitants for a solid day, then hiked back out during the evening.

Now I stood near the door of the jet. I looked at Scott and in that moment, more than any other, I saw the difference between us. I was going to jump in spite of my fear; Scott was smiling.

I saw a flashing beam of light below, signaling the aircraft. Troy had purchased one of those two-million-candlepower lights that you can plug into your car's cigarette lighter. Then Jeff's cell phone rang. "Here we go," Jeff said.

"Not yet," Scott said.

"We're going to miss—"

I never got to finish my sentence. We were falling through the night at 120 miles per hour. I can't describe the sheer terror of it. My body tensed and I was not allowing myself to breathe. At times I lost track of my brother's signal and the lights of Coeur d'Alene. I had no idea how high we were, how close we were to the ground. We could have been ten feet from it and I wouldn't have known.

Then I heard a snap, felt a tug, and we were floating toward Earth. "Okay," Scott said, "here we go."

I saw the small lake that we had seen on the map. Then I saw the buildings. Most of the lights were out.

"Ten seconds," Scott said. "Remember how to land."

Then we were on the ground. No broken bones, all our equipment intact. We shed the parachute and harnesses, then put our face masks on. "Put that shit over there," Scott said as he pointed to some trees. "We want to take it with us when we leave." I picked up the chute and harnesses and carried them over to the spot Scott had indicated, then came back to him.

There were a number of structures. One was the main residence, a gigantic structure made of logs and stone. It looked like a resort lodge. There were two smaller bunkhouses. There was a pavilion, which I assume was used for church services and hate rallies. There was a barn used for storage of equipment, and another for horses.

"I'll do the bunkhouses," he said. "You do the main house, the pavilion, and the barn."

"Not the horse barn," I said.

"No, the other one, the one with the equipment. Keep a low profile. If one of us doesn't find Skull in the chaos, we'll meet back over by those trees. Don't set fire to all sides of the building; just douse one side. We want anyone who is in these buildings to get out safely."

I walked briskly to the main house. I had three one-quart plastic bottles filled with gasoline. I doused one side of the structure with gasoline, then lit it. I ran to the barn and repeated the act, then did the same at the pavilion. I saw the sides of bunkhouses in flame. I heard Scott's firecrackers go off, so I lit mine and hid against the back side of the pavilion. It was chaos, flames and noise everywhere.

People started coming out of the house and the bunkhouses. It looked as though five came out of the house, three out of one bunkhouse, and two out of the other. A total of ten, all men. And the two German shepherds.

Skull was one of the three who emerged from the first bunkhouse. He was wearing the jean jacket with all the Aryan Resistance garbage on it. His buddies seemed confused, but he appeared alert. He made the mistake of straying from his pals and began to walk behind the bunkhouse. I knew that's where Scott was, so I slipped over to our agreed-upon departure point near the trees. The buildings were really burning now.

Skull's mouth was a bloody mess, and I could only guess how Scott had hit him. Scott was carrying something in one arm that was about the size and shape of a large briefcase. "Let's go, motherfucker," Scott said. He kicked Skull in the tailbone and we headed into the forest. When we were a few hundred yards in, we tied his hands behind his back with plastic ties and gagged him by shoving a sock in his mouth and wrapping duct tape around his head.

"What's that?" I asked Scott as I pointed to the metal object he had taken from the compound.

"I'll explain later," he said.

We had to hike downhill about four miles to make it to the road and Uncle Ray's camper. Ray knew nothing about our operation, but I had asked him to let me swap my truck for his camper for a week. Troy was driving the camper.

When we were within sight of the road, I didn't see the camper. I dialed Troy on my cell phone, and when he answered I said, "Flash your headlights for one second so we can see where you are. And don't forget to put your mask on."

He did, and that was all we needed. We walked a few hundred yards west, made sure there were no other vehicles approaching, and shoved Skull into the back of the camper. We bound his legs together with duct tape, and blindfolded him.

Skull was lying on a bed in the camper. Despite having his limbs tied together, he struggled violently at times. At other times he tried to be verbally abusive, though all we could hear was muffled noise because of the gag.

We decided to stay put for a few hours. Driving a camper at four in the morning might have attracted undue attention. We would wait until sunrise to head out.

Troy started the camper a little before six and headed into town to buy some coffee at a convenience store. Then we headed south, where we planned to catch the interstate and head down through Idaho, across Utah and Wyoming, and down into Colorado.

What to do with Skull was the subject of some debate. The consensus was, we had every right to kill him, but nobody was eager to do the deed. I knew I couldn't, and I suspected that even Scott was unwilling to go that far. The plan had been to beat the crap out of him, but he looked so helpless now, I was even questioning that. That idea had appealed to me in the abstract, but now that the opportunity had presented itself, I realized that it was more enjoyable to imagine hurting him than it would be to actually do it. It wouldn't bring my cousin back. It wouldn't bring Steve Lowell back.

As we approached Boise, I removed the gag from Skull's mouth. He was still blindfolded. "You've done a lot of evil shit in your life," I said, "and you've gotten away with it. Maybe there is a God who will make you answer for it, but maybe there isn't. Maybe it's up to us."

"I don't have anything to answer for," he said. "All I ever did was stand up for white people and the white race and the white man's way of life."

"By killing a white cop?" I said.

"Cop was in the wrong place at the wrong time," he said.

I resisted the temptation to smack him. Instead I yelled up front and told Troy to get off the interstate in Boise.

"What for?" Troy said.

"Boise's a big city. I'm sure there's a black part of town. We'll dump Adolph here in the middle of the hood and give him a chance to experience what it's like to be in the wrong place at the wrong time."

"Yeah," Scott said, "I'm sure all that White Power shit will impress the homeboys."

Eventually Troy found his way to what people usually refer to as "the bad part of town." The houses were small, many in disrepair. Unemployed black teens stared at us as we drove past. I'll go out on a limb and say they probably had never seen a white body-builder drive an old camper through their neighborhood. We might as well have painted REDNECK on Uncle Ray's vehicle.

"This looks like a nice group of gentlemen coming up on the right," Troy said. I went forward and leaned over so I could see out the front of the truck. A group of six young black men was congregated on the side of a run-down building. The windows had been boarded up and the brick side of the building was covered with graffiti.

"This will do," I said. Troy guided the camper to a stop alongside the young men. Scott and I helped Skull to his feet; then I opened up the door to the back of the camper and stepped out.

"You're in the wrong neighborhood," one of the black kids told me.

"That's no way to greet someone who is about to give you a present," I said.

"What present you gonna give us?" he said.

"Just watch," I said.

Scott cut the duct tape that held Skull's legs together and helped him step down from the camper. Skull certainly looked handsome in his Aryan Resistance jacket, but I think what really impressed the crowd was the WHITE POWER he had tattooed across his knuckles.

"You all have a nice day," I said to the black kids as Scott and I climbed back into the camper.

I closed the door to the camper and yelled up front to Troy. "Head for Colorado," I said. "Obey all the traffic laws."

54

I was putting linseed oil on the house. I do this every year to protect the wood from the effects of the sun. A big Crown Victoria approached my home on the dirt driveway. It was Valeska.

I stepped down off the ladder. I was wearing old clothes that I would throw away when I finished the linseed oil project. "If I had known you were coming, I would have dressed up."

"I just wanted to share some good news," she said.

"What's that?"

"Mongoose cut a deal."

"He did?"

"Yeah. When we searched his locksmith shop up in Lander, we did a careful check of the metal trash cans. There was burn residue in one. Our crime lab guys say they found traces of burnt leather, burnt plastic, and burnt business cards, all consistent with the burning of Lowell's credentials. We also found a record from a motel in Bozeman showing that Mongoose stayed there for one night, about a month before Lowell was killed. When we told all this to Mongoose, he caved."

"Is he talking about Skull?"

"Yes, we're going to charge Skull with Lowell's murder. It will be a death penalty case. Murder of a federal agent. It may take a week or two before he is arraigned."

"Why's that?"

"He got into it with some black kids up in Boise a few weeks ago. He's in a federal medical facility right now."

"Really?"

"He claims a couple of men burned down this compound he lives on, kidnapped him, and dumped him in a black neighborhood."

"The world is a crazy place," I said.

There was a brief pause. "Anyhow," she said, "there is one other thing I wanted to tell you."

"Sure, go ahead."

"At the back of Bugg's address book we found some numbers."

"Phone numbers?"

"No, these all had eight or nine digits. Did you notice them when you studied his address book?"

"Can't say that I did."

"It really stumped me for a while. I couldn't figure out the significance of these numbers. So I showed it to Cliff—"

"Livingston?"

"Yes. He used to be a meteorologist. Almost immediately he realized that these numbers were the longitude and latitude for certain specific locations, all in the Rocky Mountain region. In decimal form, but without the decimal points."

"Son of a gun."

"Then I remembered that Karlynn said Bugg had stashed food, weapons, and money all over the West."

"That's right, she said that."

"So on a lark, Cliff and I went to a few of these locations, and we sent other agents to check out the locations in other states."

"What did you find?"

"Just food."

"No weapons or money?"

"None."

"Well, Bugg's a big man. He probably just cares more about eating than he does about weapons or money. Some guys are like that."

"Take care, Pepper," she said. "If anyone ever needs a recommendation for a dog thief, I'll give them your name."

55

It was nine o'clock on a sunny June morning in Nederland. We had been on the air for an hour, playing everything from the yodeling tunes of Hank Williams to the upbeat reggae of Jimmy Cliff. Occasionally we played the Stress Monsters.

We limited our show to two hours each week and we never spoke on the air. We were very careful, even taking the antenna down when we weren't operating. With the fifty-watt FM transmitter Scott had seized at the Biggs compound, our broadcast covered all of Nederland, and on a good day you could hear us as far south as Rollinsville and as far north as Ward.

As we sat there on my deck, with Buck and Wheat beside us, I looked back on all that had happened since that night in November when I had stolen Prince. So much had changed. Karlynn was in Barrow and still a fugitive, but I had a hunch the warrant and indictment would go away after all the Sons of Satan had been prosecuted. Prince was living the good life with Uncle Ray down in Blanca. Luther and I had become closer friends. I had survived the rattlesnake and multiple attacks, and I found myself more open to spiritual things.

At ten we concluded our broadcast as we always did—with David Allen Coe's rendition of "You Never Even Call Me by My Name." Some have called it the perfect country-and-western song.

"Guess it's about time to take you to the airport," Scott said.

"Yup."

"China. That's a long journey."

"A very long journey," I said.

I love it when a plan comes together.